Praise for the work of Annette Blair

Gone with the Witch

"Yet another fun romp for Annette Blair!"
—*Fallen Angel Reviews*

"A spellbinding story that totally knocked my socks off!"
—*Huntress Reviews* (5 stars)

"Wonderful characters, a riveting story line, and a sensuous undercurrent are just a few of the things that made this such a phenomenal story."
—*Romance Junkies*

"This story tugged at the heart . . . A definite addition to my keeper shelf."
—*Fresh Fiction*

"I've read all of the 'witchy' tales from Ms. Blair and found this to stand on its own, but made even better having known many of the characters previously. I would recommend them all for your reading pleasure."
—*Romance Reviews Today*

"This second story about psychic triplets is just as good as the first."
—*Romantic Times* (4 stars)

Sex and the Psychic Witch

"Ms. Blair's humor and wit is evident in many ways . . . *Sex and the Psychic Witch* is . . . a delight [that] will bring chuckles."
—*Romance Reviews Today*

continued . . .

"A sexy, hilarious, romantic tale with fun characters, snappy writing, and some super-spooky moments. I've looked forward to this story since the introduction of the triplets in *The Scot, the Witch and the Wardrobe*, and it was well worth the wait!"   —*Fresh Fiction*

"More hot scenes . . . spine chills . . . outrageous stunts . . . A witchy climax that will warm your very soul. I can hardly wait until the next Cartwright triplet spins her spell. Out-Freaking-Standing!"   —*Huntress Reviews*

The Scot, the Witch and the Wardrobe

"Sassy dialogue, rich sexual tension, and plenty of laughs make this an immensely satisfying return to Blair's world of witchcraft. Fans will welcome back familiar characters in supporting roles, but newcomers will take to it just as well."   —*Publishers Weekly*

"Snappy dialogue can't disguise the characters' true insecurities, giving depth to Blair's otherwise breezy, light-hearted tale."   —*Booklist*

My Favorite Witch

"Sexy."   —*Booklist*

"Annette Blair will make your blood sizzle with this magical tale . . . A terrific way to start the new year!"
                    —*Huntress Reviews*

"This warmhearted story is a delight, filled with highly appealing characters sure to touch your heart. The magic in the air spotlights the humor that's intrinsic to the story. A definite charmer!"   —*Romantic Times*

Never
Been
Witched

Annette Blair

BERKLEY SENSATION, NEW YORK

THE BERKLEY PUBLISHING GROUP
Published by the Penguin Group
Penguin Group (USA) Inc.
375 Hudson Street, New York, New York 10014, USA
Penguin Group (Canada), 90 Eglinton Avenue East, Suite 700, Toronto, Ontario M4P 2Y3, Canada
(a division of Pearson Penguin Canada Inc.)
Penguin Books Ltd., 80 Strand, London WC2R 0RL, England
Penguin Group Ireland, 25 St. Stephen's Green, Dublin 2, Ireland (a division of Penguin Books Ltd.)
Penguin Group (Australia), 250 Camberwell Road, Camberwell, Victoria 3124, Australia
(a division of Pearson Australia Group Pty. Ltd.)
Penguin Books India Pvt. Ltd., 11 Community Centre, Panchsheel Park, New Delhi—110 017, India
Penguin Group (NZ), 67 Apollo Drive, Rosedale, North Shore 0632, New Zealand
(a division of Pearson New Zealand Ltd.)
Penguin Books (South Africa) (Pty.) Ltd., 24 Sturdee Avenue, Rosebank, Johannesburg 2196, South
Africa

Penguin Books Ltd., Registered Offices: 80 Strand, London WC2R 0RL, England

This is a work of fiction. Names, characters, places, and incidents either are the product of the author's
imagination or are used fictitiously, and any resemblance to actual persons, living or dead, business
establishments, events, or locales is entirely coincidental. The publisher does not have any control over
and does not assume any responsibility for author or third-party websites or their content.

NEVER BEEN WITCHED

A Berkley Sensation Book / published by arrangement with the author

PRINTING HISTORY
Berkley Sensation mass-market edition / February 2009

ISBN: 978-0-425-22649-0

BERKLEY® SENSATION
Berkley Sensation Books are published by The Berkley Publishing Group,
a division of Penguin Group (USA) Inc.,
375 Hudson Street, New York, New York 10014.
BERKLEY® SENSATION and the "B" design are trademarks of Penguin Group (USA) Inc.

PRINTED IN THE UNITED STATES OF AMERICA

10 9 8 7 6 5 4 3 2 1

With love and thanks to:
Lynn Haberak,
for opening her childhood home
to friendship and creativity,
and to
Catherine J. Jenssen, CJ,
for creating a home in which writers may flourish.
Live, Love, Laugh!

Dedicated to:
Summer Retreat 2007
Where this story was born

Chapter One

DESTINY Cartwright sought peace in her ritual circle but found self-censure instead. Drat the Goddess of mischievous matchmaking pranks. How could a psychic witch lust after a paranormal debunker?

What were the odds?

Talk about a lousy chooser. Not that she wanted to marry the hunky debunker: six feet of baditude in tight, torn jeans, chest-baring unbuttoned shirts, shaggy, burnished bronze hair, wide shoulders, and a five o'clock shadow.

She wanted Morgan Jarvis, architect, for sex, for a while, as a boy toy, no commitment—no after burn, aftertaste, or regrets.

She'd faced facts. The odds of identical triplets *all* finding their soul mates were nil to "No way, Jose!" Since Harmony and Storm had found theirs, that made her the single girl out.

Lightning did not strike thrice.

Yes, Morgan would probably try to debunk her every goal: psychic, magickal, emotional, and spiritual, if either of them ever discovered what they were.

Self-discovery. That's why she'd come here, to find those goals and the path she should take to reach them.

Now, in the dark parlor of the Paxton Island Lighthouse, she sat surrounded by votive candles representing earth, air, fire, and water, situated north, south, east, and west, one in the center for spirit. The crystals between each cinnamon candle refracted their flames like stars, the ageless echo of breaking waves at high tide adding an earth rhythm to her magick.

Though her particular brand of clairvoyance allowed her to see the future of others, never her own, she had envisioned this lighthouse—as lost in a fog, and as much in need of comfort as she—as the place to find her future, her psychic path, her reason for being. And if she was smart, she'd maybe spell her perverse attraction for Morgan Jarvis into the sea.

Alone, like this, she *might* be able to accomplish it, but if she allowed herself to be caught in his magnetic field, she'd get sucked right in.

She suspected that Morgan hid a soft, chewy center that he covered with a snarky rock-candy shell. She thought he might be hiding Morgan the Mystic, but after Harmony's wedding, Morgan the Mistake made more sense.

Destiny shivered as mortification threatened to singe her brows, until the moon slipped from the clouds, its beams piercing the windows, caressing her shoulders like a shawl, warm, protective, and forgiving. It offered solace and welcome with the affirming embrace.

Here, she could put her worries behind her.

Shadows danced in her circle, leaving the room's edges in darkness, including the stairs whose spindles she faced but could no longer see. Her flashlight had picked them out on arrival a short while ago, and her possessions now sat at the bottom, in large, wheeled carts awaiting transport to a bedroom upstairs.

Relief improved Destiny's spirits. She was here, not in Scotland with her well-meaning family auto-pairing her with Morgan Jarvis, so much a friend, he felt like family . . . to everyone except her.

Peace, Destiny sensed, was just out of reach.

Serenity. If only she could grasp it.

Her hyperactive cat's purring contentment attested to the tranquility surrounding them. She petted the caramel-and-marshmallow-swirl tabby. "You like the lighthouse, don't you, Caramello? I like it, too. I think it wants us here."

Destiny centered herself, a first step on this journey of self-discovery fired by a profusion of confusion over her elusive psychic goal and a riot of romantic fantasies over one maddening man.

Breathe in. Release. Breathe. Release.

Perhaps she should have saved her ritual for morning, except that—

> "Now feels right.
> In the dead of night
> I dare to invite . . .
> Profound insight."

A tentative calm settled over her, obscurity filling the dark edges of her consciousness the way it claimed the periphery of the room. She closed her eyes and searched the recesses of her mind before letting her words pour forth:

> "Earth, water, fire, air
> Angel guardians hear my prayer.

Help define my psychic brand.
For those who seek a helping hand.

"Moon, stars, high bright sun,
Light my way to souls undone.
My psychic goal with speed, reveal.
Harm it naught, I seek to heal."

Destiny opened her eyes . . . and lost her breath.

In her circle stood a man dressed as if for a centennial sail. Beside him, an apple-cheeked young girl sat in a grotto of bright white angel wings. Standing tall behind her: an angel.

Destiny's heartbeat trebled. Fear stole her breath, prickling her from the roots of her hair to the tips of her toes. She shivered and clutched her cat so tightly that Cara meowed and jumped from her grasp to circle, examine, and "talk" to the little girl.

Destiny had never seen her cat try so hard to communicate.

The child held her hand flat, well above Caramello, and the cat purred loudly, and arched as if into an actual caress.

The girl smiled, and the angel said, "Be not afraid."

Destiny about choked. Wait a minute. She tried to regain her composure. "The last time an angel spoke those words, didn't a virgin get pregnant?"

The angel remained passive, its lucent amber eyes deeply probing, while Centennial Man's eyes widened. "I don't think that could be an issue here," he quipped.

"I resent that!" Destiny fought a warm shot of embarrassment at her knee-jerk reaction and the truth of his words.

Despite the entities' lack of apparent threat, Destiny stood and pointed a large green fluorite crystal their way like a negative-energy scrub gun, because she knew—*she knew*—they were ghosts.

"Negative entities away.
Protection come to stay.
White light, elliptical in flight,
Surround me in a sphere so bright
As to sever threat and sight,
Of visions in the night."

Adrenaline pumped through her as she stepped back, but her visitors remained.

Normally, she'd feel safe in her ritual circle, except that *they* shared the circle with her.

Destiny gasped, knelt, and with a sweep of her arms, pulled candles and crystals close around her, to form a smaller, safer circle.

The ghost child's lips quirked upward on one side, bringing Morgan's rare smile to mind.

Centennial Man shook his head, as if in warning. "We're not negative," he whispered and pointed behind his hand. "That really *is* an angel."

Destiny rose and straightened, preferring to tower over them, though no human could stand taller than the angel, and she chanted her spell again, this time, loud enough to wake the dead.

A light appeared at the top of the stairs.

Another icy rush of fear. An involuntary catch in her breath. "Don't tell me there are more of you!"

Footsteps, she heard, running on the floor above. A crash. A curse.

Another male ghost? Destiny stamped her foot. "Enough already!"

A hair-raising stair creak. Two. Three.

Heavy footsteps, slowly descending a blacked-out staircase.

Words of inquiry caught in Destiny's paralyzed throat as she stood frozen in her protective circle. Beast or ghost, he could not harm her here.

She aimed the fluorite crystal high, and at the next creak—thank the Goddess for teen softball—she served it in a deadly pitch.

A man-grunt. A tumble down the stairs.

A horrendous crash against wheeled carts, her cater-wauling cat leaping into the fray, and her personal belongings flying into view turned her mind from ghosts to a flesh-and-blood man, about the size of Bigfoot, wrecking everything she'd—

"My things!"

Her heart beat a wild tattoo, yet shame for the selfish thought claimed her. A ghost would not have disturbed her carts or landed with a thud and a shivering head-crack. Unable to reach a light switch without stepping near the yeti at the bottom of the stairs, Destiny set her ritual knife on the floor to open the sacred circle to allow for her escape.

For insurance, she grabbed a large potted geranium off a nearby table. "Anyone hurt?" she called.

She heard silence but for the sea sweeping the shore out back.

As she tiptoed forward, her intruder groaned, sat up, and breached the light. A yeti, indeed, given the size of his chest and the bright of his eyes in shadow.

Destiny lowered the clay pot and crowned him before he could strike.

Like a tree trunk in a hurricane, he fell, taking at least one of her carts down with him. His torso lay in darkness, but she could see his hairy legs and ginormous feet in the candlelight.

A behemoth in the flesh, moaning like he'd been shot.

She skirted the interloper and flipped on the light.

Curled in the fetal position, amid her clothes, both hands on his balls, he wore a purple bra like a bracelet.

"Uh-oh."

Cat-scratch blood curled down his arm and dripped on his red boxers.

"Balls . . . busted," he gasped.

Destiny's fear morphed to horror. "Morgan?"

Chapter Two

MORGAN'S agony and rising nausea radiated through him, deepening his suffering. As he rode out the pain, he identified his assailant with a dizzying peek, then he closed his eyes to recover with shallow breaths and a soothing mantra: *Dead witch. Dead witch. Dead witch.*

Not that he believed in witches, but *she* sure in Hades did.

Her attack cat came over and licked his throbbing brow, meowing, or yowling, as if she were crying for him. Morgan opened his eyes and came face-to-face with the subject of all his dreams. "Nightmare," he said.

Kneeling beside him, Destiny looked as if she could *feel* his pain.

He didn't think so.

He tried to sit up and groaned, but his anguish began to level off, a sign that it might recede, and he might live, in which case: *Dead witch. Dead witch. Dead witch.*

"Can I help you up?" she asked.

"Not. Quite. Ready." Crushed cojones; that's what he got for running and hiding.

"I didn't know it was you," she said, sounding sorry, as she reached toward his brow and then stopped.

He refused to be charmed by the regretful brat who crushed his nuts. "Why, here?" he asked and blew out a breath. "Candles? Voodoo?" Damn his lost soul, he'd come here to get away from the lust of his life—to get his house in order—and here she was, like an absolution addict sitting in his confessional. Again.

She knelt to pick up her knife and snuff her candles. "The circle is open," she said, scanning the room at large. "They're gone."

"Who?" he asked, ignoring Chatty Kitty yowling his ear off.

"Who, indeed?" the temptress repeated as she knelt beside him. "Caramello is talking to you. What's with her tonight?"

The subject of his fantasies ran paradoxically gentle fingers along his scalp, raising his testosterone level to excruciating proportions. Morgan closed his eyes in renewed anguish, yet he couldn't ask her to stop.

Death wish. Sex wish. There may not be any such thing as a witch, but this woman sure could cast a spell on him.

After her sister Harmony's wedding, he and Destiny had nearly succumbed to what he believed might be mutual lust, but they didn't, which was just as well, since he'd known squat about making love back then.

With her in mind, since that night, he'd read book after book about how to pleasure a woman, make himself last for her sake, doing the exercises until he could last forever. During the self-training, he'd stayed away from her, certain that by the time she got back from Scotland, he'd be able to hide his ignorance and raise her to the heights of orgasmic satisfaction.

Instead, she'd knocked him on his ass and broken his

equipment in the process. Now, she was trying to nurse him back to insanity.

Destiny. His *destiny*, God help him, soothed every bruise she'd caused, except for the ones on his balls, which she didn't touch, more's the pity. Then again, maybe not.

Despite that, Morgan raised a knee to hide his reaction, however weakened by her attack. Sick bastard. "Ouch, damn it! That hurts," he snapped. "Ouch, there, too."

She brutalized his head, looking for and finding every bump and lump, cut, scratch, and prune. He focused on his poor, battered lap, his pecker attempting a painful call to attention.

Damn his lost soul, only she could fix *that* ache. And when she did—at some indefinite date in the future—it would take as many fixes as either of them could bear, until one of them expired of bliss—him, he figured.

Too much to hope that she might be as hot to jump his bones as he was to jump hers.

And yet he had to get her the Hades out of there. Now. Tonight.

"You'll survive," Destiny said, sitting back on her heels. "Though I'm not so sure about my things."

"Your things? You concussed and castrated me. I should think you'd be more worried about my . . . *things*!" Damn, his head hurt when he shouted.

She knelt on her heels, full of surprise. "You gave *yourself* the concussion when you fell down the stairs."

"I fell because somebody threw a boulder at my head while I was investigating a break-in."

"I didn't break in. I have a key. And all I threw was a little crystal."

He touched his throbbing eyebrow, and his hand came away bloody. "A crystal about the size of a fist?"

With a look of false innocence, she picked up a crystal off the floor. "See, I told you," she said, palm out, a speck of crystal in its center. "I couldn't have hurt you with this."

Anybody who looked that innocent had to be guilty. He searched the floor around him and found a brick of a crystal on the bottom stair. He held it so close to her face, Destiny crossed her eyes to see it.

Too bad for him, that charmed him the more.

She pushed his hand away. "I forgive you."

Morgan untangled his arm from her bra. Purple and plump, it was enough to make him think about letting her stay, the sweet, seductive scamp.

He moved the heavy metal cart handle away from the source of his pain.

Destiny stood as if that were a sign he was ready for payback.

The idea of strangling the object of his lust for showing up turned to a sick kind of gratitude. Books and practice were all well and good, but he'd rather claim the sex life he'd long suppressed with a flesh-and-blood woman. And here she stood, the source of his fantasies, in the beautiful, bountifully endowed flesh. "You forgive me for what?"

"For breaking my crystal. It's a green fluorite, which is to your benefit, by the way. They aid in cleansing the aura. Good for one as dirty as yours."

"Lucky me." Was an aura like pimples? Would it clear up if he got laid?

"Seriously," she said. "I think the crystal you broke helped when it touched you. I already see a hint of tan with a light blue band next to it in the muddy energy around you, almost as if you're happy about something. Your aura is a sensitive tan, bearing logic and a secret."

"I might once have been logical," he said, "but when I met you, that flew out the window."

"I wonder why I can't read anyone else's aura but yours?" she mused aloud, certainly not expecting an answer from him.

Damn, she was annoying. She had a mouth on her that could chew him up and spit him out. Yet the thought of what else she could do with it drove him crazy. Sass and all, he wanted it against *his* mouth, among other places.

"Gritty Spanish stucco," he snapped. He'd come for peace, two weeks' worth, while she and her family were in Scotland, to avoid the torture of her constant sexual stimulation. Who needed that? Well, he did. No, maybe what he really *needed* was to figure out what to do about this obsession he had with a self-proclaimed witch who needed to get real. A witch, by the saints! "Why aren't you on a plane to Scotland?"

"Why aren't you?"

Morgan blew out a breath. "It's *your* nephew's christening, not mine. They only invited me because King had no family, except me and Aiden, before you and your sisters showed up."

"But I'm a witch, and it's a church christening."

"Because the baby's father is Anglican," Morgan pointed out. "Your sisters, who are also his aunts, claim they're witches, too, but they're in Scotland."

"My sisters, even the baby's mother, respect my need for alone time. At Yule, I'll attend little Rory's Wiccanning with stars on."

"Speaking of alone time, I'd like some, thanks," he said. "Speaking of stars, they're floating all around you."

Destiny frowned and ran her hands through his hair again. "I think those stars are from the knots on your head."

"And my black-and-blue balls."

"Bruising those doesn't cause stars."

"No, it causes puking, but I'm better, thanks for asking."

She ignored him, as he expected. "The prune on the back of your head is probably from your landing. The one on top is from the pot of geraniums I broke over it." She winced and raised her shoulders, as if in apology.

He touched his bloody, throbbing brow. "Damn it, I just bought those geraniums this afternoon."

"Positive language, please, and why are you decorating my sister's lighthouse?"

"My best friend owned the place *before* he married your sister."

Destiny's huff pushed out her breasts. *Nice.* Morgan considered reaching for them, until she placed her hands on her hips.

"How did you get in here?" she asked.

Normally, when her mischievous eyes narrowed, a bright aquamarine glint filled them, but now they took on a stormy shade of green.

On the night of Harmony and King's wedding, when he and Destiny had kissed for the first time, and the heat of passion hit her—hit them both—he'd watched a muted gray blue roll into her eyes, like a fog, a color he'd like to see again. Fat chance.

Morgan sighed. "King gave me a key yesterday."

"Wait a minute." Destiny knelt beside him again, bringing her breasts back where he wanted them, up close and personal. "Harmony gave *me* a key last week, and she also gave me the *distinct* impression that you *were* going to Scotland." Destiny gasped. "Morgan, they set us up. They *knew* we were both coming here."

His aches and pains, thankfully, kept him from expressing his true opinion. "It'd serve them right if we killed each other."

"It could come to that."

He raised a brow. "Payback's a bitch."

Chapter Three

"ONE of us could leave," Morgan suggested, hoping she'd go, yet, true to stubborn form—his and hers—he hoped she'd refuse and stay.

True, if she stayed, he'd go up in flames, because he'd be tinder to her fire. But, ah, what a way to go.

She furrowed her exotic brows, more gull-winged than either of her sisters, and shook her head. "Harmony gave me a key first, so I get to stay."

Morgan tried to get up, using the stairs and balustrade for leverage, ignoring her helping hand, and stood bent over like an old man. "I got to the lighthouse first, so I get to stay." Hard to be assertive when you're staring at the floor.

He tried to straighten, but when he teetered, Destiny slipped an arm around him. "Oh boy. Down boy."

She helped him sit on the stairs, whether he wanted to or not. He was grateful, though he wouldn't admit it.

She sat beside him, looking as if he'd sawed her flying broom in half. "I brought the family to the airport, or I'd have been here first, and a sister is closer than a best friend, so there."

"There? Where?"

"Here," she said, examining the cat scratches on his bare chest with tender, exploratory fingers and very big eyes. "I belong here," she said, her voice suddenly scratchy.

It occurred to him that he should feel at a disadvantage, wearing only his boxers, but she seemed more fascinated than scandalized. One of her long blonde curls fell across his shoulder, the light, intimate touch in this brazenly inti-mate situation nearly unmanning him, or, more accurately, manning him.

Well, his flagpole was in good shape, hard as boss stone and ready to fly, despite any area discomfort. He swayed closer and inhaled deeply of cinnamon and sin, which had never seemed so tempting. "I've been vacationing here at the lighthouse since I was sixteen," he whispered.

"What?" she whispered, and surprised, she leaned away from him and gathered her artillery about her. "Good for you. Doesn't matter. I'm not leaving."

"Neither am I."

"This is a disaster," she said. "I have plans."

"Propose a solution. I'm listening."

"There is none, except for both of us to stay,"

Morgan shivered inwardly with dread or excitement. Who could tell? "*Bad* solution."

"There are no good solutions. Neither concussing nor castrating you worked." She helped him to stand and walk to a hard-backed parlor chair. "I suppose drowning you is out of the question."

"Smart-ass." He sat, elbows on his thighs, his head in his hands, and refused to let her see his dizzy pain and diz-zier anticipation. The two of them alone together for two weeks, him with a wish-boner the whole time. He *could* leave when the water taxi came for him on Wednesday, but he wouldn't give her the satisfaction.

"Why are you here, anyway?" she asked, watching him with concern.

"I'm planning to buy and renovate the place as a permanent residence, so I'm here to draw up the architectural design." All true. Just not the entire truth.

"Congratulations. I'll leave when you show me the deed in your name."

"Damn my soul, you're annoying."

"Don't curse. Be positive. No damns allowed. Slam, if you must, but never damn."

Morgan stood and inched back to the stairs, waving away her help and ignoring her to preserve his sanity.

Destiny whistled. "You know, I never took you for the type to wear red boxers."

"I'm in a rebellious phase."

"Red is rebellious?"

"For me it is."

"Are they silk?" she asked with enough pointed interest to raise his, er, hackles.

"No more than that bare-midriff Licensed to Thrill scrap *you're* wearing." A turn-me-inside-out *little* number that raised his hackles the more. Could her jeans *be* any tighter?

She began to gather her scattered possessions and toss them into her boner-crushing cart. He tried helping her, but when she bent over, her fine ass pointed his way. Wow. His only thought was to cup her, just there, with one hand, and use the other to test the tautness of her jeans by trying to slide his eager hand inside, starting at her cowboy boots and running his itchy palm up to—he needed a word like *heaven*, but better.

Paradise? Nah. The promised land. That's what he wanted, a ticket—better yet, a free ride—to the promised land.

Man, his boxers were about as tight as those jeans right now.

"Hey, be careful," she said. "You're hurt. You'll get blood on my clothes."

Morgan straightened. "You're all heart, Kismet."

She scoffed. "I'm messing with your head and succeeding admirably, I see. Come into the kitchen, and I'll patch you up."

Damn, or slam, his lost soul, this should be fun—like torture with perks, like her hands everywhere, except where he wanted them.

Halfway through the parlor, her cat yowled and leaped from the top of the stairs to land on his sore shoulders.

Morgan jumped and wrenched everything he'd already bruised. "Son of a—"

"Sea cat?" Destiny finished. "Is my little Caramello digging in her baby claws?"

Morgan realized that this new attempt to annoy him amused him. "Not anymore." The aptly named caramel-and-marshmallow-colored kitten was in the process of settling around his neck, front and back paws hanging down his chest from either side of his head, a bit like his grandmother's old fox stole. Now the soft thing whispered meows in his ear and licked his lobe, like they were old friends sharing a secret.

"Leave her," Morgan said, no longer caring whether he could get Caramello, the feline catapult, for assault and battery, because he was paradoxically pleased to be her confidant. The triplets' cats shared discourse with their respective triplet and no one else. Destiny, he could see, was miffed by her cat's desertion, which made Caramello's attention half honor, half payback.

The cat continued to grace his neck while Morgan wet a towel with cold tap water, held it to the bloody gash on his brow, and leaned against the copper kitchen sink so he wouldn't slide to the floor and make an ass of himself in view of Caramello's owner.

Trying to focus on anything but his pain, he eyed the bulging brown paper grocery bags on the counter. "You brought enough food for a week."

"Two weeks," Destiny corrected.

His destiny, he asked himself again, as in a form of celestial retribution for his defection? He could be in for two weeks with a seducer-type torture device who called herself a witch? Some punishment. The best he could work up was a raging round of happy, so much of it, that he saw stars again and had to grab the counter for support. *He* needed a shrink. And a drink. Whiskey, maybe a bottle or two.

"Whoa." Destiny caught him and walked him back to the living room, because the bare kitchen held no furniture beyond the fridge that came over on the ark and the stove from *Little House on the Prairie*. "Sit," she ordered.

Okay, so he'd gotten knocked around a bit. Morgan saluted and slid into the chair, only to have her cat jump into his lap, yowl for his attention, and pat his cheek with a paw.

The cat distraction didn't work. He watched the sway of Destiny's backside instead, until she disappeared into the kitchen. He picked up the cat for a face-to-face. "First thing I'm gonna do after I buy the place," he whispered, "is enlarge it and take down the wall between the kitchen and living room so when Destiny walks through the house, I can watch her ass from wherever I am."

Pedimented pillars, he was so concussed, he was discussing his fantasies with a cat. He set the fickle feline on the floor, so she lay on his bare feet like a warm, purring cat rug. He shivered. She'd upset the balance of his plummeting body temperature.

He'd hardly recovered from the lingering sensual haze of Destiny's touch when she returned with the first aid kit. "Stay," she said when he tried to rise.

"Woof," he barked, and Caramello yowled.

"What are you, a guard dog?" Destiny asked him.

"I was responding to your doggie-type command. I'm a schnoodle."

"Is that a joke?"

Hell. It was hell. Screw the positive words. He knew hell when he lived it. "A child I loved wanted a schnoodle. When I move in, I plan to honor her memory by getting one."

"Her *memory*? A child? I'm so sorry."

Morgan swallowed the guilt rising in his throat like bile. "So am I."

Destiny looked concerned, tender; God protect him from her brand of tender. "What's a schnoodle?" she asked.

"It's a cross between a miniature schnauzer and a poodle."

"That's so *human* of you, wanting a dog. Gives me a picture of a different Morgan Jarvis. Way less scary."

"Me scary? You're kidding. All this time, I thought you were the scary one. Mysterious, you know?"

Destiny scoffed and opened the first aid kit. "I think this is the longest conversation we've ever had."

Morgan coughed, a trickle of insecurity creeping in. He was getting too comfortable with this woman of experience. A goddess so far out of his league, he'd have a heart attack if they got any cozier, sex books or not. "Where'd you get the medical supplies?" he asked to turn his thoughts.

"I'm the klutzy triplet. That's why Harmony reminded me that I could find the first aid kit in the closet beneath the stairs."

Morgan willed his heart to slow. *Of all places.* "I'm surprised you went inside. It's a deep, dark cavern with no lightbulb in the socket."

"You're right. Dark as a dungeon, but the first aid kit was on a door shelf inside."

Thank God she hadn't spotted it. When, where, and how could he hide the evidence of a past that Destiny, of all people, would never understand?

"I should think you'd know where to find the first aid kit, with you staying here so often."

"I've never needed a first aid kit. I'm not the klutz, here."

In response, she raised a brow and vindictively dumped the contents of the first aid kit into his lap.

"Ouch. Victim of near castration, here, begging for mercy."

"Victim of snark here, being klutzy."

Make that one for Destiny.

Bless his loose-cannon libido, was she now going to grab each spilled item right out of his eager lap? He might be bruised, but Lazarus had nothing on his neglected manhood.

Morgan looked beyond the yellowed ceiling. *Just hit me with a lightning bolt now and get it over with.*

I know You think I deserve it.

Chapter Four

"HOW did you get here?" Morgan asked, thinking of ways to ship her out.

"As you suspect. I rode in on my broom."

Morgan covered his amusement with a cough.

She stepped back. "From you, that's almost hilarity."

I must have a concussion, then, because there's nothing entertaining about this situation. "It's too late for you to have taken a water taxi, so you must have brought your own boat."

"What's it to you?"

Their relationship had always been strained, not just because she called herself a witch and claimed she saw ghosts while he debunked the paranormal, but because she exuded sex, and he—less than a year before—had turned his back on, well, everything he'd ever been taught, which included his vow of abstinence. But, well, he hadn't considered taking up the sport until he met Destiny.

Frankly, he didn't know what he'd been missing, emotionally or physically, until he got close enough for one of Destiny's sex sparks to land on him and smolder, but *she* didn't know that, yet. And maybe this was a bit too soon for her to find out. He wasn't ready. Damn it—slam it—he'd needed her in Scotland for these two weeks.

As if to prove the strain between them, she hit the gash on his brow with a glob of antibiotic ointment.

"Ouch, damn it. Why did you do that?"

"So it wouldn't get infected."

"The least you could have done was use a soothing motion to apply it." Damn his libido, he needed to get her the Hades out of here, not reel her in.

Destiny raised a brow and formed gentle circles along his cut. To a man like him, this was as good as foreplay.

Their gazes met as she licked her barely parted, berry-ripe lips, and it was all he could do not to lean forward and lick them himself.

Besides cinnamon, she smelled of cherries, chocolate-covered, oozing juice, and in addition to his heart palpitations, he finally understood an expression that had always puzzled him. He *could* eat her up with a spoon.

"Do you need me to rub salve on you anywhere else?" Destiny asked, gazing down at his lap, her look stimulating, flirty, and dangerous as sin.

If she knew how close he was to liftoff, despite his bruising, she'd grab her bone-crushing carts and run.

Heck, maybe he should tell her and let her go, save himself from her seduction and his own humiliation.

She raised a bandage toward his brow.

He ducked—smartest thing he'd done all night. "Oh, that's rich," he said, eyeing the cartoon bandage. "Maim me then use me for graffiti? No thanks. The goop will do."

While she tended to his friendly-cat scratches, he examined her hands, gentle, long-fingered, and tipped with a polka-dot pastel version of every color in the rainbow, including several combinations thereof.

A woman who couldn't make up her mind? Or a woman who wanted it all?

"Anything in your grocery bags that needs refrigerating?" he asked, though maybe if he let her food rot, she'd go home.

"Nope, I stowed the perishables in the fridge before I started my ritual." She made her way back to the kitchen. "As a matter of fact," she called, "I have just the thing for that prune on top of your head."

"My flowerpot prune?"

Looking sheepish, she returned with two bags of frozen vegetables. "Here you go." She looked at the two bags as if weighing her options. "I think butterbeans for your head and Italian pole beans for your crotch."

"I appreciate the pole bean analogy."

She put the bag of butterbeans on his head like a hat. "Icing it will help the swelling go down." Then she placed a bag of beans on his crotch, surprising him so much he could only watch with shock as she arranged it and patted it into place. "Feel better?" she asked.

He would have felt *better* without a bag of pole beans between her hand and his concrete wishbone. "After getting kneed by a grocery cart, concussed by a flowerpot, and caught in my skivvies by a dagger-wielding candle lighter, I couldn't feel more like an ass if I tried. Why were you chanting so loudly, anyway? You woke me up so fast, I thought the place was haunted, until I remembered that I didn't believe in ghosts."

She looked quickly down at her hands, as if hiding something. "I was chanting for peace."

"Boy, did that backfire."

"You have no idea. Is your head and, ah, everything else feeling any better?"

"You bet your flying buttress," he lied. His headache

could put a teamster to bed for a week. His nuts would be black by morning.

"Good," she said, putting the first aid kit back together, raising both fear and elation in him every time she swiped something from his lap, though the frozen vegetables protected him better than an athletic cup.

"Come and help me get my things up the stairs," she said, turning and walking away.

"What things? What stairs? Why?" He followed like a drunk duck, one hand on the icy vegetables between his legs and the other holding his butterbean crown. Sick bastard. Hurt, concussed, and turned on. "Hey, I'm wounded, here."

She faced him with a wrinkled brow, wrinkles he'd like to smooth with his lips.

"You might really have a concussion," she said.

A concussion, an obsession, and a painfully throbbing dick, yet two words formed a rhythm in his head, pounding blood through his veins so fast, everything hurt: *one bed*.

He knew she'd been mad at him since the night of Harmony and King's wedding, when he walked out on their make-out session, presex, but if he'd stayed, she would have been appalled at his fumbling attempt.

He'd stayed away from her since, while he worked toward a level of sexual expertise with one thought in mind: taking Destiny Cartwright to bed and pleasuring her until she passed out. But now, with her so close, he was losing faith in his practiced prowess by the minute, which *could* be due to his injuries or his humiliation or both.

Fact: This was too soon.

Fact: He needed to take a stand on this cohabitation thing and nip it in the bud. He was so hot for her, if she stayed, he'd be screwed, and not in a satisfying way.

No denying the facts. She had to go.

She gave him a worried look. "I'll bring this stuff upstairs, myself, while you sit and rest."

He set his frozen vegetable bags on the stairs. "I think maybe you should grab that other cart and follow me." He grabbed the cart that had accosted him and dragged it through the parlor, the kitchen, and out the back door, heading for her boat.

She chased him, a turn-on in any other situation. "Morgan Jarvis, where the devil are you going with my things?"

"I'm sending you home, you hot little witch pretender."

"You think I'm hot?"

You bet your flying buttress! "No. It was a figure of speech. You're hot like a potato that gets handled too soon. Dangerous hot."

She purred. Purred! "You don't know the half of it."

"Boat. Now. Go."

Chapter Five

HE thought she was hot.

So why was he getting rid of her?

"Plucking patchouli, I'll go. Over my dead body, I'll go!"

Normally Morgan smelled of fresh nutmeg and sandal-wood, as if he'd been working on a spice plantation. Normally, his presence fine-tuned her senses and played her like a priceless violin. He could shiver her with a look, except when she wanted to beat him, like now.

"Dead or alive," he said, stiff-backed and stubborn, continuing down toward the dock. "Go any way you want. Just go."

"If you think I'm hot, then why send me home?"

Still no answer.

Panic claimed her. She had to get a grip. "You're pissing the stinging nettles out of me, Jarvis!"

In his bare feet, Morgan "ouched" his way down the

crushed-shell path; his determination despite his pain would be impressive if this were any other situation.

She caught up, grabbed the cart, and pulled it in the opposite direction.

Morgan dug in with his bare feet. "Son of a witch!"

"Listen, Blue Balls, you want the *B* word not the *W* word for your *itch*. Mix them up again, and I'll show you the plucking difference in a way you'll never forget."

As if the sea was on his side, its wind cut through her like a blade of ice, and she shivered.

"I'm not the one shuddering in my shoes," he said, too cocky for his own good.

"Because you're too stupid to wear shoes."

"Because you woke me from a sound sleep, which will not happen again." Did he really *not* want that to happen, again?

He did want it. She could tell. He did. He so did. "You, Cartwright, are going home."

She crossed her arms. "You, Jarvis, are an ass."

"Positive words, please," he said, mimicking her with a twinkle in his eye that made her want to stuff her fist down his throat.

"I'm *positive* you're an ass."

"Say *apse*, but never *ass*."

The cart fell over on the uneven shell path. "Double bargeboard!"

"What are you talking about?"

"Architecture. You use witch-speak to be positive; I use architecture. It's that or profanity. Take your pick."

"I'll take architecture for a thousand."

He laughed. Morgan Jarvis had just laughed. She felt good about that. Hopeful. "Stop trying to get rid of me. You're shuddering in your bruised body, and I'm the witch who can break you."

"Gritty Spanish stucco, you can't even get the cart away

from me," he said. He tried to lift it, to prove himself right, but his string of curses told her that his bruised body had taken another hit. He put it down fast, his curse having nothing to do with architecture.

They returned to playing tug-of-war, but at least *she* had her shoes on. "I've never wanted to turn a man into a slug, more. I'm staying, I tell you."

"I'm repacking your boat so you can leave. Now. To-night."

Prickles of rage raced up Destiny's arms and legs, weakening her, allowing Morgan custody of the cart. He picked it up, succeeded this time, and ran with it, "ouching" all the way.

Beyond the red haze of fury, Destiny considered her options. *No boat, no way home.*

He reached the boat at the same time she reached its mooring behind him and untied it.

Morgan lowered the cart as the tide stole the boat from beneath it.

Her cart sank like a thug in cement shoes.

Her heart sank, too.

She shoved him for forcing her hand. "My clothes, slam you!"

Unprepared for her assault, he teetered, lost his footing, and fell into an icy October sea.

"Morgan!" she screamed. She hadn't meant to drown him, but when he popped back up, her anger returned. "You deserved that for sinking my clothes."

"Truce. Help me out. It's freezing in here."

"I don't think so. Ice water's good for blue balls and dented brains."

"The sea salt's not helping my cat scratches!"

He fought the tide, up and under, up and under, sputtering and cursing, words she didn't know he had in him, pure man smut. Really turned her on. "Wha'd'ya know," she said. "You got a mouth on you."

He conquered the undertow and swiped water from his face. "And I'm about to get my jollies." He grabbed for her ankle, but she stepped away and stomped on the hand clamping him to the dock.

Destiny shivered. If he ever got out of there, he was gonna kill her. "You owe me a thousand dollars for new clothes," she called, backing toward the house, planning to stake her claim and lock him out, to save her delicate hide.

"Did you spell me into this?" he shouted, swimming against the tide.

"Careful, debunker. You sound suspiciously like you believe I could."

"I wouldn't put anything past you after this stunt."

She stopped. "This *stunt* was yours. Take your own boat back to Salem. I'm locking you out."

"I don't have a boat. I took a water taxi, and it's not due back until Wednesday."

"Too bad you can't stay at the castle or the windmill. They're fumigated and sealed."

"Lookee here." He swung something thick and white, lasso-style, above his head. "Lose the attitude, brat, if you want what I just found."

"My skirt!"

"*Somebody's* things are popping up all around me."

"My clothes!"

"Oh? Are they yours?"

Strangulation came to mind as she watched him ignore them. "Morgan Jarvis, you grab my clothes."

He got his hands on the dock's edge again, and she couldn't stomp on them this time, which annoyed the stinging nettles out of her.

"You want these things floating around me?" he asked. "Here's the deal. Let me in the house, and I'll bring the clothes with me."

"*You* tried to throw me out first." True, she came to get away from him, but that was a moot point.

"I apologize," he said, so close he made her jump, and scream, and step on his hand by accident.

Prepared, he'd pulled away, giving her an evil, teeth-chattering grin, retribution written all over it. He was pulling himself along the edge of the dock, coming closer and closer to her.

"Get my clothes!" she snapped.

"Lock that door, and you can't have them."

"Damn. Witch's promise."

"Is a damn witch's promise as good as a hot witch's promise?"

"Yes, damn it—slam it. My clothes are going out with the tide. Please, Morgan, get them."

"A deal with a sorceress, or so she claims. One of my former teachers just turned over in his grave." Morgan hooted and went fishing for clothes.

At least he was in good spirits, stronger, too, probably because his cracked head and sore balls were numb with cold.

"I'll throw your things on the dock," he said. "Leave them. I'll get them when I get out. No need for both of us to freeze to death. One of us should be able to function."

She went in the lighthouse to get a blanket for him, and when she saw her second cart, she was happy that he hadn't grabbed the cart with her art supplies and portfolio. True, some of her clothes would be lost or ruined, but most would be fine. Salt-stiff, wrinkled, and scratchy as nettle shirts, but nothing a good washing or dry cleaning couldn't fix.

Good Goddess, her magick supplies. They were packed beneath the blanket. She would have lost them, too, if he'd taken the wrong cart. She needed them to find her psychic path and—barn door closed too late—throw her attraction to Morgan in the sea.

She guessed she'd already done that by throwing him in the sea.

Why hadn't he gone to Scotland as planned?

Wait. Why had she gotten a vision of the lighthouse when it was practically Morgan's? He'd been coming here for years. Did the universe want them together? Where were the ghosts she'd seen? She looked for them as she went back outside.

She wanted to ask if he'd ever seen them, but he hated ghost talk, because, according to him, ghosts didn't exist. Then again, neither did witches.

Outside, he was climbing the ladder up the cement foundation that jutted into the sea and kept the land beneath the lighthouse from floating away. The ladder led to the boat shed.

Morgan came out the back door, dripping icicles.

Destiny wrapped her blanket around him and eyed her wet clothes strewn about the dock. "I don't suppose we have a clothesline out here somewhere?"

He went back into the shed and came out with a wheelbarrow, which he filled with her clothes. "There's rope in the lighthouse. I'll string you a clothesline at the base of the light tower steps, between the stair rails and lantern hooks."

"We have to hang them tonight," she said, "so they don't get moldy, or so stiff and wrinkled they'll stand on their own. I'm gonna look and smell like a slimy stinkhorn in those things."

He looked her up and down. "You know my answer to that."

She huffed. "Go home?"

"No. Go naked."

She raised her chin. "Care for another swim?"

He gave her a full-bodied shiver and pushed the wheelbarrow of wet clothes to the house. "I'll leave these in the tower, put on dry clothes, and be back to help you hang them." He stopped in the kitchen while she got the mop from the corner. "Do you know how to make tea?"

She patted the cast-iron monster dominating the kitchen. "On a stove out of *Cabin and Wagon Train Magazine*? Surely you jest."

"I've been using it for years. It's ready for morning coffee. Strike a match, and touch it to the kindling in here." He opened a door and pointed. "This is the firebox." He took an empty, blue enamelware coffeepot from the stove's top shelf where it sat beside an old aluminum coffeepot. A warming shelf, she surmised.

"Fill this with water. Heat it. Pour it in a mug. Find a teabag. Think you can do that?"

Part of her wanted to hit him with the damned pot that he used as a kettle. But the absurdly attracted part of her wanted to warm him, in a very big way.

She yanked it from his icy hand. "Call me Annie freaking Oakley."

Chapter Six

CAST-IRON stoves, salacious thoughts, and Popsicle hunks did not a romantic scene make, Destiny told herself. "You're turning a nice shade of blue," she said as the puddle he stood in got bigger. "In a minute, you'll match your balls. Go change. One cup of hot hemlock tea coming up."

He looked back at her, raised a finger, shook his head, and left the kitchen. She took a pail, mopped his saltwater trail from the kitchen into the tower—amazing place—through the parlor, along the floor *around* the beautiful old Persian rug—he respected antiques—and up the stairs to the top.

No way was she gonna mop in on him naked. She left the mop and bucket so he could take it from there after he was dressed.

Twenty minutes later, his teeth still chattering, Morgan looked pretty dumb in layered sweats, hoods up and tied tight, no two pieces the same color. "You look like a tall, color-blind elf."

Gloves on, teeth chattering worse than ever—a delayed reaction, she supposed—he could barely hold his mug.

"If you catch pneumonia, I'll never forgive you," Destiny said. She bit the inside of her cheek and set the doormat on the floor near the firebox, so he could sit near its warmth. She put another blanket from her cart around him and took off his gloves so he could warm his hands on his mug. Caramello came in and curled up in his lap, yowling as if commiserating with him.

She petted her cat on Morgan's lap. "Night swims in October are a little out of your league, I take it?"

He shivered so hard, he jarred Caramello, and she ended up on the floor, but she climbed right back up. "I think she's trying to keep me warm."

Destiny scratched Caramello behind her ears, her hand knuckle-deep in the silky caramel-and-marshmallow-swirl coat. "Not that you deserve this, Cara," Destiny said. "Scratching Morgan the way you did."

In response, Caramello licked her nose and purred louder.

"Good girl." Destiny poured herself a cup of tea, took out a bag of bakery-fresh chocolate chip cookies, gave Morgan one, and sat on the floor beside him. She sipped her tea and found the silence comfortable between them. When she shivered, he scooted over to share his blankets with her, changing the dynamics and making conversation imperative. "So why *have* you been coming here since you were a kid? You and your parents take separate vacations?"

He shrugged. "If you met them, you'd understand why that would have been preferable. Suffice it to say that I was on my own at an early age. Why did you come here instead of going to Scotland or staying in Salem, for that matter?"

"I had a psychic vision of the lighthouse, okay? I believe that I have to be here to find my psychic path." She elbowed him. "Okay, so you're not big on trust. It doesn't matter. We both wanted to be here, and we are."

Morgan shook his head and unzipped one of his hood-
ies. "We both wanted to be *alone*, and we're not, at least
until the water taxi comes on Wednesday."

She offered him another cookie. "I'm here for two
weeks. Are you thinking you'll leave on that taxi? Why
Wednesday?"

"You're gonna think this is lame, because in a way it is,
but I call my parents every Wednesday afternoon. Since
Paxton Island still doesn't have phone lines or cell phone
access, I go into Salem to call. My parents and I don't get
along, but they're old and they're mine, so I check on
them."

"You don't get along, but you call?"

He shrugged. "You only get one set of parents."

"I wouldn't know. I never had a set."

Morgan gazed earnestly into her eyes. "I'm sorry."

Something shifted in the time-space continuum. "Why?
It's not your fault about my parents."

"No. I'm sorry I tried to make you leave. You're right, I
have a problem with trust. But around you, it's myself I
don't trust." As if he'd said too much, he set down his mug,
stood, and pulled a wad of rope from his jacket pocket.
"Come on, let's get your clothes hung so we can shut the
lights on the longest day in Paxton Lighthouse history."

They walked through the same small connecting room
from the house to the tower that Destiny had mopped.
Morgan called the connecting room the keeper's room.
The wide base of the tower made it possible to hang
clotheslines in a kind of spiderweb effect, from the stair
rails to the lantern hooks and back again, all around.

Without old-fashioned clothespins, Destiny draped her
wet things over the ropes. Morgan watched for a minute
and pitched in. "Thanks," she said.

"It's the least I can do." He shrugged. "I threw them in."

"I untied the boat."

"You what!"

"Stop yelling! I didn't want to go. No boat, no go."

He got a rather incredulous look on his face. "You *wanted* to stay here with me?"

"Well, I wanted to stay *here*. We can be alone with our thoughts, do our own thing, take separate walks, and eat our own food. Sure, we'll be forced to talk, sometimes."

"Right. Sometimes." He turned back to her wet things. "You brought enough clothes for a month."

"Who are you to talk? You're *wearing* enough clothes for a month. Half of what I brought is gone. Good thing I doubled up."

"I'm sorry. I thought I was putting them in the boat, not the ocean. You know that, right?"

"I guess."

"Thanks for the high opinion." Morgan went to hang clothes on the opposite side of the tower's circular stairs.

Hanging her salty underwear, she caught movement out of the corner of her eye: the ghosts sitting on the fifth stair up, watching her.

Centennial Man nodded.

"I saw your picture in the house," Destiny said. "You were the lighthouse keeper, weren't you? Your uniform reminds me of a train conductor's, especially the hat."

"I was the last keeper," he said. "The woman beside me in the picture is my wife, Ida. She's buried here on the island, but I'm not."

"Is that why you're still here?"

"I *did want* to be buried with her, but I think there might be something more to my being here. I'm guessing the angel knows, but she's not talking. Not to me, anyway."

Destiny looked from the keeper to the child. "Is this your little girl?"

"I never had children," he said with a heavy sadness. "My name's Horace."

"And my name is Meggie," the little girl said. "I'm here with my brother. He needs to remember."

"Hello, Meggie, I'm Destiny. Is Horace your brother, then?"

Meggie denied that with a shake of her head, pigtails swinging.

"Destiny?" Morgan called. "What did you say? I can barely hear you from here." He ducked under a clothesline and caught a pair of her panties in the face. "Yellow," he said, straightening them. "Your underwear seems to call my name."

Meggie giggled, but Destiny could tell that Morgan hadn't heard. The way the child looked at Morgan, with that half smile, one side up, like his, really made Destiny wonder. She turned to her unexpected housemate. "You've been staying here on and off since you were sixteen, and you never met one ghost?"

He raised his hands and let them fall to his sides. "Do you and your sisters do *nothing* but chase ghosts?"

"We don't chase them; they find us. Besides, these ghosts aren't negative like the ones at Paxton castle were."

"These? You think there are ghosts here?" He scratched his earlobe. "You ever think of writing for the Sci Fi Channel?"

"These ghosts are friendly. Meggie is only a child."

"Meggie?" Morgan paled, a tic suddenly pulsing in his cheek. He put distance between them as if by instinct. "Who told you?"

"Who *could* have told me?" She had no idea what they were talking about, but drawing him out might help.

He fisted his hands and considered her question. "No one. No one knows," he said, almost to himself.

"There you go. Maybe . . . I'm psychic. Maybe I *can* see ghosts." Destiny hated how hearing Meggie's name had about stabbed Morgan in the heart.

"What?" Morgan asked. "Do I talk in my sleep? You came upstairs before your ritual, didn't you?"

"If that's what you prefer to believe, sure," Destiny said.

"You were talking in your sleep. You said *Meggie* and *schnoodle*."

Morgan looked sharply up at her, but he failed to comment on her perception.

She'd bet that Meggie had been the child who wanted the schnoodle. Meggie, the ghost child, watched the two of them now, her anguish mirroring Morgan's. Soul-deep pain. Longing. A lifetime's worth.

She wouldn't push for more answers. She couldn't hurt either of them by trying, not tonight. "I think we're done here," Destiny said, wiping her wet hands on her jeans.

Morgan gave a clipped nod, mouth grim. "I've had enough melodrama for one night."

Destiny watched the angel close Meggie in the grotto of her embrace.

Chapter Seven

NOBODY had spoken Meggie's name in years, because that's what his parents wanted—which his sister didn't deserve. And now, he was trapped with a beguiler claiming Megs was here. He'd managed to bury his emotions over the years, and now this soul-deep grief had risen to the surface.

Destiny's hypothetical child ghost couldn't possibly be his sister.

Morgan banned the thought and followed Destiny up the stairs, a warning playing in his mind, her fine ass at eye level swaying to a different tune.

With each step came a scary-thrilling thought: *One bed. One bed. One bed.* The slow-climbing cadence made him think of a doomed prisoner on his way to the electric chair. Or, in this case, the electric bed.

Ghosts, he could run from. They didn't exist.

Emotions, he could run from. Better not to let them take over.

Doomed, he could live with; he had for years.

But need, the simple human need to touch someone with love. He wanted—God, he wanted. Not only to take Destiny to bed, he wanted her to teach him to play. If he could sip at the well of her adventurous spirit, he might find a blade sharp enough to sever the unnamed weight threatening to swamp his life.

How could he be so fascinated by one of a three-pack? Identical triplets. Destiny looked exactly like Harmony and Storm, and yet Destiny, the mysterious yet audacious triplet, had perfected the art of grabbing life by the balloon strings and sailing that helium rainbow to the clouds. For Destiny, he yearned. With her, he wanted to take to the clouds and soar as well.

Destiny could be annoyingly feisty and cheerful, though she wasn't quite as self-confident as he'd once suspected. He'd glimpsed vulnerability in her tonight when she'd crossed her arms and backed away from the dock.

He'd recognized her search for a life path in the way that she seemed to uselessly grasp, as if for purpose. He recognized it, because he owned its twin—poor word choice, but apt.

Perhaps, somehow, they could each discover their own purpose, entwine them, and become manna to each other . . . like his mother might accept him and his decision to become an architect, and stop nagging.

And pigs might fly, and *not* crap all over him.

It irked him to be attuned to Destiny.

Destiny. Fate. Karma. Providence—though certainly not divine. By whatever name, he'd recognized her the first time he saw her as somehow fitting him, like a piece of his life puzzle. Big puzzle. Huge. Useless. Half his pieces tossed in the trash.

Two seconds after meeting Destiny, their first meeting, they'd sized each other up, circled with palpable mistrust, and scoffed when the other spoke, which might have been attraction, or the fear of it. Story of his life.

Had it been attraction, dislike, or jealousy? He'd intercepted Destiny's triplet connection, recognized and envied it with a rage of regret, because he'd lost its like, his twin connection, when Meggie passed.

He'd mocked Aiden and King for correctly picking Harmony and Storm from the triplet lineup, but damned if he didn't think he could spot Destiny as his in the clone line now.

But love connected Aiden and King with Destiny's sisters, married love—not an option for him. Who would have him anyway?

Not Destiny.

He could admit his connection to her. Lust. The kind a man got from being parched in the desert his whole life. Down-and-dirty lust that could only be cured with down-and-dirty sex. Temporary fix. Good enough.

Sex for fun. He wondered if she might be up for it.

Not a good time to ask with a bed staring them both down.

"I can sleep here," she said, indicating the bed in the first bedroom they'd come to. Too much to hope, he supposed, that his prayers had been answered.

She ran a loving hand over the ornate brass headboard. "I love old brass beds."

"You want this bed?"

"Sure. It's gorgeous." She tested the mattress by pushing on it, unknowingly wiggling her ass his way again. "Nice and soft."

"Looks firm to me. Oh, you mean the mattress. Okay by me. Do you sleep on the right or the left? Or we could share the middle."

"Never mind, smut brain, I'll pick another, since I take it this one is yours?"

Morgan left her cart where it stood and followed Destiny in silence from room to room, some rooms with chairs or tables, one that was book-lined, one he'd made into a studio for his drawing table and architectural supplies.

She stopped in the doorway of the last bedroom. "Shriveling scrying balls! Only one bed? Harmony said the place was furnished."

He didn't understand her exclamation, but he didn't think he'd like his balls shriveled, whatever she named them.

"And not a sofa in the place," he added, crossing his arms so he could cross his legs, because he'd already come to the conclusion she was working her way up to: one bed, two people.

She lost the starch in her stance. "Sleeping bag?" she asked with hope, her voice so soft, she was giving him another rare peek at her vulnerable side, which derailed his train of thought and allowed him to stand straighter.

"Sorry." Morgan let her lead the way back to his room.

Since the starch returned to her spine on the way, he wondered what ploy he was in for. She looked at the bed, at him, claimed the bed by planting her fine ass on it, instead of him—he should be so lucky—and folded her arms. "Bummer," she said. "You're not gonna be very comfortable on the floor."

He straightened, caught by surprise. "I beg your pardon?"

"You're a gentleman, so you will, of course, sleep on the parlor rug. That's got to be the softest—"

"It's threadbare. This rug is at least newer and thicker, and you're not as heavy as me, so you won't feel the hard—"

"It's practically *beneath* the bed," she said, examining it, "except for a body-sized scrap. I most certainly will not like it, because I'm not sleeping on it. I'll take the bed, because I know a gentleman like you would insist, thank you very much. You could sleep on the floor. In one of the other bedrooms, because you're a man and I'm a woman?"

His body sure in blood-pumping Hades knew that; it was trying to sit up and beg. "I'm sleeping in *this* room," Morgan said. "It's the coolest in the summer and the warmest in winter. In the autumn, like now, it's nothing short of spectacular. For that reason, I took that bed apart and moved it here, from a hot and stale front bedroom, piece by piece, thirteen years ago. The ocean may be cold at night—to which I can personally attest—but we're having a great Indian summer, and with the daytime heat still heavy in the air, the breeze in here is unmatched."

He realized he was rambling, but he was also ticked and getting warm, finally, and *she* might be growing a conscience, judging by the way she nibbled the side of a polka-dot thumbnail.

He removed a layer of sweats, almost embarrassed to have another layer beneath them.

"Okay, you can stay in this room," she said with less of an edge, "but this rug doesn't look half as comfortable as the one in the parlor."

His frustration had done nothing but rise enough to shoot off the charts since she woke him and beat the crap out of him, so at this point, anger seemed a wasted effort. "If we listen, I think we can hear them snickering," he said.

She leaned forward. "Who?"

"King and Harmony in Scotland. They planned this."

"The rats! It would serve them right if we got along."

His head came up, as did his suspicion.

She shrugged. "Not that it's possible."

"Right." Of course, right. "Did your sister tell you to bring your own bedding, at least? Because that's mine on the bed."

"Yes, she did, but she didn't say to bring a bed, the brat. Fortunately for both of us, my bedding's right here in the cart that didn't drown." Destiny pulled out her blankets and sheets and handed them to him.

"You brought three blankets?" he asked. "Counting the one I soaked when you put it over my shoulders. Did I say thanks?"

She nodded. "I was planning peaceful picnics with my paintings and my thoughts. One blanket for the sand—"

"You planned to be a sand-witch?"

She raised a disgusted brow and unbuttoned her jeans, while the devil in his sweats stood to cheer. "One blanket for grassy picnics, and one to sleep beneath. With no washer, three made sense." She slipped her jeans down her legs to reveal a pair of bikini panties as sea green as her tee. Yawning, she climbed into the center of *his* double bed.

As she did, he read, When Hell Freezes Over, printed across her green silk ass. And didn't he know it.

"Hell is not a positive word," he said. "Your rules."

"It is when it makes my point."

"How convenient." It sure was making his point, and he meant that in a purely sexual way. His mouth went dry, and his palms began to sweat. For a minute, he couldn't believe he was looking at his fantasy in the flesh. He blinked to erase the hallucination or wake up, but Destiny remained curled up right there in her underwear before his greedy eyes. "Look who's sleeping in my bed."

"Gentlemen prefer witches," she said with an ass wiggle, the stripped tease.

Morgan looked beyond the ceiling toward the celestial abode of his former boss. *Good one, taunting me with my own wicked fantasies, but I'm still not going back.*

He yearned, he drooled, and he ached to climb in with her, if only she'd let him practice his newfound skills. He supposed he could ask. But how? *I have a brass boner that likes your ass? I have a loner boner; won't you play with it? Would you care to taste my T(rex)bone? Want a little steak sauce with that?*

I can make you scream with pleasure. Now that's the

kind of thing men said—men who lost their virginity in fifth grade and never finished school.

Talk about being between a rock and a hard-on.

She lifted her head. "Aren't you going to get ready for bed?"

"Aren't you going to brush your teeth?"

"Brushed before I left home. Haven't eaten a thing. Not letting you claim the bed while I brush again." She opened an eye and looked over her shoulder at him. "Are you going to stand there watching me all night?"

He'd probably like that. For a man like him, it'd be like foreplay.

Morgan didn't know where else to look, or what else to do—literally—so he turned to action. The brass bed weighed a ton in pieces, so there was no moving it to give him more rug, but enough of it stuck out from beneath the bed to give him a bit of padding. He folded two blankets, one atop the other, to add to his "mattress," then he used one of her sheets as a blanket to keep his loose-cannon dick under wraps.

It didn't take a minute to realize this was like sleeping on a slab of concrete. The floor creaked when he moved.

His bed creaked when she moved, and every time it did, he heard it say, "Dumb ass."

He'd never noticed the squeaky springs, and he'd certainly never seen their underbelly in moonlight. Hadn't wanted to, though he might have agreed to it, if it meant getting Destiny in the sack. But he preferred to be in there with her.

"Dumb ass. Dumb ass. Dumb ass." He was ashamed of himself for being mocked by his own bed and for taking it lying down to boot. How much torture would he put up with?

"Light?" she asked.

Damn—slam! He raised his chin so he could see the

switch, far away, three feet above him, and upside down. "You can reach it. It's on your left."

As he watched, she slapped the wall behind her a few times, putting so much energy into it—not!—she didn't so much as jiggle a bedspring, and still he felt like a dumb ass.

"Can't find it," she said, yawning again.

From day one, she had a way of inflicting a unique form of torture on him, like wood slivers beneath his fingernails. Torture Destiny style, times ten. Nobody had ever managed to piss him off quite so thoroughly and seductively. Maybe there was something to her claim to magic.

Morgan got up to turn off the light but made the mistake of looking down at her; silver star earrings, butterfly pendant between her breasts, seahorse cuff bracelet on her right wrist, tiny butterfly tattoo on her left ankle. A goddess. A paradox. A pain in the ass!

He yanked one of his pillows out from beneath her head.

"Hey!" She frowned at him over her shoulder. "You know, you've got kind of a red haze overwhelming your aura. You should calm down."

"That's it! Don't look now, but hell *is* freezing over." He slapped her on the ass a good one. "Move over, brat."

Chapter Eight

"YOU'RE a bully," she said.

"I'm a man, and this is my bed. Move that sassy ass, or I'll move it for you." Spanking that ass sounded pretty good, too. Did that make him a sicko?

Obviously, sharing the bed didn't appeal. The pillow that smacked him in the head was his first clue. The goddess of Destiny standing on his bed raising her fist was his second.

She tried for a right hook, but he caught her around the waist and threw her over his shoulder. "I've been battered enough for one night, thank you very much." He carried her from room to room, upstairs and down, occasionally finding it necessary to keep her ass in place. He didn't mind a bit. "Stop me when you see a floor that looks comfortable," he said, "because *I'm* sleeping in my bed. Now, you can sleep there with me, Wonderbrat, but you can't sleep there alone."

She wiggled in his arms. "You son of a sea cock! You just want to have it all your way."

"You bet your flying buttress. My mother would have a heart attack, by the way, if she heard a woman say *cock*, but mine is quite happy, thank you, because you're getting me hot with all that wiggling."

She stilled.

"Is cock a positive word?" he asked, because she seemed taken by this conversation.

"I like cocks," she said. "Generally speaking, yes. Cocks are positive."

He cleared his throat. "I can't use the plural, but I am fond of my own."

"I can't say, since I haven't seen yours yet."

Yet? His knees about buckled. "I'll introduce you some-time."

"We'll see."

At least that wasn't a firm no. With her still over his shoulder, and her ass in his peripheral vision, they stood in the keeper's room, surrounded by shelves of oil lanterns, measuring cups, pitchers, a box marked Wicks, two fun-nels, three cans of kerosene, and a fire bucket. "Does this room suit you?"

"Spell you!"

"Aw, use the *F* word, I'll take you up on it, and neither of us will care where we sleep."

She gasped. "I never use the *F* word. Say *pluck* if you must, and only in an emergency."

"Did I say that out loud? Sorry, you bring out the beast in me." Morgan stood the stunner on the floor for the sake of his sanity.

She straightened her Licensed to Thrill bare-midriff T-shirt and When Hell Freezes Over panties, the vast ex-panse of curvaceous skin between them a fine, bronze tan.

"You're acting like a frustrated bear," she said, recall-ing his attention.

A frustrated male bear, he agreed mentally, because he needed to get laid.

"I am not sleeping on *any* floor," she said, swinging her hair for emphasis.

"Neither am I. Glad that's settled." He took her by the hand and tugged her back to *their* bedroom. "What's the difference between me three feet away or one foot away?"

"Six inches," she said.

He gave her a double take. "You must have failed math."

She smirked. "You must have failed sex ed."

"Ah, now I get your drift, Kismet. You figure if I face you from a foot away, we'll be six inches apart?"

"Right. This isn't a king, you know."

"Nor a queen, and *neither* are you. You've underestimated my inches, by the way, but what say we keep my impressive manly length *safe* from your womanly wiles and hang a curtain between us?"

"*It Happened One Night* style? You're kidding?"

"Get over it. Sure we'd be stuck in the same bed, but sleeping separately, more or less. I'd do my best, but I am a man."

"Your point?"

"Exactly."

She slithered close enough for her bare midriff to touch him, and he sure wished he'd taken his shirt off. She ran a hand around his earlobe. "You think I'll turn you on?"

"Of course I don't *think*. I *know* you will. You already have. I hardly expect to sleep for the discomfort, but at least my back won't be broken, too."

"Try to scale our 'wall of Jericho,' and your cock might be."

"Warning taken. Cock shrinking in complete understanding."

He wished she didn't have such a hopeful glint in her eyes. "Is there any rope left in the house after our giant spiderweb clothesline?" she asked.

"Let's go see. After you," he said, him down to his last

pair of sweats, and her in her skivvies. Why were they never both in their skivvies at the same time? He flipped on the light at the bottom of the stairs simply to improve the view of her going down.

Already, he'd had enough of being a gentleman.

Gentlemen slept on floors. Gentlemen never got laid.

In the closet beneath the stairs, he found more rope.

"Holy monkshood," she said. "I guess you have been here a lot, if you can find anything in that black hole."

"Monkshood?" he asked, stopping, so she plowed into him. He turned to steady her. "What does that mean?"

"It's an herb that witches used years ago to make flying ointments, in the way that marijuana makes you fly. I hear that spilling blood on monkshood flowers makes war magick, but I'd never do that."

"More than I needed to know," he said, but the unvarnished reminder of her witchy delusions helped him recover his equilibrium. He didn't know which was more disturbing, the truth about the magickal herb, or his fear that she might suspect his past. Not that he'd been a monk . . . precisely.

After they fastened the rope to the bed's footboard and headboard, taut and straight, she helped him throw one of her blankets over it to form a wall between them.

She stood on the bed and looked over it at him. "It happened one witch," she said.

"Is that an invitation or a promise?"

"It was an observation. The walls of Jericho stay up, thank you very much."

A few minutes later, Morgan settled in the bed like a stiff in a casket, *stiff* being the operative word. Soon enough, he discovered that bed-sharing involved heat, hundreds of degrees higher than normal. Since said heat was not about to be translated into sex—when had it ever?—he got up to shed the rest of his clothes, down to his navy boxers. He also opened the second window.

Destiny's giggle at the sound of his actions turned him hot with embarrassment, until she began to chant.

> *"Not that he stares at my ass,*
> *Or drools o'er my boobs,*
> *No caress 'neath a breast.*
> *Lip-locking or Frenching.*
>
> *"Beneath curtain fencing,*
> He *probably won't duck.*
> *That's as may be,*
> *But I wish myself luck."*

Morgan raised himself on an elbow, confused yet captivated. She needed luck? For what? Resisting him? She would call that a spell, he knew from past experience with her and her sisters, but it hadn't sounded so much magical as practical.

With her words, the seductress had given nothing—or everything—away. He couldn't believe she *hadn't* caught him drooling or staring. And though he'd made a couple of cocky admissions, she must have taken them as jokes.

Pluck him; he could *still* hide his feelings like a pro. The ability to hide his struggle between his faith and his humanity probably stemmed from growing up with a mother who made Hitler look like a wuss.

He wished there was something he could say right now, but Destiny would be better off assuming that he didn't want to pin her to the bed and pluck her senseless.

Despite the size of Celibate Charlie, and after all the books he'd read about pleasing a woman, he didn't think he was ready for a hands-on—scratch that, he'd mastered the hands on. It was the man-on-woman type exercise that he wasn't ready for. Ah, who was he kidding? He was so ready, the imagery alone had Charlie doing stretches to prepare for the big event.

Morgan lay carefully back against his pillows and didn't move a muscle . . . that he could control.

An hour later, the bed hadn't creaked once. Destiny had either fallen asleep, or she lay as wide-awake as him. Unmoving.

Despite her final words, he felt the need to find some common ground between them. He cleared his throat. "I did know a little girl named Meggie once."

The bed creaked, a sign of interest, because she'd probably turned his way. "Was Meggie a relative?"

Her words had been so charming, he'd forgotten she was psychic. Damn. "What makes you think that?"

"Her smile," Destiny said, "reminds me of yours."

"I don't smile." Morgan turned to face away from her, despite the walls of Jericho. "I suppose you think you know?"

A big creak, a full-body shift. Deep interest. "What am I supposed to know?" she all but whispered.

"That I had a sister named Meggie."

"Oh, Morgan. I didn't know. Honestly. She died so young. I'm sorry."

Morgan shifted, uncomfortable in his own skin, never mind the bed. "My family fell apart," he said.

"If it's any consolation, Meggie looked at you with a great deal of love."

He cleared his throat again. "I almost wish I believed you saw her."

"Meggie looks about twelve years old," Destiny said. "Her long, burnished blonde hair is the same streaked shade as yours. She's wearing a red plaid jumper that looks like it might have been a school uniform. The bows on her braids are the same plaid as her jumper."

Grief rushed Morgan, hit him in the solar plexus. She had described Meggie's last school picture to the hair ribbons. He fisted his hands, swallowed, and rubbed his chest. "Get the hell out of my head."

Chapter Nine

HIM telling her to get the hell out of his head wasn't exactly a positive statement, but Destiny didn't think this was the time to say so. Somewhat heartsore as a result of his abrupt dismissal, Destiny allowed that if she lost one of her sisters, she might not be half as nice.

"I'm not in your head," she said, softening her tone, "but Meggie's *here* for a reason, or she wouldn't have shown herself to me.

"She said she needs her brother to remember, and at first, I thought she was talking about Horace."

"Horace?" Morgan asked, grasping at the subject change like a lifeline, though she couldn't see him beyond the curtain. "Another ghost? Is he as young as Meggie?"

"No, he's about my age, handsome, with a sense of humor, and a thick head of dark hair. Virile," she added, to tick Morgan off and replace sorrow with ire, sure she could hear him gritting his teeth. Jealousy. Good sign.

"What the Hades is this Horace guy doing here?"

"He was the last lighthouse keeper, and he looks yummers in that uniform, I'll tell you, but he doesn't know why he's here."

The bed creaking and Morgan mumbling about plucking lighthouse keepers were the last sounds Destiny remembered. She woke to find Morgan doing push-ups on the floor, on her side of the bed, Caramello riding his back, kitty paws around his neck. She wished she'd brought a camera.

Destiny bit the inside of her lip, she was so charmed. "Good morning," she said. "You're working up quite a sweat."

"You snore," he snapped. "So does your cat. And what's with the noises you make while you sleep?"

"What noises? My—no man has ever complained about the noises I make in my sleep." She'd nearly said her sisters didn't, but in a perverse way, she liked baiting him.

He stopped flexing his muscles and gave her a nasty look. So he did care where she slept and with whom? An interesting sign from a man she'd been sparring with and lusting after from day one. A man who'd been running since day one.

"You whimper and you sigh," he said, "like you're having great sex—and your cat slept on my chest, braying like a drunk donkey."

Destiny sat up, shook her head, and ran her hands through her hair, sure she had a bad case of bed head. "I see you're a morning person." She got up and found one of his pajama tops to use in lieu of a robe.

"Your hair's a mess," he said, "but it's never looked so beautiful." He stood wiping the perspiration off his face and chest with a towel he'd thrown over the foot of the bed. She wished she had the balls to push him back on the bed and make him sweat some more.

She stretched, because she liked the way he watched her, as if he was interested, exactly where she wanted him.

"I noticed that the downstairs bathroom has a gorgeous old tub but no shower. Is there a shower up here?"

"If you want a shower, there's one out back. I built two additions in the spring. One for the shower. One for the hot water heater. But I haven't connected the heater to any of the inside plumbing, yet."

"So, *outside*, out back?"

The twinkle in his eyes turned her knees to jelly. "Yes outside. It's in that wooden cubicle between the back door and the tower."

"Well, then, I guess I'm off to the shower."

"Don't use *all* the hot water. I'm next."

It was the most luxurious shower she'd ever taken, given its huge, wide showerhead with thick pellets of hot, soft water sluicing over her chilled body. The last time she'd felt this decadent outside, she'd been walking naked into the sea—sky clad—as she and her sisters prepped for a ritual cleansing with King, Aiden, and Morgan looking on.

Still, this felt more so, because she was here at the lighthouse *alone* with Morgan. She didn't dare look toward the upstairs window, in case he was there, because she wouldn't want him to step back too soon.

She shivered at the erotic image of what she wished watching her might do to him.

With water this soft, her hair would fall into its naturally curly pageboy, but who cared? Nobody would see her except Morgan, and the truth was, he probably wouldn't care if she wore a bag over her head.

She finally looked up, but Morgan wasn't watching, more's the pity. Sometimes. She used to wonder if he had a sexual bone in his body, but he'd actually referred to the possibility yesterday, which gave her hope.

Well, actually, she knew he had one sexual bone in his body. She'd noticed it when she woke up, before he stopped doing push-ups and turned away from her to reveal his gorgeous back, almost as amazing as his golden chest and perfect pecs. But every man got a morning boner. She'd like to see him with an afternoon boner. Or one that popped up just because *she* walked into the room.

When she went back upstairs, Morgan went down to the shower, and as soon as she heard the kitchen door slam, she went looking for the window that overlooked the shower.

She stood as far back as she could to watch him without him seeing her. Naughty thing. Oh my. She'd slept, literally—un-freaking-fortunately—with a hunky god with a bod to die for. Small waist with a line of golden hair arrowing from his belly button to one mighty fine specimen of bone hood. She put her hand over her mouth. His balls *were* black and blue. She'd think they must hurt, except that he washed his boner with vigor, which made her doubt his suffering, though he looked as if he suffered.

Destiny fanned herself, she got so hot, but he stopped, damn it, slam it, before fulfilling her fantasy, and when he turned his back on her, both arms on the wall, head beneath the shower, and she saw his tight butt, she squeaked.

He turned around and looked up.

She took a quick step back.

She'd never seen such a perfectly beautiful man butt. She hadn't expected to see a butt cheek tattoo, either. Hidden depths there. Slam it, he moved. Whoa, a tattoo on his thigh as well, a larger one, more colorful, though Destiny couldn't make out either design.

He turned off the water.

What? He was done? Sweet shivering man flesh, that was fast. She hadn't started to dress yet. "Yikes!" Destiny sprinted to the bedroom and threw on her clothes so fast, she got whiplash from setting a new record.

Of course, skipping her underwear helped.

By the time she pulled down her red In Your Dreams tee, her face was so warm, she opened the bedroom window and stuck her head out to cool off, so he wouldn't see the evidence of her peeping tomfoolery coloring her cheeks.

"What the Hades are you doing?" he asked.

"Drying my hair," she called back, tossing her hair in the fresh sea breeze.

"Nice view," he said.

"You're right. Great view of the ocean from here."

"I meant the view from here."

"Huh?" She pulled her head back in so fast, she smacked it on the window sash. "Ouch." She rubbed her sore head. "My backside? *You* admired my backside?"

"You're pleased, though you're trying not to show it," he said. "You don't mind if I ogle you? Scratch that. You *like* that I ogle you." His perception caught her unaware and radiated through her in a series of ripples that turned to delicious shivers in sensitive and unexpected places.

"Nice shirt," he said. "And it's correct. You did make an appearance in my dreams last night."

They stood staring, eating each other up with their gazes, until Morgan grabbed his sneakers. "I dreamed that you were trying to drown me. I'm going for a run. Don't wait up."

"Wait up? It's six in the morning, three freaking hours after we went to bed. I should go back to sleep is what I should do."

"Go for it."

She'd rather have him in the bed beside her, but he wasn't ready to hear that. What was with him? One minute he's interested, the next, not?

When she got downstairs, Horace, the lighthouse keeper, stood leaning against the front door, arms crossed, as if waiting for her.

"I'm going for a walk," she said. "Do you want to join me? I'd love to ask you some questions."

"Your wish is my command."

"Honestly?"

"No. I'm a ghost. I can move small objects with my mind and satisfy you with a conversation. That's it."

He couldn't be flirting. Could he? She raised a brow, opened the door, but he insisted she precede him. A gentleman ghost.

"You've got more spirit, for a spirit, than the flesh-and-blood man I'm living with." They set off through the tall marsh grasses, Horace leading the way.

"You're underestimating him," Horace said. "He's been through the fires of hell and back, but that's not my story to tell. It's his. As a man, he's very much aware of you, on both the spiritual and physical planes."

"You're joking. He doesn't know I'm alive." Though he had noticed her backside and mentioned her role in his dreams, though they might have been nightmares for all he'd explained.

"He most certainly does. I'm a man. I know these things. I can't tell you anything about him, but I can tell you about the lighthouse."

Meggie and her angel appeared beside them, flitting and flirting butterflies seeming to follow in Meggie's wake. "I can tell you what Morgan *likes*," she said.

"You're Morgan's sister?"

Meggie nodded.

"Who's your angel?"

"I named her Buffy," she said. "She's been with me my whole life and death. You can talk to her, but she doesn't say much more than, 'Be not afraid.' She mostly only talks to me and Morgan."

"Morgan talks to her?"

"Not anymore. He's in hiding."

Destiny started a bouquet by picking bits of dry summer grasses and blooming fall wildflowers as they walked. "Morgan's hiding from his guardian angel?" she asked as they cut through a wildflower field, Meggie gathering more butterfly followers.

The little girl smiled, again like Morgan, one side up. A smile Destiny had at first thought mocking and later, self-deprecating. "Morgan's hiding inside himself," Meggie said. "He can't move on with his life until he makes peace with his past, accepts his fate, and remembers who he is."

Destiny picked a straw flower and twirled it between her fingers. "You know, your brother taking part in the whole angel/ghost thing doesn't make much sense, given the fact that he's a paranormal debunker."

"That's what he's hiding behind, his debunking. That's why you're here. He needs you, Destiny."

Destiny shivered and stopped walking. Her psychic purpose couldn't be to help Morgan find himself. Could it? "If that's my job, why are you here?"

"I can tell you what Morgan likes, because if you know, it'll be easier for you to get through to him, but I can't tell you anything about your future."

"Funny," Destiny said. "I can't tell you anything about *your* future, either."

Meggie's eyes twinkled. "Mine's a done deal, wouldn't you say?"

Right. Ghosts had no future. A familiar warmth climbed Destiny's cheeks. "Unless—do you believe in reincarnation?"

Meggie directed her expression inward with a cat-who-lapped-the-cream expression. "One can only hope."

Horace resettled his cap and nodded. "I could do with another chance, myself. I'd like a big family next time around."

"Do either of you know why you're still here at the lighthouse?"

"To guide a ship through the fog?" Horace guessed.

"Like always? I don't know, but Meggie and I, we've been here a long time, and this is the most fun we've had. Right, Meggie?"

Morgan's sister skipped faster. "Right!"

Destiny found it suddenly difficult to swallow, imagining what Morgan must have suffered at his little sister's death. "Okay, Meggie. Tell me what your brother likes, because leading him to what he likes will probably bring him back to the time he's trying to forget, right?"

Meggie looked up at her angel, and the angel's love for the child warmed the air, overflowed, and touched Destiny: utterly powerful, beautiful, and, surprisingly, given the fact that Meggie was dead, life-giving.

Chapter Ten

SWEATY from his run, Morgan took another shower and changed into a fresh chamois shirt, unbuttoned, and jeans, buttoned for his own safety. From a front upstairs window, he watched Destiny hiking back toward the lighthouse carrying a bouquet of wildflowers, bittersweet, and oak sprigs, and trailing butterflies for a good tenth of a mile behind her, her wide-brimmed red hat flopping in the breeze.

Though walking alone, she spoke with animation to, well, several nobodies, judging by the movement of her head from side to side as she addressed the shadows. A kook with invisible friends, though her mention of Meggie last night had carried more coincidence than he cared for.

He met Destiny in the kitchen where she set the live flowers into an inch of water in the copper sink, and the dry ones on the cabinet beside it. Then she filled a bowl with

Lucky Charms, poured milk over them, and took her break-fast out to the dock to eat while she dangled her feet in the water.

He ate Wheat Chex over the blue-cotton-skirted sink and watched Destiny out the window. "Sick bastard," he said, washing the bowl. Why didn't he just go out there and sit beside her like he wanted to?

He went up to the room where he'd set up his drafting table and architectural supplies, because it pulled in the best natural light, and got to work on his design for the lighthouse.

He noticed a while later, when he got up for an apple and a glass of milk, that Destiny had set up her easel out-side. He went out to take a peek at her work, surprised at the scope of her talent.

"What?" she asked.

He shrugged. "You're looking at a gorgeous seascape, but you're painting a purple house with a blue It's a Boy flag out front.

"Oh, I don't paint what's in front of me. I paint what I see in my mind's eye."

"That's scary."

"No, we had a grandmother who painted Paxton Castle in great detail from the Salem dock, where she could never have seen the detail. That painting helped bring my sisters and me here to the island in the first place."

"Double scary."

"The baby boy in this house is a big deal. I sense a life-time dream come true and lots of celebrating."

When a big, fat raindrop hit her painting, Morgan helped her gather her things and led her up to the room where he worked on his art, his architecture.

"I won't bother you," she said. "I need silence to work, too."

He didn't like working with anyone else in the room, so

why had he brought her here? He said nothing and helped her set up by the second window. For the rest of the morning and into the afternoon, they worked in silence, while his awe of her talent grew, along with intimacy and a palpable sexual awareness, on his part at least.

At suppertime, she began to chop vegetables and bread chicken, while he opened a can of beans. "Is that what you're going to eat?" she asked.

"I eat a lot of beans, here," he said. "No problem. I'll go upstairs so you can have your own space."

"Oh for heaven's sake. I'll cook for both of us. I like to cook. My sisters and I practically raised each other, so we've been cooking forever. Just find some kind of dinner table, okay?"

"There's nothing in this house that resembles a kitchen table. Never has been."

She took her pots off the monster stove's fire and went into the parlor. "There's a table. Bring the one we used last night."

"That skinny side table?"

"Bring it."

When he got it there, he was surprised to see Destiny get beneath it. "Morgan hold up the two wings, while I unhook and swing out the legs." She worked some kind of miracle down there, stood, and wiped her hands on her jeans. "You can let the table rest on the legs now. There you go. It's a gateleg table, now our dinner table. Two straight parlor chairs would work with it."

Morgan brought the chairs and set them in place. When he took a bite of her chicken cordon bleu and pan-roasted vegetables, he saw her in a new light. "This is better than restaurant food."

"I should hope so."

"But you acted like such a spoiled brat when I first met you."

"I did not. You disliked me on sight with no instigation from me."

"Maybe the snarky shirts you and your sisters wore had something to do with it. 'I'm a Witch with PMS. Any Questions?' Plus, you'd just outed your triplet status and made us all feel pretty stupid for not figuring it out ourselves."

"King and Aiden didn't seem angry. I'm thinking the problem was you, not me."

Mentally, he slapped himself upside the head. It had been the *triplet* connection. Jealousy, plain and simple. He shook his head. "Maybe you're right. I'm not good with women."

Destiny choked on her tea. "Sweet stinging nettles, what did you say?"

"I did *not* say that out loud."

She put down her fork. "You know what, Morgan? I'm beginning to think that we don't know each other at all. Let me introduce myself. I'm Destiny Cartwright, the middle triplet. Abandoned at birth by our mother and raised by our alcoholic father, we are so *not* spoiled. If not for finding our half sister Vickie after we got thrown out of college for nonpayment of tuition, we'd have ended up living in our van. But Vickie gave us a home and part ownership of the Immortal Classic."

"I like Vickie," Morgan said. "And now I respect her."

"Me, too. Anyway, I'm here to find my psychic mandate, my reason for being. My sisters have already found theirs. And frankly, I'm feeling a bit like the loser triplet, because Storm, the baby of the family, found her psychic goal before I did. Now, tell me about you."

"Morgan Jarvis, as you know. Your brother-in-law King's roommate senior year of high school. I'm an architect working on the castle and the windmill, and I'm planning on buying this place."

"My cup runneth over with knowledge," she said facetiously, picking up her fork. "So your life started when you became an architect?"

Morgan considered her question and nodded truthfully. "As a matter of fact, it did. Tell me about your walk. You seemed to be having a fascinating conversation with some imaginary friends?"

"I was walking with Horace. He told me some interesting things about the lighthouse. It's forty-six feet tall and holds secrets and treasures that nobody else knows about."

"I doubt that. I've explored every inch of the place."

"Okay, tell me about the cellar."

"It doesn't have a cellar."

"Wrong. Under the house is a maze of pilings. There's also an old cistern under the floor in the northeast corner. The maze leads to an escape hatch beneath the tower."

"Your source is suspect."

"You're jealous of a ghost."

"Ghosts don't exist, and I have my debunking equipment with me to prove it."

"Never mind. I can prove it." She got up from the table in the middle of her delicious dinner and went to the closet beneath the stairs. Morgan nearly had a heart attack.

"Here, I found it. Come see. A captain's chest, just like Horace said. It belonged to Nicodemus Paxton, who built Harmony and King's castle."

"That doesn't prove that your phantom lighthouse keeper exists," Morgan answered with relief. "Come and finish this nice dinner you made."

"Hey, this is weird," she said.

Morgan stood, ready to jump from his skin if she didn't finish her thought, but he didn't have to wait long.

She came into the kitchen carrying the hanger with the cassock on it, its stiff white collar stuffed into its pocket. "What do you suppose this is?" she asked. "It looks like something a priest would wear."

"Thanks for dinner," Morgan said, going out the kitchen

door, unable to explain to Destiny what he was running from, and why, because he didn't quite know, himself.

"Are you some kind of priest?" she called after him.

He stopped. "No, damn it!" he shouted and started running.

Chapter Eleven

DESTINY expected Morgan back before she finished the dishes, but he remained absent. She filled glass containers—beakers, cruets, jelly jars, and measuring cups made with swirls of color, of milk glass, or of opalescent glass—with the assortment of flowers and grasses she'd found. After distributing them to every room in the house, and setting her candles in old, unmatched candlesticks on every mantel, she wandered like a forlorn idiot, though her Samhain decorating cheered her somewhat.

She decided that she needed to occupy her mind, so she went to the room where she'd left the giant pickle jar of Chinese lanterns, maple sprigs, and marsh grasses, the room where books lined the walls. You could learn a lot about a man through his reading material, so she got nosy.

No doubt about it, Morgan's how-to books dominated his collection, five to one, and his fiction tastes varied widely, revealing hidden depths.

One stack of books, on a bottom shelf in a far corner,

however, caught her eye simply because they'd been placed binding side in and shoved much farther back than the rest. She took them out, read their spines, and came face-to-face with a possible explanation for the priestly garb she'd found beneath the stairs.

This particular set of how-to books were about sex, mostly about how to keep a woman happy in bed by giving her multiple and long-lasting orgasms. Go, Morgan. The book about how a man should cultivate this skill through practice looked dog-eared and well-read. Hmm. A man who practiced his staying power. Destiny grinned while her body heated deliciously. She shivered.

In a clerical tome, which outnumbered his sex books—another clue—she searched for a picture of the priestly garb she'd found and finally identified the item. "Cassock: close-fitting, ankle-length garment worn by the clergy in the Roman Catholic church." The picture looked the same: black, long sleeves, buttons down the front. A stiff white band centered the thin, black, stand-up collar.

In Morgan's makeshift art studio, Destiny began to paint a picture of a male version of Meggie: Morgan wearing a cassock as a boy, a bit, but not much older than Meggie had been when she died.

How could she see Morgan wearing a cassock at such a young age, when she usually saw the future, not the past? She continued painting, hoping to see more of his past, of his and Meggie's pasts together, but those visions eluded her.

She heard a heavy step on the sloped plank path from the marsh toward the lighthouse—sloped, because the lighthouse sat on an oval stone base about sixty feet around and twelve feet deep, according to Horace, three-quarters on marshland, hence the plank, and one-quarter extending beyond the natural beach into the sea.

In case it was Morgan, Destiny left the painting in an empty drawer of an old bureau in the studio and scooted into the bedroom, hoping she would look like she'd been asleep for a while when he came up.

If he came up.

He poked around downstairs, and when she finally heard the creak of the stairs, she closed her eyes.

He came in and stopped next to her side of the bed. She heard him breathing. Difficult to keep your eyes closed and pretend to sleep when the person you were playing possum for stood watching you.

She swallowed the hitch in her breathing as he traced her silver chain down to the butterfly between her breasts, around its filigreed wings, and back up to her nape. The butterfly, her symbol for fate, destiny—for coming out of one's cocoon—seemed to have a strange effect on Morgan, as if he was shedding his inhibitions at this very moment.

When he stopped, she might have cried out, if she wasn't trying so hard to let him think she slept to allow him to be himself. He went to the foot of the bed, flipped the blanket off her feet—she peeked; she couldn't help it—and he stooped down to examine the butterfly tattoo on her ankle. He traced that, too, and she closed her eyes to let the wonder of his touch radiate through her.

When his hand traced higher, and higher still, keeping her breathing steady became a problem. His finger slid up along the side of her knee, rising toward—

Shocked, she squeaked, and sat up. "Where were you going with that finger?"

"The lure of the unknown," he said. "I wanted to see how far you'd let me go. I know you just came to bed. I sat outside on one of the stone benches watching you paint until a short while ago. For a psychic, you sure are dense about being watched."

For a sexual being, he sure was dense about taking up the practice.

He'd been watching her. Maybe she got such a good vision of him, because he was as tuned into her as she was to him, though she wouldn't tell him so. He'd probably block her the way he blocked what he was supposed to remember, according to Meggie.

Destiny raised herself on an elbow. "I pretended to sleep because I didn't want to make you uncomfortable if you didn't want to talk. I was giving you an out."

"Thanks. I'll take the out. What does your bed shirt say?" He took his own shirt off.

Nice chest. She could usually see a part of it beneath the open shirts he liked to wear, but she liked seeing the whole thing. Touchable. "Blonde and Bitchin', my shirt says."

He lowered the blanket to her waist to double-check. "Not so long ago, I would have thought it should say Blonde and Bitchy, but I've revised my initial impression. And your panties? What do they say?"

"Why don't you just pull my blanket off entirely, and you can read my ass yourself?"

He took her up on her offer, and she rolled to her side to give him a peek. "Bite Me," he read. "Does that mean your ass is none of my business, or is it a delightful invitation for me to nibble on that fine portion of your anatomy?" He palmed her bottom and primed her at the same time.

"Bummer," she said. "I interpreted it as an insult, not an invitation."

He retrieved his hand and went to his side of the bed, so she could no longer see him. "Too bad," he said, dropping his jeans. She heard them hit the floor. Then his shoes landed, one by one, and he lay in the bed beside her, the walls of Jericho keeping her from seeing any visible evidence that he'd be inclined to accept an ass-nibbling invitation.

"Are you going to rhyme us another good night prayer?" he asked.

"Sniffling sneezeweed, have you come a long way. You're dense, though. Very dense."

> *"He sees more than I think*
> *And wants more than he'll say.*
> *I see more than I say*
> *And want more than he'll give.*

> *"When it comes to sex,*
> *Tenderness beats skill.*
> *Hands 'neath the curtain*
> *Are a sign of goodwill."*

Half a beat, and his hand met hers beneath the curtain. He held tight. "Do you mean what I think you do?" he asked.

"My spells are my prayers. You were right about that. And this one is open to interpretation. Some are not, but this one is."

"Thank you." A minute later, his breathing evened out in sleep.

He'd hardly slept the night before, but sweet sassafras tea, he'd left her wanting.

She didn't know what he'd thanked her for, the spell or her offer to give him sex lessons—in the event she correctly understood his need, and he caught her less-than-subtle offer. Everything about him seemed to be a matter of psychic speculation and as open to interpretation as her spell.

Closing her eyes while aching for him and holding his hand, however, opened a window in her mind to his past—so odd when she normally saw the future, though she and her sisters each carried a bit of the others' gifts.

She might need to glimpse Morgan's past to help him remember it, so he could move on to his future, her area of psychic expertise.

With any psychic gift, linked thoughts, and especially linked hands, or the sense of touch, strengthened vision. Him touching her in the bed, earlier, might have dialed up her vision. It had certainly dialed up her desire.

She saw him wearing his cassock, a boy, a minute or so older than Meggie, kneeling in the grass, tracing her name and date of birth chiseled into a huge pink granite gravestone—topped by an angel lacking Buffy's features, though similar in stature—towering over the cemetery.

Morgan the boy doubled over and sobbed, guilt welling up in him, in Destiny, choking them both, until her own racking sobs overwhelmed her.

She found herself caught up in Morgan's arms. Him, comforting *her*, rocking her, kissing her brow, offering solace when *he* had suffered so deeply. "What is it?" he asked. "Des, tell me what's wrong."

"I should have told them what I saw," she sobbed against his strong and sturdy chest. "She'd be alive if I told. I'm sorry. So sorry."

Chapter Twelve

DESTINY felt Morgan go still. "Who'd be alive? Who, Destiny?"

"I—" She opened her eyes. "Morgan? I don't know who. I was lost in a mist. Time had shifted, and you were—"

"*You,*" he corrected too quickly, "were having a nightmare." He kissed her brow, the walls of Jericho behind his back. "Are you all right? Do you want a glass of water?"

"No, thank you."

"Wanna push me in the ocean again? Would that make you feel better?"

"Yes," she said, because she knew he wanted her mind away from her dream. Or her vision of the past?

The relief in his easing grasp and the slowing beat of his heart confirmed as much. "Okay if I let you go now?" he asked.

Destiny wanted to say no, but after the books she saw, she sensed that, when it came to intimacy, Morgan needed to make the first move.

"Yes, you can let me go now, if you want to. I'm fine, thank you. It's pink granite gravestones that give me the creeps."

His muscles beneath her hands became taut again. He let her go and returned to the opposite side of their wall, creaking the springs and mumbling beneath his breath about pink granite angels and walls he didn't want toppled.

Tired as well from the short night they'd had last night, Destiny felt herself nodding off. She slept fitfully, exhausted, but not in a good way, with dreams or visions skipping in and out of her mind, giving her incomplete peeks into the sequence of events that had brought her here. She saw twins and a fanatical uncle, the priest who baptized them.

She woke with a gasp. A clue, maybe. Unlikely. Possibly.

She changed positions, kicked off the blankets, and woke again, this time with one of Morgan's hands cupping her breast. Loving the tactile experience, her nipple growing into his palm, she closed her eyes.

The next time she woke, she came wide-awake, because they were snuggled crotch to bottom, with nothing but the walls of Jericho, her Bite Me underwear, and *maybe* a pair of his red silk boxers between them.

Dawn hadn't quite made an appearance as she felt herself being poked and spooned by an aroused male. This was real. This was Morgan making the first move, if he was awake, and even if he wasn't.

"Gee, who could that be?" she whispered. "I like."

Morgan didn't answer.

Destiny wiggled her butt to test his cock; yes, his rigidity and its resting place beneath her bottom gave the impression of length, or perhaps that was witchful thinking.

Morgan groaned at her movement, but asleep or awake? Who cared? She wallowed in her power and gave his fine, firm dick the wiggling run of its randy life.

Morgan moaned and changed position. He *must* be awake. No sleeping male would move *away* from that kind of pressure on his boner. A sleeping man would instinctively move toward it.

She shouldn't be so proud of herself for getting him hard, because she was as ready and willing as him, with no relief in sight. And he should at least call her a tease. Something. "You wanna relieve that ache?" she asked, but he didn't answer. Maybe he was embarrassed. Hesitant. "Tenderness means more than skill," she repeated, and still he didn't move.

"Fine, but you should know that I'm hot, and it's your fault." Destiny huffed and tried to get comfortable, all but throwing her frustrated body into an assortment of positions, mostly to annoy him, until she saw his leg on *her* side of the bed like an escaped refugee beneath their blanket wall.

Hot damn. This she could work with.

She threw a leg over his, pushed her hot, flowering mound against his thigh, raised her knee, and let it ride his pulsing boner, barely northwest of the blanket border.

Comfortable for the first time since Morgan had come to bed, Destiny sighed and drifted in ecstasy as he slipped a hand down her back and into her panties to cop a feel and cup her. She did the same, a hand beneath his boxers, found his buns, as soft as a baby's cheek, but she did a bit more exploring than he'd dared.

She cupped and palmed every inch of his perfect butt cheeks, then she stroked him between his legs all the way to the root of his desire.

Once she found that delicious spot, she rubbed it, just there at the root, no higher, in small circles, then up and down the slightest bit, until he moaned again and splayed his hand to cup her butt tighter, pulling her moist mound against his leg, pushing her knee tighter against his burgeoning sex.

She wanted to come. He wanted to come. And they were both too wise to yank down that freaking blanket. Evidently, he wasn't *emotionally* ready to take that step. She could respect that. But physically? Oh brother, was he ready.

She couldn't help herself. Her need to give overrode her need to get. She rocked against his boner with her knee and matched the rhythm of her hand at the base of it. Yes, he'd learned staying power. What an incredible turn on. But she was in control, and they both knew it. He rode the wave of her manipulation until he began to rock against her mound, and though they couldn't see each other, she came and didn't hide her pleasure.

After she did, he rocked faster, as if he wanted her to come again, so she obliged. Amazing with a blanket between them, but maybe that's how he needed it to be for now.

She closed her thumb and forefinger around the base of him, squeezed, released, squeezed, and slid her hand upward, not far, but he moaned. She took it slow and did it again. He moaned again. She came again. This might be the best sex she'd ever had. Kinky. Nearly blindfolded. No kissing. Just the glorious, mysterious basics.

He must have felt the wetness of her come on his leg, because he moved as if he'd been challenged and rode her so she came again.

Destiny sped her movements, closed two fingers around his base, sliding, sliding, three fingers, her whole fist, picked up speed, and she soared one last outrageous time. At the same moment, something warm hit her knee, her leg. As he groaned his pleasure, his arms tightened around her, and his brow settled against hers, with only the blanket wall between them.

Destiny drifted into sated sleep and opened her eyes to full light, glad to be alone, warmed by her memories, and on fire over her brazenness. She hoped the experience had the same exacerbating effect on Morgan's libido as it did on hers.

Hot, ready, and distracted, Destiny found that preparing to dress took more thought than usual. She planned her wardrobe before showering. She didn't have a T-shirt based on Meggie's information about Morgan, so she decided to make one to fit the bill. Then she decided to take it a step further. Easier said than done. Her clothes at the base of the tower's circular stairs didn't give her a lot of choices. Most were still wet though no longer dripping. And the rest? Yech.

Wrinkled and stiff from salt water, but dry, her peach Instigator T-shirt would work. How appropriate, since at this moment, she embraced instigation. Destiny turned the shirt inside out and went to their makeshift art studio for her acrylic paints.

She was glad he said he wasn't a priest, because seducing a priest would be bad karma. Never mind that she'd kept picturing him wearing the cassock; he'd denied it. So there.

She'd wear her shirt without a bra—his lucky day—so she put it on and painted a hot pink pastel heart around each of her hard nipples.

Hard from remembering and anticipating more of same.

Carefully, so as not to smudge the paint, she raised the shirt over her head and flattened it on Morgan's drawing board. With pastels and concentration, she painted, Cassock Wearers Welcome, above the hearts, added an I between the hearts, then Dare You beneath that.

Okay, so subtlety didn't enter into this, but sexually speaking, Morgan seemed as thick as a California redwood, and according to Meggie, he hated to turn down a dare.

Destiny mentally rubbed her hands with wicked glee, cackling like a cartoon witch, except that the apple she offered was hot and wet, free of poison, full of sparks, and aching for a sweet, tasty nibble.

She figured that wearing a suggestive shirt wasn't quite like making the first sexual move. It was like opening the door so that Morgan might feel comfortable stepping inside to make *his* move—his first true move.

Down in the kitchen, near the lingering, coffee-making warmth of the prairie cookstove, she spotted the corner of a picture frame on the top shelf of the Hoosier cabinet, a perfect spot to leave her shirt, paint side up, to dry.

By the time she'd showered, wrapped a towel around herself, and gathered the mums, Chinese lanterns, and silver dollars she found in the backyard, her seductive shirt was done to a T.

Destiny loved working with acrylics, especially on fabric, because the paint dried quick as a wink. A tease like her needed a quick wink now and again.

After she dressed and applied her makeup, she put on the woven straw hat she'd bought to help fight breast cancer, took a container of yogurt from the ancient fridge, mixed in a handful of frozen cranberries and a teaspoon of flaxseed, grabbed a spoon, and went outside.

She found Morgan whistling a Sousa march as he painted the molding that formed squares on the front door, Caramello perched beside him on a wooden bench, talking up a storm.

"Good, gorgeous morning," Destiny said. "Isn't it?"

"Good morning, gorgeous," Morgan said, turning a fine beet red as he leaned a hand on the paint can cover, paint side up, in an effort to appear nonchalant.

Once his indifference was blown, and he'd wiped his hand, he cupped her nape, pulled her close, lowered his lips to hers, and kissed her like she'd never been kissed in her life. His way of acknowledging the night before with thanks, she imagined. Fine with her. For a man with his limited sexual experience, 'nuff said.

Regaining his bearings—not an easy task, judging by his fumbling—he noticed the message on her shirt for the first time, and gave it a double take, an intrigued spark entering his eyes. "Cassock wearers get their own statement shirts?"

"Statement shirt? It's a freaking engraved invitation. Cassock wearers can remove said shirt as well."

"You're wearing it inside out."

"Just for you." She spooned some of her yogurt into his mouth.

He made a sound of surprised appreciation. "You know anybody who wears cassocks?" he asked, returning to his painting.

"Scads of men."

"Any of them ever take you up on that invite?"

She sighed. "Only in my dreams."

Chapter Thirteen

"YOU'D better go find one then," he said a minute later. "Can't let that shirt go to waste."

She froze and nearly dropped her yogurt. Huge disappointment. He'd played as much of the game as was in him in the light of day.

Backpedal, Cartwright. Don't let him see you drool.

"I thought you looked lonely out here," she said, determined to draw him out.

He indicated Caramello adoring him from the porch rail. "Chatty Kitty here's been keeping me company since I got up, though she went ballistic when she followed me into the shower and I turned it on. She can jump a six foot wall, did you know that?"

"She's a regular catapult." Destiny petted her arching cat while trying not to let Morgan's embarrassment affect her. "Why do you never talk to *me*, Caramello?"

"Must be my animal attraction," Morgan said.

Destiny elbowed him. "First time I see your cocky side.

Your *emotional* cocky side," she added quickly. "I like it better than your cranky side."

Morgan eyed her shirt. "By the looks of that shirt, and the bra you're not wearing, you're bucking to see more of my . . . cocky side."

She stepped closer. "Well, this invite is special."

"So it is, which leaves me out."

Caramello jumped into the space between them.

Destiny scratched her cat behind the ears, knuckle deep in soft, lush fur. "I think my Cara's in love with you."

"And she's jealous of you." Morgan raised Caramello for an eye to eye, and her cat got all feline flirty and über-chatty. Humph. She did have a rival for Morgan's affections. Good thing the cat had gotten shut out of their room last night. Cara wouldn't have liked what they were doing.

Like a catapult, she would have tried to stop them.

"Thanks for soothing my nightmares last night, by the way. I hope you were able to sleep . . . after."

This time only his ears got red. "Like a baby," he said, his gaze locked on hers. Their first true eye to eye since the best sex of her life. "You?" he asked.

"Like a babe. Yeah, that." She looked around, wondering what color *her* face had turned. The patch of Chinese lanterns growing between the porch and the plank walkway in front of the lighthouse looked brighter this morning, the trees in the distance like a watercolor wash of red, orange, and yellow. "Prettier than a painting," she said. "I love this place."

"I love it, too." But he had given his attention back to his project.

"Coral is a great color for the door trim," Destiny said as she took a turreted, multilevel Victorian birdhouse off the porch rail. Painted in shades of sage, cream, and egg-plant, it looked like a regular painted lady of the San Francisco variety. "This is gorgeous, a truly talented work of art. Where did you get it?"

"It's my design and my handiwork. I build birdhouses for fun."

"You? Building birdhouses? Now there's a hobby that doesn't fit my image of the stern Morgan Jarvis."

"You? Cooking? There's a hobby that doesn't fit my image of the mysterious Destiny Cartwright." He wiped his paint-stained hands on a rag. "Hidden depths, the both of us," he said. "I think the coral accentuates the brick perfectly."

Deeply hidden depths. "Coral would be my choice." It *had* been her choice, once upon a painting.

Morgan wiggled a brand-new paintbrush before her eyes. "Finish your breakfast, and I *might* let you help with the molding on the back door."

"How grateful am I?"

They finished the trim on both doors by eleven.

"No more manual labor for today," Morgan said as they made sandwiches for lunch.

"What's this?" he asked when he saw her painting hanging on the kitchen wall.

"It's a swarm of ladybugs on a coffeepot. See the spout?"

"I can tell what it is, but it's new to the room. How'd it get here?"

"I found the frame on the top shelf of the Hoosier cabinet and knew it'd fit this old painting I had in my portfolio, so I went and got it. Do you mind?"

"I suppose you found this picture in your head, too?"

"Sure. Years and years ago. The date's covered by the frame, but I was a kid."

Morgan looked around and realized that the kitchen had come alive with fall flowers and old antique kitchenware no longer hidden from view but perfectly displayed. "Your ladybug painting looks as if you painted it with this room in mind. Like the fall flowers in that six-pack of milk bottles on the sideboard. You have an artist's eye."

"Thank you. I run a vintage clothing and curio shop. I have an eye for the rare and beautiful as well. The bottles were empty and crying for color. They're gorgeous antiques."

"Des, they're milk bottles."

"In their original metal stand, I might add. Do you know what I could get for that set at my shop?"

"Does it matter to you? The money, I mean?"

"No, because they're beautiful where they are. They have a history, *here*, and I'm already in love with them."

"You fall in love easily. They're glass."

"They're history, I tell you."

Morgan took a carton of milk from the old refrigerator with its motor chugging and vibrating the round case on top. "History matters to you, doesn't it?"

She slathered mayo on the bread. "Our history is the foundation of our destiny."

Morgan knocked over a glass. "God, I hope not."

Destiny held the glass still while he poured. "Not fond of your history, are you?"

"Let's just say that I never look back."

"Let's say that you hate to look back. Let's admit that you blocked your past, which is sad, and yes, I can tell because I'm psychic, but I'll save that argument for another day. Why are you painting the trim on the lighthouse, if you plan to remodel it? Seems like a waste of effort."

"Keeping a historical building attractive and fresh is never a waste."

"Aha! You *do* care about history."

Morgan looked surprised. He shrugged. "Let's say, I care more about the history of buildings than my own history."

"Sure. Let's lie."

He gave a frustrated grunt, and she stuck out her tongue.

He reacted with shock then sadness.

"Morgan, I meant to be playful not rude."

"Oh, I know. It's just that somebody I used to know liked to do that, and it surprised me."

"Meggie?"

"I hate when you know things you shouldn't."

"I don't know how to block my gifts, and I like it that way." She unwrapped a package of cupcakes, the healthy kind, with chocolate frosting, a white swirl, and a five-year shelf life.

"Paint preserves wood, and my renovations will comply so seamlessly with the integrity of the original structure that everything will look original. It'll take another expert to tell where one begins and the other ends."

"You consider yourself an expert?"

"King, Aiden, and I flip houses for fun and profit. We buy old monsters, turn them into vintage beauties, and sell them, clean and quick."

Destiny had frosting all over her fingers, until Morgan took her hand and raised it to his lips. He kissed each chocolaty fingertip. Then he licked the frosting off, finger by slow finger.

Her heart pumped harder than when the ghosts had appeared in her circle, while the texture of Morgan's tongue did funny things to her insides, sending ripples through her, stroking and touching her everywhere.

She shivered. She flowered. Yikes. A proliferation of stimulation, if only he'd follow through and ravish her. Outdated word, but it fit her mood. Besides, ravishment at an ancient lighthouse sounded so romantic. Idiot witch.

When he finished, he licked his lips, and traced the *I* on her shirt between her breasts with a slow finger. "You dare me to do what?" he asked.

"You? Are you a cassock wearer? If so, I dare you to do . . . anything you'd like."

"Those hearts surround your unencumbered nipples perfectly," he speculated, watching her nipples pucker with arousal. "Like you might have been wearing it when the artist painted them. Odd that. They remind me of bull's-eyes."

"Do they?" She cleared her throat. "They do?"

He raised a hand toward her breasts, and she nearly lost her breath. Just last night, he'd cupped her *naked* breast. Cupped her bottom. Made her come. They'd made each other come, but the action had been all but hidden, like a fantasy acted out in one's mind, though better.

But now, he stopped short of cupping her and simply thumbed the tip of a nipple. One freaking nipple.

She squeaked in shock and disappointment, and he picked up their paper plates and carried them to the dock.

Destiny growled in frustration.

By the time she joined him on the dock, she grabbed her sandwich and tried to ignore him. "I'm not speaking to you."

"Why? What did I do?"

"What didn't you do? My other nipple feels left out, never mind the rest of me." Heck, one touch, and she opened like a flower.

"You're scaring me, Kismet. I *want* to accept what you're offering."

"Then do try to get your head screwed on straight and figure the swell out what it is I'm offering."

Chapter Fourteen

DESTINY took off her platform cork slides and slipped her feet in the water beside his, and *he* played footsie with her as he explained his plans for the lighthouse, which sounded totally familiar.

She couldn't figure him out. He hadn't said no to her invitation, but he hadn't said, "Swell yes!" either. Sure, Morgan was a man who needed to think things through. She'd seen it in his work at the castle and here at the drawing board. She just had to give him time to make a decision.

She finished her sandwich and got up. "I'm going for a walk." He watched her take the wheelbarrow and leave, but he didn't say a word. She went to Paxton Castle, here on the island, her sister and brother-in-law's place, and mounded her barrow with pumpkins and gourds from Harmony's garden. She also grabbed some fresh herbs from the kitchen herb garden for cooking. On the way back, she gathered an abundance of fall treasures left by the Goddess: rose hips, poppy pods, bittersweet, and holly.

She parked the pumpkin-and-gourd-mounded wheelbarrow on the porch as a decoration in itself. Then she braided wreaths of bittersweet with seed husks and rose hips, and hung one on a nail beside the front door. Perfect.

She took pumpkins and wreaths into the house. A pumpkin went on each mantel, upstairs and downstairs in the center chimney structure, and she hung wreaths wherever she found a naked nail.

The last wreath went in the studio, then she went to Morgan, seated silently at his drawing table. "Hi," she said.

"Hi."

As he reached behind him, she placed her chin on his head, massaged his shoulders, and ran her hands down either side of his chest.

He leaned against her and caught her hands, kissing the palm of each. "Nice," he said. "Did you have a good walk?"

"Did you have a good think?"

"I thought about Meggie."

"Probably because she's sitting here watching you." Destiny winked at Meggie, who grew wide-eyed at being exposed, more or less, and she watched her brother for his reaction. Her angel, as always, remained expressionless.

"Whatever," Morgan said, letting her go and getting back to his work.

Meggie wilted, and she and Buffy disappeared.

Destiny worked at her easel there in the studio so she could watch the play of muscles on Morgan's wide-shouldered, slim-waisted torso. On him, subtlety was a waste. Vexing vetiver, blatant suggestions were totally lost on him. It made her wonder what he'd do if she painted Take Me, I'm Yours in scarlet on the bedsheets or across the walls of Jericho.

If his bedroom wall didn't retain its beautifully hand-painted wallpaper of pale pink and sage dogwood branches, she'd paint an invitation in foot-high letters where he could see it from his side of the bed.

A buzzer rang, a rusty sound, and a rude interruption.

Morgan looked up. "Who the heck could that be?"

"Be?" She looked out the window toward the front porch. "Looks like a deliveryman, but I can't read what it says on his jacket." She followed Morgan down the stairs.

"Who delivers what to an island?" he asked, opening the door.

"We deliver kayaks to an island," the stranger said, "or in this case one kayak. A two-seater."

Frustration rushed Destiny. No! Not a way off the island. Not now. It was too soon. She was just beginning to make some headway. She bit her lip and folded her arms. "A means of escape for you, maybe, but *I'm* not going anywhere."

Morgan rolled his eyes. "Then I take it you didn't order the kayak?"

"Sure," she said. "I cast a transportation spell so *you* could get off the island."

The man from Show-Boats looked from one of them to the other. "What?"

Morgan looked down, shook his head, and maybe his shoulders shook a little, too. "I didn't order it either," he said.

The guy checked his paperwork. "Are you King Paxton?"

Morgan gave her an I-told-you-so look. "No. That'd be at the castle."

"Nobody home at the castle, and I need a signature. Frankly, it'll cost Mr. Paxton a hefty sum to get us out here a second time. We saw the windows open upstairs and thought you might be willing to take delivery."

"I'll take the kayak," Morgan said.

"And I'll take the hat," Destiny added.

The man tipped his Red Sox World Series Champs hat her way before he went to help his crew unload the kayak. Morgan followed him outside, and Destiny watched out the kitchen window. The delivery crew left a huge bright red kayak right there on the beach beside the foundation wall.

She went outside. "Won't that float away at high tide?"

Morgan regarded her with speculation. "I'll pull it higher up on land later. I thought you might want to go for a ride around the island. Ever since King and Harmony fell down the rabbit hole into the hot-springs in the amethyst cave, I've wanted to look for a way to reach it from the beach."

Damn, that sounded like fun, *if* that's what he honestly planned. She crossed her arms. "I am *not* letting you take me back to the mainland."

"Give it up already. I'm sorry for my moment of madness."

"The one that ruined and lost my clothes?"

"Yeah, yeah. Go put on a hoodie, slacks, a jacket, and some sensible shoes, and bring spares. You can have your own paddle." He raised one in the air for her to see. "Big sucker. If you don't like the direction I'm heading, you can hit me with it. I'm making you the backseat driver."

"I'll use it if I have to."

"I don't doubt it for a minute."

"Just so you know. They teach you kayaking in the seminary?"

"Kayaking 101. They teach it right after exorcism and before ordination."

"So, you are a priest. Have you ever handled a kayak before?"

"No to the priest. Yes to the kayak. I've been out with King and Aiden, but we rented kayaks back then. King's been planning to buy one for a while."

"Do you think he'll mind if we use it? I mean, it's brand-new."

"The money we saved him by accepting delivery can be our rental fee."

"Works for me. I'll be right back." She did want to go. It looked like fun.

"I'll pack the supplies," he said as she was leaving.

Suspicion stopped her. "What kind of supplies? Wait. Don't those things flip over?"

"I'm packing precautionary supplies. I was an Eagle Scout. Strong survival skills." He tapped his temple. "Smart."

"Dumb," she said as she turned back to the house. "Too dumb to accept the sexual invitation I handed you on a nipple platter."

"I heard that!"

"Okay, now try translating it into a language you *understand*."

No easy solution to finding warm clothes for her. He came to get his own in a blink, but her thick, warm clothes were still damp. The base of the lighthouse stairs wasn't exactly a warm, sunny spot. But after he left, she solved her problem by stealing some of his sweats.

"Took you long enough," he said when she went to meet him.

"I wanted a padded bra so I'd float when we tip over."

Morgan nodded, gave her an almost smile, handed her a personal flotation device, put her extra clothes in a water-proof bag, and stowed it. "Here," he said, taking something from his pocket. He removed her soft-brimmed velvet hat from her head and replaced it with the Sox Champs cap.

"How did you get it?"

"The guy was bribable, and I know how much you like hats."

"You noticed."

"Hard to miss when you wear one to bed."

"I do not."

"Let's put you in the life vest and get you in." He helped

her put the flotation device over her head and managed to cop a feel along the way. Wandering widdershins, he might figure out how to think straight yet. Hope reigned supreme. He fastened her into her vest, and she felt like a Barbie doll, like his toy, with him playing dress-up.

He winked and helped her into the boat. The thing that hugged her waist like elastic, he called a spray skirt, designed so the spray couldn't get her too wet.

He backed the kayak into the water and climbed in at the last minute. "Oooh," she squeaked. "This *is* tippy."

"Only while I was getting in. Shush and enjoy the scenery."

She held her paddle, in case he needed a good smack, and enjoyed the scenery. He looked back and did a double take. "Feel free to paddle at any time."

"Oh, you need help getting us there?"

"Double the weight, double the paddling."

"I beg your pardon, but we do not weigh the same."

"Shut up and paddle."

"I'm dipping in my oar," she said. "In, out. In, out. The Eagle should consider doing the same."

Chapter Fifteen

"THIS is scary," Destiny said. "Maybe we should go back."

"Nah, we should paddle away from the shore so we can arrive at our destination by crossing the waves rather than letting them roll us."

"I think home."

"I think the open sea."

"Bad idea." But he'd already turned them so they could take a circuitous sea-jaunt jug handle toward their appointed destination. It made a weird sort of sense, until the water began to swoosh and swirl and the kayak lifted out of the water.

Destiny screamed, and Morgan shouted.

The swirling water around them seemed to explode with a whoosh! and they were drenched and dripping.

A dolphin came up beside them and laughed. Whew. But another came up on the other side. Frolicking dolphins rocked them like paper dolls in a paper boat.

"Morrrrgannn."

Four, maybe five dolphins, played beneath and around the kayak, raising it up and plopping it back down, splishing and splashing, whooshing and thrashing, while the pointy-nosed clowns came up to make fun of them.

Destiny pulled the paddle carefully from the water on the right so as not to hit one of the dolphins, but the other end got Morgan in the head.

That was the crack she heard, right before he slumped forward.

"Dear Goddess, I've killed him!"

Destiny unfastened her splash skirt and stood to reach for him, but two dolphins jumped up beside them . . . and rolled them over. Destiny surfaced to find the kayak floating upside down and no Morgan in sight. She dove beneath it and found him opening his splash skirt to get out. They surfaced together. "Are you all right?" she asked.

"Grab the kayak," he shouted. "Where are the paddles?"

She grabbed the kayak. "I've got a paddle. Where's yours?"

Together they righted the boat. Morgan unsnapped a couple of watertight bags containing small sauce pots and handed her one.

"Time to cook?" she asked.

"Time to bail, so we can get back in."

The air nipped at her wet face and frozen fingers. "You said this wouldn't tip. Good grief, you're bleeding."

He felt the back of his head and came away with bloody fingers. "Did you hit me with your paddle?"

"I didn't want to hit a dolphin."

"So you knocked me out, instead?"

"Bail," she said, and the dolphins laughed. "Good thing they don't eat people. They don't, right?"

"I don't know. You look pretty tasty to me."

"Cute."

"Let me get in first," he said. "Then I'll help you in. I have experience."

"You lie. You said it wouldn't tip, but you have experience getting back in after it does? This water is freaking cold."

"I know. I've tested it twice since you got here. Am I bleeding, again?"

"This was not my fault. *You* chose to move us away from shore and toward Dolphins R Us."

He helped her climb back in while she felt like a beached whale, then she landed with a thud and only felt dizzy. She fastened her splash skirt but didn't know why. She couldn't get any wetter.

"If we roll again," he said. "Just hold your breath and don't get out. I know how to roll us back up."

"If you had said that back at the lighthouse, I wouldn't be here."

"That's why I didn't say it."

"I'm cold."

"You're whining."

"The wind is blowing, and I'm freezing my ass off."

"It's a fine ass."

"You should know. You slept with it in your hand for most of the night."

"Ditto," he said, though he didn't turn around and from where she sat, she saw his ears get red.

Such cute ears. Progress in the sex department, anyway. "I wanna go home."

"Look, there's the waterfall. That's our destination."

"But I'm *wet.*"

"That's why you brought dry clothes."

"Boy am I stupid for thinking second layer."

He pulled the kayak way up on the beach in a small lagoon that you wouldn't notice if you weren't this close.

"It's not quite low tide," he said. "We've got a few more hours of easy sailing."

"That was easy sailing?"

He helped her out of the kayak and took out their dry clothes. "Do you want to change here on the beach, behind the rocks, or wait until after we swim in the hot springs?"

Her teeth chattered. "Are you sure there are hot springs?"

"No." He pulled her closer to the cliff to break the wind. "That steaming waterfall, however, is coming from a hot spring about twenty feet above us. There *should* be a natural opening in the rocks somewhere along here, according to my personal geological theories. Are you game?"

"I'm wet and freezing," she snapped. "You nearly drowned me."

"You clocked me."

"I did have your permission, in the event you were not going in the direction I wanted."

He sighed. "Let's find a cave where you can change."

"Let's."

His theory seemed to be correct, at least in the cave aspect, because he found one that seemed to go upward and onward. Shivering and teeth chattering, they changed with their backs to each other. This was no time for sexual exploration.

"Let's explore," she said once she warmed up.

"Being warm and dry sure improved your disposition," he said.

"Watch it Eagle Boy, you're treading icy water."

"Eagle *Scout*. By the way, cave exploring is called spelunking."

She pulled up her hoodie and shoved her wet hair inside. "And I'll bet caves don't have bats like kayaks don't tip."

He tugged playfully on her hood, and a rush of lust ran through her. At the moment, she rather liked him. "Who knew I could have fun with Eagle Who Lies Through Teeth About Tipping Kayak."

He took her hand and tugged. "Let's go, Sea Witch."

She stopped to catch her breath. "Are we climbing, or is it my imagination?"

"We're climbing. Look behind us."

"Wow," she said. "Behind us is below us."

"We may come to a rock wall any second but—do you hear water running?"

"I do. Oh, please let it be hot."

"There's an opening between the rocks, here, but it's too small. Not sure I can get through."

"Oh, let me try. I'll just go for a quick hot swim and be right back."

"You *want* to greet the cave bats by yourself?"

"You're mean." She shoved him playfully, but he didn't expect it and let himself fall against a rock that turned out to be loose.

"Shit!" He pulled her against him and covered her head with his body.

Destiny braced herself, but no rubble fell, not a pebble. She opened her eyes, and they both looked around. "The opening's bigger now," she said. "And the sound of running water is louder."

"So it is." He tested the rock he'd hit, and it moved back and forth. "Nature's swinging door," he said, pulling her through the larger opening and taking a minute to get his bearings.

"Sweet Palace of the Earth Goddess," Destiny said. "This will be wonderful for your aura, Morgan. In nature, there are ions that invigorate and cleanse the aura. Take some deep breaths. It'll help."

Morgan raised a brow, but she huffed, so he took some deep breaths.

"There. That didn't hurt, did it? And your aura is brighter." She looked around the cave, totally in awe. "Harmony told us about this place, but it's more gorgeous than I imagined. She was right. It is spiritual. The stalagmites and stalactites are like male servants who don't come to life until the Goddess needs them to do her bidding."

"I don't remember Harmony saying anything like that, and I helped pull her up the rabbit hole."

"She *didn't* say it. I did. That's how I feel. And look, there's the giant amethyst geode that's part of the cavern wall."

Destiny went and chose several bright, beautiful amethyst clusters from the crystals on the floor beneath the geode, for spell work. She slipped them into her hoodie pocket. "The crystals you *find* are sacred and more powerful than the ones you buy," she said. "Amethysts bring peace of mind and the understanding of death and rebirth. As a psychic, I use them to clear spiritual and psychic blocks. They ease psychic stress and amplify intuition."

Morgan blinked. "With you, I never know which/witch end is up."

Destiny nudged him. "Disbeliever."

"I disbelieve nothing," he said, as if disbelieving his own statement. "Now *I'm* freezing my ass off."

Destiny shivered. "I'm not cold."

"Right." Morgan took her arm. "Let's follow the steam to the hot spring."

"Cool."

"No, *hot*."

"It looks like a cauldron on the bubble."

"A cauldron? Nice image. Like frogs and lizards are boiling in there?"

"Let's get naked, go for a swim, and see what develops."

He scoffed. "Promises, promises."

"Do not mock me. I've issued hand-painted invites. You're primed, and the big guy's on the rise." She threw off her jacket and made sure he got a peek at her Great in Bed sweatshirt. She turned around to take off her panties, so he'd catch Smile If You're Horny across her ass.

She looked back at him. "Hah! You're horny!"

"I was smiling about the tattoo at the base of your spine. What is it?"

"You can examine it, at length, later, in warmer climes, but it's a white owl, a symbol of those who need to acknowledge the shadows of the past while looking toward a new phase of light and happiness."

Morgan grunted. "Easy for you to say."

"Not at all. Remaining in our comfort zone is easy, but it isn't growth, and forward movement is our goal on earth, no matter our spiritual path."

"I guess it is."

"Are you gonna get naked or not?"

She jumped in. "Sweet scintillating seduction," she shouted, her words echoing around them. "This is decadent!" She shivered. "It's steamy, stimulating, sultry, and seductive." She floated past him so he could get a good look at what he was missing. "Step in, Morgan the Horny, for a sensual taste of delight."

That fast, he stripped and stood there facing her, letting her eat him up with her gaze, despite his full-body blush. A god of Mount Olympus, an Adonis, erect and proud. She couldn't wait to get her hands on his sinewy, sumptuous body.

"You look like you *belong* in a Goddess Palace, but I'm glad you're mine, for now, I mean, as a sex toy, you know. You, Morgan Jarvis, are as sexy as sweet scrumpy cider."

"You, Destiny Cartwright, have teased me about as much as I can stand." He jumped in.

Finally, he was gonna take the bait!

Chapter Sixteen

HE swam around her as if in some kind of ritual mating dance. Above and beneath the water, fingertips touching, toes, torsos coming closer and closer then moving away.

The most beautiful man she'd ever seen knew best how to hide beneath a cassock—according to her vision, not his admission—beneath a growl, a frown, and his grumble-stiltskin temper. His anger, however, could not be removed as easily as his cassock. Deep-rooted anger simmered inside him. Something from his past festered, infecting every aspect of his life.

He hurt, and she wanted to heal him.

She wanted *him*. For sex, for playing and adventuring, for tipping kayaks, spelunking, lunches on the dock, sharing their art, talking, long walks, for sleeping beside . . . and for sex.

Not a good sign for two people as different as a witch from a cassock wearer.

Bloodless bloodhounds from hell, he could be on sabbatical for all she knew. Did cassock wearers take sabbaticals? Except that he'd said he wasn't one. Nor a priest either.

If he avoided sexual commitment now, imagine how he'd run if he knew she was falling for him. Oh no. Goddess, no, she couldn't let herself fall, and she certainly couldn't let him suspect that she was in danger of it. He wasn't emotionally ready for anything more than sex. Who was she kidding? He hadn't exactly said yes to sex, yet, either.

She swam away from him toward the opening in the cliff where the spring overflowed into a waterfall that caught rainbows in its mist before it reached the ocean. "I see the kayak," she said, rising up in the water to peek out. "Is the tide changing?"

"We have time," Morgan said, coming up behind her, slipping his arms around her waist, kissing her shoulder, her neck, his boner beneath her bottom tickling her so close, so very close to the center of her need. He nibbled her ear and nipped the lobe, ran a hand through her hair, down her spine, around her owl tattoo, and along her hip toward the place where she pulsed with want.

He found her with his hand, almost by accident. She could tell, because he nearly pulled away. She gasped as he did, so he touched her after all, tentative at first, until he thumbed her, examined her with a finger, as if counting her folds and memorizing her. He found her slick and willing. Unerringly, he found her clit and raised her up, and up, and higher still, until he made her fly.

She turned her head into his neck while he methodically pleasured her, taking his sweet, determined time like no other. Not that she'd had many partners, but more than him.

For her, it had been a while, and this man, this book-taught genius, brought her a degree of pleasure that had her clawing at him and shouting his name.

She tried to reach for his splendid cock, but he pulled away. "This is for you. Just for you," he said. "I need—I need to *know* that I can please you more than last night's . . . experiment."

She tilted her head. "An experiment, Professor? More like a sexsperiment."

He granted her point with a nod. "You don't have to understand. Just accept me."

"I do. Oh, Morgan, it's better than anything, better than a superlong vibrating kangaroo made of battery-filled plastic."

Something like a grumble or a snigger formed beneath her ear, down deep in his chest. "One more time," he whispered, tickling her neck with his breath. "We have to catch the tide before it takes the kayak off to missing-clothes heaven, somewhere deep beneath the sea."

She gave him his way. A glorious way. A kiss to die for and an extended orgasm that outlasted her. That final rise, a climbing-out-of-her-skin orgasm shot through her until she fell limp and heavy in his arms. "I can't float anymore," she whispered against his neck. "If you let me go, I'll drop to the bottom like a rock."

"I've got you," he said, swimming them back toward their clothes. "I won't let you go."

If only, she thought. "I'm too exhausted to get dressed."

"I'll help." He dried her off with his spare jacket, and she leaned against him as he pulled up her panties, stuck her bra in his pocket, and slipped her shirt and hoodie over her head.

"Hey," he said. "This is my hoodie."

"Yeah, thanks."

He gave her an endearing look, proud almost. "You're welcome. Sit so I can get your socks and boots on you."

"Nobody ever helped me like this," she said, pointing her foot and watching the play of muscles on his naked back as he slipped her socks on her then struggled to push her boots on over them.

He shrugged in his perfectly fitted man skin. "Close your eyes and rest while I get dressed."

"Oh, I don't think so. I wouldn't miss an inch . . . I mean a peek. Great hawk tattoo on your butt cheek, and is that an angel on your thigh?"

"I know it seems irreverent, but I needed to put them where they wouldn't show in bathing trunks."

"The angel makes sense," given Meggie's companion, "but why a hawk?"

"I like hawks. They . . . speak to me." He shrugged, pulled on his jeans, and stuffed his boxers in his pocket. Be still her heart; he was going commando. She hoped she'd get to unzip him and let the big guy out into her hands later.

She tried not to show her thoughts. "Hawks move between realms, connecting both worlds. People with hawk totems see the future."

"So *you* should have the hawk," Morgan said. "Not me."

"You're the one who chose the symbol of prophetic insight, not me," she countered. "Funny thing is, people who don't develop their psychic skill have a tendency to over-analyze and lose their way." She tilted her head. "Remind you of anybody?"

"Nope. C'mon, let's go."

He walked her to the cave's swinging rock door, keeping his arm around her all the way down the granite incline. Her knees lost their wobble, though she could sleep for a week. "I've never experienced what you made me feel in the hot spring, Morgan. You deserve a gold medal."

He stood straighter. "You sound drunk."

"I am, as if I blue-ribboned in the everlasting orgasm

competition. I could be stopped and ticketed for exceeding the legal limit for extended sexual satisfaction."

"We'll paddle slow, in case there are sex cops in the water."

"*You'll* paddle slow. You *lost* the other paddle. I gotta close my eyes."

He got her into her seat, pulled a blanket from storage to wrap around her, even over her hair, and closed her spray skirt.

"Oh, this is bad," she said feeling drifty. "Now I'm satiated and warm, and very kindly disposed toward you. Not kidding, I'm gonna sleep. I haven't been this sexually satisfied in ages."

He stood straight. "Seriously?"

"Look at me. I'm too drunk to lie. Not one of my battery-operated boyfriends can hold a candle to you. You're the best of the best, human-wise, as well, Boy Scout."

He grinned and pushed the kayak toward the water while she fought her heavy eyelids for control. The way the kayak rocked made her feel like the baby on the treetop.

The next thing she knew, cold fingers reached for her, and gravity had a field day. Salty bubbles filled her mouth. Whooshing deafened her.

The bough had broken and dropped her in the sea.

Air, icy, stinging, slapped her in the face. Her neck snapped. "I'm awake!"

Dripping wet, Morgan turned and grinned. "It's about time. You slept through a flip and roll."

"Did we live?"

"I'll let you know later. Go back to sleep."

"Okay."

Then he was urging her out of the boat.

She opened her eyes long enough to see the lighthouse.

When he got her standing, he peeled her wet clothes off her and carried her to the shower.

She woke around nine the next morning, bare-assed

beneath the blankets, her hair in a tangle of wayward witch curls, because she'd fallen asleep with it still wet from the shower. She got up, put on a pair of Bad Girl on Board panties, buttoned herself into one of Morgan's tan cotton shirts, and followed her instincts to their makeshift studio.

He looked gorgeous sitting at his drawing board, jeans unsnapped, chambray shirt open to reveal a sliver of gorgeous bare chest, sleeves rolled up, his attention on his work, with no idea of how edible he looked. Yummers.

Chapter Seventeen

DESTINY cleared her throat to catch Morgan's attention.

He looked up to take her in, from her bare legs to her electric-shock hairstyle, and he couldn't seem to get enough of looking at her. "You slept through the night," he said.

She might be no closer to finding her psychic goal, but she sure was closer to seducing him, and he'd damned well better cooperate. She turned, lifted her shirttails, and flashed her Bad Girl panties his way.

The twinkle in his eyes said it all. "Are you hungry?" he asked.

Were they talking about food? "Yes. Are you?"

"I am." He picked up her portfolio. "May I?" he asked. "I didn't dare without your permission, but after seeing the ladybug painting in the kitchen, I wanted to see more."

Uh-oh. The lighthouse. "I'm shy about showing my work." It wasn't true, of course, but he had a shock in store if he kept going.

"You? You're not shy about anything. I received more

than enough proof last night and today. Please, Kismet. Let me see what your mind has seen. I'm fascinated."

"And disbelieving."

"That's what intrigues me about your work; the realism in your visions make disbelief difficult."

And there was the rub. She accepted the inevitability— karma or fate?—glad the painting of him as a boy in a cassock still sat in a drawer. "Go ahead," she said.

He opened her portfolio and whistled. "You're good." He flipped through her paintings, made several positive comments as he viewed them with the eye of an artist. His suddenly frozen stance and haunted expression told her that he'd found the lighthouse painting. "Destiny?"

"I know."

"No, you don't. You can't."

"Yes, I do. You told me about the renovations you planned."

His head came up. "What?"

He hadn't found her painting of the lighthouse, then? "What?" she asked, stepping toward her portfolio. "Oh, I forgot about the angel." Holy angel's wings, she'd painted a picture of Buffy, Meggie's angel. "No wonder I forgot," she said. "Look at the date. I was a kid when I painted that one, too." Seeing it put a psychic and predestined spin on her choice of the lighthouse as a place in which to heal emotionally and find herself spiritually and psychically.

Morgan cleared his throat of more than a slight tickle as he gazed at her with a dull, wounded expression. "Des, you painted this angel the day Meggie died."

Destiny stared at the painting, tears blurring her vision, until she got a flashback of one of her misty dreams: two babies being christened together. "Oh, Morgan, Meggie was your twin!"

Her words about broke him. He fisted his hands, swallowed hard, and shook his head, not in denial of the fact but in denial of his ability to respond.

Of course, he couldn't speak, but she didn't need him to.

She combed the hair at his temple and let her fingers linger. "That's why her smile made me think of yours."

He turned his face into her caressing hand and kissed her palm. "I can't imagine what the ghost of a child would have to smile about," he said. "*I* can rarely think of a reason."

"Caramello talks to your sister the way she talks to you. Meggie likes it."

Morgan's eyes widened then narrowed, and Destiny couldn't tell if he chose to deny or accept his sister's ghostly presence. Either way, fate, or her psychic goal, had been hiding here all along. She'd been meant to come here, either for Meggie, or Morgan, or both.

Then again, making Morgan remember seemed to be Meggie's goal, so maybe she'd simply been fated to help. The trick would be in finding out how.

Morgan cleared his throat, turned away from her, and slipped the angel painting to the bottom of her portfolio. He straightened his spine, the muscles in his arms and hands tense again.

Ah, *now* he'd found her painting of the lighthouse.

He brought it to the window, portfolio in hand, to get a better look. He turned to her. "Do you have any other surprises for me in here?"

"Maybe you should stop looking."

"Destiny, this is a painting of the lighthouse the way I want it to look in the future, after I remodel it, and it's dated four years ago."

"I'm aware of that. I painted it before I set foot on this island for the first time, before I knew this lighthouse existed."

"Are you sure?"

"Absolutely. I painted it for one of my college art classes."

"This is my home the way I envision it, the way I haven't finished drawing it, painted in the colors I envision, *coral,* big surprise, and white on brick, and modernized to fit my architectural vision. *Four years ago*, you painted the picture that I have in my mind now, at this moment, of a restored and enlarged lighthouse I haven't yet purchased?"

"Psychic," she said. "Put that in your pipe and debunk it."

"These multilevel decks overlooking the water with granite fountains and the boathouse; they're barely formed ideas! Look at this, you put a nautical-designed stained glass window in the round tower window. I've already had that design commissioned. You even put *peach* geraniums in the coral window boxes I planned to build. Coral, of course."

"But I didn't paint your design *exactly*," Destiny said.

"Well no. Thank God, or I'd think you *were* psychic."

"Good Goddess, you've got a thick head. I am psychic, or your ideas wouldn't have been preserved on canvas *before* they came to you."

"But you painted the tower as nothing but a heap of scattered bricks, which clearly is not the case. So there is a flaw in your gift."

Morgan, grow up. "Time is the only flaw. The tower hasn't collapsed . . . yet."

Chapter Eighteen

DESTINY'S lighthouse painting made Morgan ill. Panic increased the vague and nauseating miasma of grief and guilt pulling at him, making it heavy and heartbreaking.

For an unending minute, he nearly gave in and let the heaviness swallow him, but he rallied, fought the pull, and shoved it away. "You're wrong about the tower," he snapped. "It won't collapse. It can't. It's as structurally sound as the day it was constructed."

"Morgan, that's my vision of the future. Face it. The tower could collapse."

"But only after I finish the remodeling, right? According to your painting?"

"Not exactly. Psychic visions are open to interpretation. If my sisters were here, we'd be arguing those exact details."

Not set in stone, then. His trembling insides calmed. "Arguing in what way?"

Destiny took the painting. "Storm, who sees the present,

might argue that this is telling us the tower will fall *now*, and make the renovations necessary."

Morgan nodded. "Go on."

"Harmony, who sees the past, especially with her sense of touch, would touch the bricks, walk around inside the tower, and tell us something about its past that might affect its future, possibly explaining away my vision or explaining why it will, or it must, happen."

"I think you're all three certifiable."

"Morgan, I don't want to be right. I hope to the Goddess that I'm wrong. But this is what I saw in my mind's eye. No more. No less. I don't usually find the objects representing my painted view of the future, but sometimes, like now, I do."

Morgan winced inwardly. *Like Meggie's angel.* He knew what Buffy looked like, because Meggie had drawn Buffy's picture for him once, almost the same picture as Destiny's, down to the same childlike style. Meggie said that Buffy guarded them both, and, good grief, had he believed Meggie back then? How could his sister have *seen* their guardian angel? How could he have believed her? "I suddenly have the mother of all headaches," he said. "How many of your visions come true?"

"Blessed thistle if I know. I don't drive around looking for ladybugs crawling on coffeepots. I capture a moment in my mind's eye, paint it, and move on. I usually forget about it afterward. I don't track the results."

"Usually?"

"Well, yeah. Sometimes, they end up *in my face*, like Meggie's angel. Like this lighthouse and your plans for it."

He took her hand, a simple act, but a privilege he appreciated like the intimacy to do so. "Let me prove to you that the tower is structurally sound."

"If that would make you feel better, fine. After a shower and breakfast, I'd love to. I've been dying to go to the top.

I love heights. And maybe once you see that I'm right, you'll admit that psychics *do* exist."

He was so antsy that poor Destiny still had a piece of toast in her hand when he whisked her into his inspection. He took her for a thorough examination while he explained what he checked and why. He went over every aspect of the lower structure, starting at the foundation and working his way toward the birdcage lantern light at the top. He looked for bad wiring, cracks, chinks, mold, and mildew. He emptied his architectural bag of tricks looking for a problem, any problem.

He checked flooring, joints, walls, angles, framing, as he searched for damage or the potential for it. "Pipes and electrical are up to code," he said. "No faulty wiring, no rust, lead paint, or leaks. The bricks don't even need pointing."

"They look pointy enough to me," Destiny said.

As they climbed the tower's circular staircase, she glanced back down. "Look, Morgan, the stairwell looks like the center slice of a nautilus shell. Eighty-eight circular steps. What a gorgeous sight."

"You think so? Look up."

"That's the biggest and most amazing thing I've ever seen."

"It's a light," he said.

As she circled it, he checked framing, angles, and more electrical wiring. "See," he said, "no water or air leaks, and the seals and grounding wires are in perfect condition. Everything is up to code. This tower is as sound as if it were built yesterday."

"Okay, okay. So you still don't believe in psychics," she said, "but you're missing the beauty here."

"I'm not comfortable in towers," he said, thinking of Meggie but pushing his wave of nausea aside.

"You're not comfortable in towers, and you're buying a lighthouse?"

"I love this light station," he said. "That's the name for the light keeper's home. But I feel trapped in the lighthouse, the name of the tower that houses the lens."

"You're nuts," Destiny said. "Look at this. This gorgeous light is an architectural work of art, of science, of brilliant minds from a time without the precision tools we now have at our disposal. It's absolutely breathtaking, but, explain it, please."

"It's a revolving second-order Fresnel lens, a classic beehive design with bull's-eyes, made in France around 1880, and electrified around 1900. The prisms refract and reflect the light, depending on where they're placed on the lens. They focus the light rays into a beam that can be seen from about twenty nautical miles away.

"The prisms are harder than flint glass; we can't touch them, because they break easily. You have a good eye. This is a world-class piece of history. Your favorite hobby. It takes two men to open the lens, like a lotus flower, just to change the bulb. It stands six feet high and weighs about thirty-five hundred pounds."

"I'm in awe," she said. "And so are you. I can tell that you love it."

"I do. I love the intricate workmanship of the lens, its sheer beauty, but I'd love it better if it wasn't in a tower," he admitted. "Not that I'll ever move it."

"I'm sorry I doubted you."

"I've forced myself to overcome my aversion to towers, so I polish the brass on the light whenever I come to stay. The light station has always welcomed me and allowed me to relax and forget the problems I left behind. The fact that it has a tower attached to it seems—"

"Like fate to me," Destiny said, finishing his sentence.

"If you started coming here as a teen," she added, as if she were looking far into *his* past, which he hated, "then losing Meggie must have been one of the driving forces behind you coming here in the first place. Do you still talk to Buffy like you used to, or did Meggie get sole custody when she passed?"

Buffy? Nobody but he and Meggie knew their angel's name. He'd swear they didn't. So how did Destiny, who claimed to be psychic, know, unless she was?

Morgan rubbed the back of his neck. Every time she said something scary like that, he felt sicker. He hadn't been able to leave his problems behind this trip. His past was beginning to plague him, even here, though maybe he should blame Destiny. But how could he, when she was the . . . cure . . . he'd always needed?

Get a grip, Jarvis.

She wasn't a cure. She was a reminder of the horrible memories haunting him. Dreadful mistakes. Some from his deep past, like the toppled tower, with symbols of more recent errors, like the cassock.

"So," Destiny said, watching him. "This is you relaxed? Because, frankly, I think sex would relax you a whole lot more."

Chapter Nineteen

"DON'T look so scared," Destiny said as they made their way back down the tower stairs. "I'm not going to attack you. I was speaking about sex for fun not fright."

Morgan stopped. "Scared? I'm not afraid of sex."

Destiny noticed the way he belatedly caught her query. "I don't doubt it. You wouldn't be reading so much about it, if you were."

Morgan covered his face with a hand and massaged his brow a minute before he scrubbed his face with both hands, and looked her in the eye. "You've been looking at the books in my library."

"You're a man with eclectic tastes, Eagle Scout, and you'll try to teach yourself just about anything, won't you? I take it education was the mechanism that helped you forget?"

"What do you suppose I was trying to forget, smart-ass? Never mind; forget I asked."

"Heck if I know. Sweet sassafras tea; whatever it is that Meggie says you need to remember, I suppose."

"I hate when you do that."

"What? I'm trying to put together a puzzle, and you're hiding pieces from both of us. You can tell me what's bothering you, you know. I may have gotten the vision to come here because I'm supposed to help you."

In the keeper's room, as they left the tower, Destiny got an inclination to go to the closet beneath the stairs. She went in and found a pair of old leather suitcases and took them into the parlor.

Morgan followed her.

Destiny laid the cases on the floor and opened them. "Look at the gorgeous old clothes."

"Why would you be the one to help," Morgan asked, obviously still ticked, "whatever it is you *imagine* that I need help with?"

"Oh, I don't know," Destiny said, unpacking a woman's pristine white linen day dress. "Because I'm the only one who can see and talk to Meggie? And Horace and Buffy, of course. And you *can't* talk to them."

Horace appeared before her. "That belonged to my wife, Ida. She sewed the dress, made the lace, and hand stitched the embroidery. The other case is filled with my things."

"Cool," Destiny said.

"What?" Morgan asked.

"Never mind. I was talking to Horace. Come on, Morgan. Tell me what's been driving you to come here for so many years."

"You're the psychic; you tell me."

"Hah! It doesn't work that way. Besides, I think you're psychic, too."

Not only didn't Morgan laugh, he took exception to her suspicion, judging by his frown. So much for teasing him into some kind of smiling admission. She supposed that getting further into bed with him would be too much of a freaking karmic complication, anyway, so why did she want him so badly?

As if he could read her, he pulled her into his arms and lifted her off her feet to swing her in a circle. "Speak psycho to me," Morgan said.

Horace disappeared as quietly as he'd arrived.

"Psy*chic*."

"Right, that," Morgan said. "Impress me."

"Okay. I sense a connection between you and the cassock. Put it on so I can paint your picture wearing it. You're certainly stodgy enough to be a priest."

He set her down like a hot potato.

She lost her balance and ended up polishing the floor with her ass. "Thanks a bunch." She rose and rubbed her bruised bottom.

"I'm not stodgy, but I'm not putting on that cassock."

"Hah! That *proves* you're stodgy."

"Hey, how do you know what it's called?"

"Stodgy?"

'No, smart-ass. How do you know it's called a cassock? Witches don't usually have cassocks in their vocabulary."

"You have church books in your library. Tons of them. I looked it up after you took off the other night."

"Ah. I didn't count on the witch factor."

Destiny got the cassock from the closet beneath the stairs. "Here, put it on."

"I refuse."

"If you put it on, it'll be a first step in facing your past, which your sister Meggie sincerely wants you to do."

"Let's get this straight right now," he said. "I'm doing this for Meggie, in the highly unlikely event that she could possibly be haunting this lighthouse. I'd do anything for Meggie. Are we clear on that?"

"Clear as a lighthouse fog bell."

Morgan snatched the cassock off the hanger with such force, he bounced the hanger into a lampshade that fell off the lamp and rolled to his feet. He looked down at the shade and up at her. "Meggie would have loved that. We used to bounce things off each other to annoy our mother."

"*That's* why Meggie's giggling right now."

"Cut it out, Kismet."

"She says to tell you that the coffee ice cream is on her. Do you get that?"

"Jesus!"

"Now she's wagging a finger at you."

"Slam, that's exactly what she would do."

"Try it on, Morgan. For her."

He tugged the priestly garb over his head, so it fell on its own over his shirt and pants, then he took the white collar from the pocket and snapped it in place without looking or half trying.

"Are you happy now?" he asked, hands on hips.

Meggie seemed to be. She nodded and disappeared.

But her? No. Not happy at all. Her breath became short, and her legs turned to jelly, as if they couldn't hold her anymore.

Good Goddess, he looked so out of place. It belonged on him, but it didn't. She'd assumed, feared, the priestly garb would fit, but seeing it on him clogged her throat and blurred her vision.

Somewhere on his life's journey, he'd taken a wrong path. A direction that possibly did more harm than good. She ached for him, but she didn't know why.

It seemed inaccurate somehow, him wearing something so foreign. He looked beautiful but sad. Attractive but forbidden.

He knelt on the rug beside her.

She didn't remember getting to her knees, but it didn't matter, because Morgan's arms came around her. He rubbed her back, kissed her cheek, her brow, her lips. Tender, his kisses. A rise to passion. She'd forgotten their power, the power of his desire. Now he held nothing back.

Suddenly, he acted free.

His kisses were for the long haul. Scary that, but her fear paled in comparison to the emergence of her desire. She stroked his brow and searched his expression. "Is it against some rule for me to admit that you look sexy in a cassock?"

He barked a self-mocking laugh. Her pulse raced from his touch, from his expression and her own arousal, and yet she needed his words to confirm the suspicion she preferred to scorn. "Why does it fit you so well? Why do you know how to wear it?"

"Shh. No more tears, and I'll answer your questions."

She buried her face in his neck and felt better.

He dried her tears with the cassock's hem. "It is mine," he said. "My parents put me in a seminary boarding school when I was thirteen, shortly after Meggie passed, though I didn't begin studying for the priesthood until after I graduated from high school."

She pulled away. "So you . . . *are* . . . a priest?"

"I did it to please my parents and pay for my sins. A big mistake."

"Is that why you never made a proactive pass at me? That's what was wrong then, the night of Harmony and King's wedding when I dragged you home, got you drunk, and gave you a lap dance, so you'd kiss me. And, oh dear, us in bed, and yesterday at the hot springs."

He smiled and tucked a lock of her hair behind her ear. "I've wanted you more than I've wanted to breathe—before, after, during, and since each of those occasions."

"But you're a priest."

"An *ex*-priest. I left the priesthood nearly a year ago, came here, took off the cassock, and hung it beneath the stairs."

She couldn't hide her relief. "Are you happy with your decision?"

"Very."

"So, we can have sex?"

"Destiny, sweetheart." He planted small feathery kisses on her face, tender and meaningful, because each came from his heart. Not a mating dance, but an expression of affection. With his lips, he nibbled and kissed his way down her throat, but when he came to the place where her V-neck met her cleavage, her butterfly necklace resting there, he stopped and looked up at her. "I'm as experienced and horny as a twelve-year-old," he said, regarding her pointedly. "Except that I'm a thirty-year-old. Do you understand what I'm saying, Kismet? I've never been witched."

"Are you plucking kidding me? You've *never* had sex?"

"Not with another person, except for our recent experiments."

Destiny bit the inside of her cheek. This was serious, and she wouldn't want him to misunderstand, but his virtue made her utterly hot. "Morgan, your body already knows what to do. You've been reading all those lovely how-to books—and thanks by the way for paying such close attention to your partner's pleasure. Those pages are positively dog-eared. But if there's anything I can teach you, it's how to make love."

"I don't understand," he said, "how two people can make love, if they don't love each other? Not that I don't care about you. And not that I don't want to have sex with you."

"See, that's your cassock mentality speaking. People get the words *love* and *sex* confused, like I just did. This, between us, will be sex, plain and simple. Really, it's independence all the way for me. I mean, I care about you, but I'm not in love with you, though I want very much to have sex with you. Do you want to have sex with me?"

"Am I human? Hell yes. I mean, swell yes!"

Chapter Twenty

"GIVE me a minute to get ready," she said, going first to the clotheslines at the bottom of the tower then into the bathroom. She wanted him to find her wearing quality, sexy, stud-hardening lingerie and the proper statement shirt.

She wore his shirt over her outfit so she could surprise him.

"Let's start by getting you out of that cassock," she said, returning to the living room, "because your aura has gone from bad to worse since you've been wearing it. It's getting dark and muddy. You really shouldn't be wearing it."

"Who insisted that I put it on?"

"Meggie?"

He kissed her and she fell into the kiss even as she undid all hundred and three buttons.

"Can you hear me purring?" she asked, as he stepped free of it. "Oh, no, that's Caramello. She won't like me taking you away from her. We'll have to leave her some treats in the kitchen as a diversion and run up to the bedroom. Are you game?"

"Wait," Morgan said. "You say you've seen Meggie. Not that I believe you, but you've said some . . . insightful things about her, and, in the unlikely event you're right, and she's here, I wouldn't want her to *see* us having sex. I mean she's only twelve, or she was when she died. Bargeboard," he said pulling out of her arms and running a hand through his shaggy-stud hair. "I don't know what I mean or what I believe."

"Okay, now we're losing the mood," Destiny said. "First lesson: losing the mood—*bad*. Enhancing the mood—good."

"The mood is intact." He caught her up in his arms again. "I've never had sex. I've been in the mood since puberty. Nothing could kill it, except worrying about destroying Meggie's innocence by indulging."

She cupped his cheek. "You don't believe that Meggie's here, but you want to protect her, in the event you're wrong, which you are. I understand and respect that. Would you like me to protect us from prying eyes? Something simple, no voodoo or slaughtered chickens."

"You're mocking me."

"No, well, maybe a bit, but mostly I'm trying to cheer you. Let's get all our distractions in a row."

To divert Caramello, they put shredded sliced turkey, sprinkled with Parmesan cheese, in her food dish and set it beside the kitchen door.

"In a way," Destiny said, "I no longer feel the need to defend myself and my beliefs. I mean, you were a priest. No wonder you don't believe in magick."

Morgan zipped the bag of turkey and put it back in the fridge. "I know I've sounded judgmental. I frankly worry that judgment is in my genes, but I'm trying to change."

"Caramello's taking the bait," Destiny said. "Run."

They barely made it to the bedroom hand in hand and

out of breath, before Caramello was scratching and yowling at the closed door.

Morgan applauded their success, winked, and cupped
his hands around his mouth. He trumpeted appropriately,
and together they tugged the blanket so the walls of Jericho would come tumbling down.

They dove into the bed from either side, met in the
middle, and their kisses got hot fast, until Morgan pulled
away. "You were going to insure us some privacy from the
curious gaze of an innocent? Please, Des."

Her every fiber humming, nerve endings standing on
end, Destiny tried not to be frustrated as she sought control
of her body and emotions, which she needed to do to cast a
spell properly.

She sat up but looked at Morgan lying in bed in his
open shirt and skintight jeans, waiting to make love to her.
Given the sight, she couldn't come up with one nonsexual
word. "You're a distraction," she snapped.

"Thank you, ma'am."

She sighed and stood with her back to him, so she could
concentrate, which would also help her keep her hands off
him long enough to cast a proper spell.

She took her amethyst-tipped wand from the nightstand
drawer and grounded herself with thoughts of Meggie's
innocence, her smiles, and giggles. Then she waved the
wand to encompass the room:

> "A curtain displaced
> Two lovers embrace.
> Sphere of white light,
> Shelter from sight
> The pleasure we share
> In this bed we dare.
> I give this man my vow,
> Be it here, be it now,

To protect from strange fears,
She of tender heart and years.
Stay innocent; stay sweet
While two hearts meet."

Destiny turned to Morgan, who was watching her, gratitude in his gaze, touched by her words. "Thank you," he whispered, almost as if he believed.

"I should be thanking you," she countered, one knee on the bed as she unbuttoned his shirt to reveal her Orgasm Donor T-shirt. "You just took a big step toward understanding my gifts. Have you had a personality transplant?"

He took her hand from the mattress, knocking her off balance so she fell forward and landed on top of him. "I'd embrace any belief to keep Meggie safe," he said, settling Destiny over him like his own personal blanket. "I can't say that I know what to believe anymore, but I do know that I'm happy for the first time in years. Nice shirt."

He took her lips in a kiss that spoke of yearning, deep and long denied, not only for sex but for the touch of another. His hands were all over her in a celebration of freedom. "I want more than sex," he whispered, proving her right. "I want you. I ache for you, Destiny."

"And I ache for you." She loved the feel of his body beneath hers, the thrust of his ready hips, the strength of his erection encumbered by his jeans. She loved his roaming lips exploring her eyelids, her brows and nose, as if learning the shape of her face, her ears, the arch of her neck, then he went back to her mouth and drank like a man parched.

He ran his hands down her spine, cupped a butt cheek in each, and sighed in contentment. "This is where you belong, in my arms."

"I've often thought so."

They stayed like that for minutes or hours. Who cared?

Front to front, like two peas in a tight pod, touching also with hands and lips. She learned that arousal filled his amber eyes with flecks of green and brown.

Outside the door, Caramello's cries quieted.

They kissed until their hearts pounded and their sex pulsed, until rocking against each other with their clothes between them wasn't enough.

"This is the most wonderful experience of my life, and I know there's more," Morgan said near her ear before kissing it. "My body is crying for more. But what exactly is next? How do I move? What do I say? Because right now: 'Pluck me please, or I'll come without you,' is all I can think of, and that can't be right. I mean, I want to kiss you forever. I've dreamed of it for months, but my body has other plans."

She laid her head on his chest and sighed. "I'm so comfortable as your blanket, I could go to sleep."

His torso stiffened beneath her.

"Guess you don't like that idea," she said with a chuckle. "Want me to move, do you?" She raised her head and rested it on her hands, her elbows on his chest. "What would you do if I refused to move?"

He growled and rolled them together so he ended on top.

Destiny punched the air. "Wahoo, you figured it out by yourself."

"Call it desperation."

"Call it instinct. We could start now and put slot A into slot B," she said, "or we could take it slow and easy and make this one swell of a day."

"I'm an ex-priest. Surely I have a *hell* of a good time coming to me."

"Yeah, that kind of good time, with you coming your brains out."

"Guess *hell*'s a negative word?"

"Not in this context, it isn't. Get up. Stand. There you

go." His confusion charmed her, though he did as told. "Don't look so anxious," she said. "I'm not taking away your toys. I'm playing the leader, so follow where I lead."

"I always thought you were mysterious," he said. "And it turns out that you're deep, and playful, and sexy as sin. Turns out, I *like* sin."

She knelt at his feet and ran her hands up his jeans and along the outside of his legs, around to his fine man butt. Then she started from the beginning again and ran her hands slowly along his inseam. He groaned when she stroked the power beneath his zipper. "You've been practicing going the distance, according to the rules in your books, right?"

"Yeah, but it's a whole new ball game when you're not playing sexual solitaire."

"Relax. You're all tense. And try to hang on. Good wordplay, by the way, because I'll be playing with your balls." She unbuttoned his jeans slower than a snail going uphill, just to torture him and make it last. She slid his jeans down his legs until they puddled at his feet.

She pulled off his shoes, then his jeans, which gave her clear access to the hairy, muscular legs beneath her palms. "Nice," she said. "Not at all like a yeti's."

"What?"

"Tell you later." She kissed her way up his legs, feeling him become more tense by the kiss.

"You're killing me here, Cartwright."

She peeked up at him. "It's called foreplay, you soon-to-be-ex-virgin. Get into the spirit. This is just the beginning. You get to torture *me* next."

"Alleluia!"

"That certainly upped your, er, spirit. Now close your eyes and enjoy." She kissed her way from his knee to his poor, confined cock pulsing beneath his boxers to be set free.

She kissed him through the fabric, and he bucked so

hard, he knocked her on her ass. "Hey! Are you paying me back for your concussion?"

His grin about stopped her heart. "I'm new at this. That was a surprise. I liked it!" He growled. "Do it again."

"Okay," she said, "but be prepared. Your pecker is mine to do with as I please."

"I've died and gone to the promised land."

"Not yet."

Chapter Twenty-one

AGAIN, she kissed him through his boxers, and Morgan tried not to buck as hard. He loved her attention, but he wanted her as insane as him. When she slipped her hands into the back waistband of his shorts—raw pleasure shivering him to his marrow—and cupped his bare bottom with her silky palms, he couldn't stand being passive another minute.

He opened his eyes to watch and double his pleasure. Having the subject of all his fantasies pleasuring him was one thing. Watching her about made him come.

He combed his hand through her hair and cupped her head while she slid his boxers down his legs, his boss stone cock staring her in the face.

She looked up at him and winked. "Congratulations to me. Congratulations to me," she sang to the tune of "Happy Birthday," while she admired his pecker. "Hel-*lo*, Big Boy."

"You're not disappointed?" he asked like an insecure fool.

"Disappointed, Stud?" she said with a wink. "I'm so impressed, I'm salivating everywhere."

His sex danced in excitement.

She licked his happy dancer, and he tried to control his reaction, while shivers of elation thrummed through him. If he died tonight, he'd die happy and satisfied, because all his dreams would have come true.

She closed her hand around him, and he shouted with shock and utter pleasure. She squeezed, and he blew out his breath. She moved her hand along his length, and he stopped her. "I don't think I can go the distance."

She sat back on her heels. "This *is* your first flight," she said, as if giving him permission to blow it before they began. "If you don't count our recent practice runs."

"Thank you for understanding. I'm a rookie, and you're a pro."

"I am *not* a pro!"

"I didn't mean a hooker." Morgan's ears caught fire; that's how embarrassed he was.

"Morgan Jarvis, I'll have you know that I only have sex with men I care about. You're my fourth . . . relationship."

"This is a relationship?" He could feel his cock shrinking. Going into hiding, as it were.

"Of course, it is. We're friends, aren't we? We've been attracted from the first, haven't we?"

Morgan swallowed. "Have we?"

"Sure, or we wouldn't have cared enough to watch, follow, bait, research, attract, and generally annoy the wandering widdershins out of each other. We would simply have walked away."

"But we couldn't walk," he said. "What do you mean, research?"

"You asked my sisters about me, and I asked your friends about you. It's called research."

"Questions. Right," he said. "We're in a relationship." Which made him feel better about this whole sex thing. "I

like the way you're bringing the big guy back to life—
brother do I—but I'd like to get to first base for the first
time in my life without a precipitous foul out, if you know
what I mean."

"Then let's go for the homer. Once you've hit your first,
it'll get easier to go the distance. Nothing to do but dis-
pense with the clothes."

To Morgan's shock, she pulled her Orgasm Donor shirt
over her head, and slipped her jeans down her legs. The
panties she still wore were the same purple as her bra and
made of lace so he could see her blond nest quite well beneath them.

Turned out, he had a stronger heart than he thought.

"Here," she said, pushing her breasts his way. "I'm bet-
ting you need some bra unhooking practice."

He tried. He honestly did. But those beautiful breasts—
the very things he wanted to get at—were in his way. "Are
you mocking me with those twinkling eyes?"

"Of course not, but you'll lose your badge for sure if
you can't do this. Every Eagle Scout knows how to unhook
a bra. Do what you do best. Get logical, Professor."

"Okay, not sex. Logic." Morgan stopped thinking with
his hyperactive cock. Logic said to fold the bra at the point
of connection and pull both halves in opposite directions.

"Wahoo!" Destiny cheered and jumped, like a cheer-
leader on speed, so that no matter how often he grabbed for
them, he couldn't get those puppies into his hands where he
wanted them. As if to prove him right, she spread her legs
and raised her arms as if she were about to do a real witch
cheer—her, um, pom-poms, jiggling before his glazed
eyes.

> *"Three cheers*
> *For the eagle,*
> *The hawk,*
> *The scout.*

"No sport like sex
For a virgin ex.
Tattoos to schmooze.
Nothing to lose.

"A home for your cock,
Like a sheath or a sock,
But warmer and wetter.
Nothing feels better."

Morgan thought he might short circuit from sensual overload. Still wearing only her purple lace panties, she ended ass up, legs spread wide, and bent over double.

Then she bounced up and turned to face him. His knees nearly buckled at the sight of her full breasts—had they inflated when she bent over like that? Oxygen, please. Her taut nipples with their wide russet aureolas made him so hungry, he wiped his mouth in the event of drool before he finally grabbed those puppies, two hands full. "Mine," he said.

She slid her panties down, barely, first one side, then the other, inch by inch, walking them down her legs so slowly as to make his cock jump to attention. Then this dynamite woman stood before him. Destiny. His for the taking. Dreams did come true.

She lay on the bed and opened her arms. "Climb on."

"A virgin could have a coronary from such an invitation."

Mounting his favorite woman meant mounting a rebellion of the first order against the mistakes of his past.

Destiny took him in hand, slid him into her tight, slick center, and pulsed all around him, and Morgan understood that a man could travel beyond the promised land during such an experience.

"The eagle has landed," Destiny said, raising her hips to pull him deeper.

Pleasure roared in his ears. Satisfaction, or the ultimate promise of it. A silk sheath, pulsing around him. "This is like nothing, nothing I've ever—"

"Don't move," she warned, barely stopping him in time. "This stage is not for the faint of heart, First-Timer. Get used to the feel of me gloving you before you try anything fancy."

"But I'm aching to move, Kismet, or I'll die, I tell you."

"If you wanna last more than one surge, take a couple of deep breaths. Cup my breasts, kiss me."

He surged without meaning to. "Your words made me do that, and I just realized that I got foreplay, and you didn't." He'd die if this ended in a rush. "I'm afraid this'll happen without you."

"Hey, you think this is our only shot? We have the rest of two weeks. You are so screwed."

Screwed and unglued. No words ever sounded kinkier. "And, Kismet, you're the one who's screwed. Once I get the hang of this, watch out." He kissed one of her nipples as if it were sacred, with reverence and a great deal of emotional and physical investment. He closed his mouth over the nubbin, suckled, gave it a tug, and pride filled him when Destiny moved her body beneath his, along his length, making them both shudder in hot expectation.

"You liked that?" she asked.

"Very much. Do you know how nervous I am? I suppose a man shouldn't admit that."

"Are you kidding? I hate conceited jerks who think they're God's gift to women." She cupped his face and raised her hips. "Your honesty is a turn-on."

"Seriously?"

"You can't tell?"

"How would I? I have no basis for comparison."

"You have a lot to learn. I'm so glad that I get to teach you. Take a walk on the wild side, and let's take that boner out for a spin." Destiny wrapped her legs around him, and that's all it took for him to surge and retreat—again and again—rush after rush of unbearable sensation. He watched Destiny's eyes glaze over while she watched him, and he wondered if his expression said as much about his arousal and sexual excitement as hers did.

A huge swelling of pride filled him. He was finally having sex with Destiny. And she liked it as much as he did!

He went for her other breast and made love to her with his mouth while her hips rose in welcome, and the muscles deep in her womb pulled and squeezed him as if she were milking him.

He was only a man. How strong could he be?

A man, a first-timer, could only take so much. Worried that he couldn't satisfy her, Morgan tried to take it slow, make it last, and as his reward, her hips took over, and she convulsed around him. Excited, he concentrated on lasting, and she had two more orgasms in quick succession, which gave him superhuman confidence.

By the saints, he wanted to see how many he could give her before holding back killed him.

Chapter Twenty-two

ONE hundred and thirty one; that's how many orgasms Destiny had . . . or so it seemed. If he could pat himself on the back without breaking stride, Morgan would try, but he'd settle for his button-busting pride.

He knew how to make it last for her, and he tried every book trick he remembered, aiming for her pleasure, not his own, though, in doing so, he experienced a pleasure beyond the physical. Besides, he'd get the final ride. Unless . . . "Please don't pass out on me."

Instead, she climaxed again. "I can't believe how amazingly, *long*, you've lasted."

"Damn, and I thought you were going to say you couldn't believe how amazingly long the big guy is."

"Oh, *he* is, but as a thirty-year-old virgin, you should have gotten your jollies in the first ten seconds."

"I'm getting a kick out of playing you. I may be as big as Bigfoot, but you're a goddess. I think you could kill your lovers with your voracity." He didn't like thinking about her having other lovers.

"I know. My sisters have always been jealous. I won the orgasmathon when we were kids. Storm says I'm just an easy lay."

"Whoa. What's an orgasmathon?"

"We counted our orgasms and compared notes later. Why?"

"Because I got a concurrent triathlon type picture in my head that could keep me going for a decade."

"Hey! We were just normal horny teenage girls. We didn't get kinky until we got older and had dates."

"What kind of kinky?"

"Never mind. Am I too greedy?"

"No comparison, but you're turning me on like crazy. You're the best lover I've ever had."

She laughed and came at the same time. "I'm the only lover you've ever had."

He leaned back and found the smooth skin of her ass with both his hands, which gave him a new way to move in her, and gave her a sea swell of an orgasm. She sat up to face him and increase the friction.

Later, she lay back down and placed her ankles on his shoulders so he could pump deeper and harder, and she cried his name in an extended orgasm that shocked her and made him clench and hold to his . . . dignity.

"This should be more for you than me," she said. "If I do pass out, I'll never forgive myself."

"Every rookie should have such a sex goddess as his coach, because I don't feel like a first-timer. I feel like Morgan the Magnificent. Bigger than life. A superhero in the sack."

"You are. You're a natural. And I've never been so sexually satisfied in my life."

"Wanna come again?" he asked.

"I'm game if you are."

He'd die of embarrassment if *he* passed out before his turn came.

"Okay," she said after taking the sexual world by storm, "I'm starting to see stars. How about one more time but with the two of us in sync? This time, when I start to come, let yourself go, and we'll come together."

"Are you sure?" he asked, his body already reacting to her suggestion.

"Boy Scout," she said, "I wanna live to do this again, after a reasonable recovery period."

He patted the sweat from her brow with the corner of a blanket. "How *long* is a reasonable recovery period?"

She slipped her hand between them to stroke him, and he lost it.

"Twelve minutes," she said, distracting him.

He hadn't been prepared for the satisfaction of pleasuring her. He certainly hadn't been prepared to let go, to reach the ultimate pleasure, that final thrust as he spilled his seed, the ultimate sensation lasting longer than his breath, the unbearable and surprising aftershocks—hers and his intermingling—drawing pleasure from pleasure. He especially hadn't been prepared for an *emotional* connection. By the saints, sex with Destiny poleaxed him, but before he could make any sense of it, he collapsed.

"You okay?" she asked. "Because I don't think I have the strength to give you CPR."

He rolled off her so as not to crush her, found her hand, and squeezed. "Never better. Wanna do it again?" The urge to chuckle, or run, was the last thing he remembered until he woke hours later.

He could seriously care for the woman sleeping beside him, he thought—not for the first time—though the rush of heart and soul that accompanied his yearning hadn't been present previous to taking her to bed or her taking him or whatever one called what had taken place between them, besides a high-octane inferno.

He adored the sight of her body in moonlight. He ached to touch, so he did, softly, gently, so as not to wake her. He kissed her hip, her mound, sweet with the musk of their sex, her belly button ring—a surprise, but not, like the toe ring—her ankles, calves, thighs. She slept through every touch and kiss.

When she mumbled his name and turned on her side, he got a breast in the face. Nothing he could do but accept the gift and close his lips around it, and as he did, he nestled his awakening cock against her soft, pliant body. He slipped a hand between her legs to unfold her petals, one by one, and find her slick, sleeping center.

Sweet, warm, willing, she opened to him, spread her legs in sleep, allowed him access. When she whispered his name and arched against him, she might as well have taken his heart in her hand and claimed it as hers, he was that humbled. Even in sleep, she wanted *him*.

He suckled her and worked at her core until she began to rock against him, sighing and moaning, finding his mouth and Frenching him the way she'd done the night of King and Harmony's wedding, but this time—this time— he knew exactly what to do.

On their sides facing each other, Morgan pulled Destiny's leg over his and slipped inside her sweet, sweet haven, but he let her take over the rhythm. When she rose and climaxed, she opened her eyes and gazed at him with a world of tenderness.

Lovers. He'd never understood the intimacy before, the vulnerability in sharing a sexual bond. Powerful. Mighty powerful. Scary powerful.

Could be mistaken for love.

"What?" she asked. "Again with the 'no foreplay for me'?"

He kissed her and surged inside her. "You slept through it, but that's okay. I'll start again from the top."

"See that you do."

Chapter Twenty-three

DESTINY woke alone and stretched like a sated feline in the sun, disappointed that Morgan no longer slept beside her. Speaking of cats, she heard Caramello yowling in the distance, talking to Morgan.

Destiny got up and followed the sound to the open window overlooking the shower. Yummers. Morgan, getting naked for a shower, Caramello playing Chatty Kitty beside him. He pulled the chain to release the steamy stream of hot water, and her cat yowled, bounced from wall to wall, then scrambled up and over the top of the enclosure with Morgan laughing his ass off.

He'd told her about it, but it was definitely more fun to watch.

Speaking of which, be still her heart, how gorgeous was Morgan? Laughing. Easygoing. No grudge, no frown. Morgan the major sex god.

Hot damn. No more wasting time. She wanted to share that decadent shower with him, so she ran downstairs and out the door, naked and uncaring. "Don't start without me," she called as she rushed in and jumped him beneath the silky spray.

He caught her with a grunt, her ass in his hands, her legs around his waist. "Care for some company?" she asked.

"Well, hello." He kissed the triquetra on her breast. "What does this one mean?"

"The triquetra is the Celtic symbol of three in a heart to symbolize triplets—me and my sisters."

"If they each have a tat like it, I don't want to know." He eyed her, challenged her to keep the information to herself, and when she did, he scooped a nipple into his mouth and took her back to their world of wonder and pleasure. Mr. Mammoth came into his own; she could feel him growing beneath her bottom. Slam it, she'd aimed too high. She didn't want the big guy beneath her but inside her.

One-handed, she brought him up to target and took him in. No man had ever filled her so completely, stretched and challenged her—and she was talking heart as much as flesh, with a good deal of spirit and emotion thrown into the mix.

She was talking *crazy*.

Good thing she *wasn't* talking.

Shut up a you mind, she told herself, paraphrasing their old, Italian grocer. She guessed she was the mind-talking triplet, but who cared when you were shivering and showering with a god and coming in his arms.

They came together in a quick, cataclysmic mating and ended sitting on the raised slat floor, all soapy, beneath the warm, life-giving spray. "Sorry," Morgan said, catching his breath. "Lost my legs. Did you bring vitamins?"

"I did."

"You brought everything you'd need in the event you sapped the life out of me. You *do* see the future."

She hooted and shoved him. "About time you figured that out."

"So you knew I was here?"

"Here in the shower? Or here at the lighthouse?"

"The lighthouse."

"No. I can't see my own future, and since you would have been part of it—since you were already here—I didn't know. I came looking for my psychic purpose, a clear mind, and ordered priorities." *You among them,* which she didn't admit.

Morgan gave her a nod, as if he approved her goals. "Did you find everything you came looking for?"

"Not everything, but I did find *more* than I expected."

"Because you taught an ex-priest how to have sex."

"So you know everything there is to know about sex? You're finished with your lessons?"

"'Fraid not. I'll need lessons every other hour for the rest of our . . . two weeks."

She'd caught his hesitation as he lathered her breasts with wicked enthusiasm.

"There are *other* parts that need washing, you know, but no soap around the vaginal area. Causes itches that can become infections."

"New information. Thanks. The big guy wants a place to go."

"You're all heart."

"What can I say? Jumbo likes his new venue."

"Which is why he needs a good wash."

The object of their discourse rose to attention, and Destiny took him in hand for a good scrubbing. Slowly at first, one-handed, while she oh-so-gently cupped Morgan's pretty blue balls, and he looked ready to float to the firmament. "They don't hurt anymore?" she asked.

"What? Who?"

"Your balls."

"Oh them. They've never been treated so well. They wouldn't take kindly to being kneed or cart-busted again, but they're recovering fine and appreciate your attention."

"I watched you in the shower the other morning," she confessed. "You were washing the big guy quite vigorously, but you didn't finish to *my* satisfaction, nor your own, I noticed. I wanted to see your face while you came."

The big guy firmed and thickened in her hand, overlapping her palm by another inch at least. Obviously turned on at the thought of her watching, or washing him, Morgan let himself go, his eyes glazing over, while telltale brown flecks appeared in their green gold depths.

"I want to watch you, now," she said. "I'll wash Studly Big Bone, here, until you can't hold off any longer. I want to see his stream and watch your face while you experience the ultimate pleasure at my hands. I couldn't watch last night, I was too busy climaxing myself, but this is different. This is for you. Last as long as you want. The longer you do, the more outrageous your pleasure, but you can't close your eyes. I want you not only thinking about me, I want you looking at me."

Morgan groaned and leaned against the side of the wooden shower stall while she worked him. "I haven't thought of anyone but you while coming since the day I met you. You looked daggers at me."

She raised a brow. "I didn't like the way you made me feel."

"You didn't like me debunking you."

"I didn't appreciate you saying you didn't believe in psychics, when it seems like you *are* psychic."

"Maybe I am, because I predict that this is going to be the best shower I ever had."

"You can take that to the bank, Morgan the Magnificent."

She lathered his cock, brought him to the brink, and then she rinsed him off and took him into her mouth.

Morgan yelped satisfactorily while Destiny continued to attempt to surprise him. When he seemed to be near to spilling, she stopped her torture to prolong his pleasure and stroked his lovely, pulsing boner between her breasts and used it to tease her nipples taut and hard.

She knew when to lather him again by watching his face. When she picked up her pace, he became taut, his eyes bright, and he gazed into her eyes. She about climaxed just watching his stream.

"That was the most beautiful sight I've ever seen," she said, pulsing like crazy. "Watching you about put me over the edge."

He settled her head against his shoulder, found her center, and gave her as good as he got, and there in the sunny shower, he watched as she came with every bit as much arousal and focused interest.

She kissed his chest and twirled the hair around one of his nipples. "At some point, we should actually take a shower," she said a few minutes later.

He shrugged. "I suppose."

"I'm too tired." She yawned. "Let's be lazy today."

"What do you have in mind?" he asked with a suggestive brow wiggle. "A day in bed?"

She pretended to pass out. "A breakfast picnic?"

"Do we have to stand up?" he asked. "Hey what's this tattoo on your thigh?"

"Oh, that's my Celtic seahorse. It suggests guidance to another world."

"Well you've sure guided me to another world, an incredible new world, a polka-dot paradise like your fingernails, suggestive like your shirts, delicious like your cherry scent, and as sublime as the texture of your skin beneath my hands and tongue. Sweet and calming like the sounds you make when you come in my arms."

She blushed. She couldn't help herself. "Picnic?" she repeated. "Please."

After they finally showered, when she opened the kitchen

door, bugs flew out at them. More crawled on the kitchen door, the curtains, and countertops. Bugs everywhere.

"Ladybugs," Morgan said. "I've never seen so many in one place."

Destiny followed him inside but left the kitchen door open so the bugs could leave when they wanted. "The place is crawling with them. Aren't they cute?" One landed on her hand, and she remembered that in France, people believed that if a ladybug landed on a girl's hand, it meant she was getting married. Yeah, right.

"Ladybugs are good omens, signs of good luck," she said. "They remind us that life is short, so we should release our fears, enjoy and trust in destiny, if you'll pardon the pun."

But Morgan wasn't smiling. He stood stock-still staring at his blue French enamelware coffeepot covered in ladybugs.

"Yikes," Destiny said, taking her painting off the wall to compare it to the real thing. "It's my painting come to life."

"I was afraid you were going to say that." Morgan couldn't seem to pry his gaze from the sight.

"Funny," she said, "I always thought the item in my painting was a watering can."

"I use mine as a teakettle but sometimes a watering can," he said. "It could be either, I suppose."

Destiny shook her head, a bit dazed by the sight herself. "It's neither; it's a French enamelware coffeepot. I own a curio shop, remember? Morgan, I can tell you're freaked, but I painted that years and years ago. It could have taken place anywhere at any time, and many times. I might never have known it happened. It doesn't *have* to be this scene."

Morgan grunted, but she knew he wasn't listening.

"The tower is structurally *sound*," he snapped as he walked away.

Chapter Twenty-four

HE couldn't get over the fact that he'd seen her painting come to life. A simple thing—a swarm of ladybugs covering a coffeepot—which Destiny saw in her head as a child, except that it happened now, down to the color of the coffeepot.

Down to the right colors, like in his unspoken, unfinished plans for the lighthouse.

All he could see in his mind's eye was her painting of the tower in ruins. The thought that psychics might exist gave him a sick headache. Destiny was getting ready for a leisurely picnic that would probably include sex, and he felt like jumping out of his skin. Well, she could cure that. Sex with her could cure nearly everything, except for the unnerving thought that psychics might exist.

He knew damned well they didn't.

Damn, slam, he needed to relax. Sex would help. With Destiny, he could get addicted. How had he relaxed for the first thirty years of his life?

There you go. He had never relaxed, not when sex was a one-man show.

As he pulled on his jeans, he spotted the calendar with Wednesday circled. What the flipping day was it? He buttoned his jeans, turned, and walked into the bedroom door. "Ouch." Creeping crenellations; good lesson. Never think sex and walk at the same time. He opened the door, and Caramello raced inside—the reason it had been closed in the first place.

She passed him, slid across the floor at warp speed, and hit the wall. Yowling she took a slippery turn to chase him and got caught in his legs, tripping him, until he picked her up. "There. Are you satisfied now?"

She chatter yowled her appreciation and rubbed her head against his neck.

Morgan shook his head and carried the lovesick cat into the kitchen. "What day is it?"

"Wednesday, I think."

"I was afraid of that. Can't do a picnic. I have to call my parents."

"There's no landline or cell phone service on the island."

He tapped her nose. "Precisely why I'm going to town to call them. I'll take you to breakfast. The water taxi's coming in ten, no, twenty minutes. Get dressed and come with me. Get a move on."

"I could stop and see Reggie and Jake, and see how Reggie's managing with the shop. Sweet sassafras tea, I could get some fresh clothes that aren't stiff and scratchy from seawater. Unless you're still trying to get rid of me." She batted her lashes like a sex kitten. *His* sex kitten.

He kissed her, didn't want to stop, but resisted her pull. "No, I'm addicted to you. If you stayed in town, I'd have to stay there with you, because there's still so much for you to teach me. So you'll be coming back with me later, and I'll hear no arguments about it." He set out to slap her fine ass but turned it into a caress. Then he took her by the shoul-

NEVER BEEN WITCHED   145

ders and turned her to face the stairs. "Get a move on before I throw you on the parlor rug and have my lusty way with you."

"Hold that thought," she said, running up the stairs.

The water taxi arrived on time. Destiny did not. "Hurry up," Morgan called up the stairs. "You're gonna change when you get home anyway."

"That's true," she said, coming down, trying to pull her hair into a ponytail.

Morgan grabbed her hand and dragged her out the door.

"Wait. I lost my scrunchy. I won't be able to put up my hair."

"Good, I like your hair down and dancing in the wind the way it is."

"It's a mess."

"Yeah, wild, like you coming in my arms in an outdoor shower."

She stopped and crossed her arms. "So you're saying my hair makes me look like a wild woman?"

Morgan picked her up, carried her to the water taxi, and waited until they were under way to speak. He sat them out of earshot of the driver. "I'm saying you look alluring—"

"Sinsational, fantasmaglorious, seductive?" she offered. "So do you."

"Yes to how you look," he said. "Me? I'm just a prime stud."

She raised her brows.

Somehow, her expression became a source of pride. He grinned, not even sure why she looked that way.

Destiny shook her head as if he might be a lost cause, but a *charming* one. Oh, the power.

He owed his growing self-confidence to the scorching sorceress because of her scintillating sex lessons, which set him free of his sanctified shackles, made him less inhibited and more himself. He'd finally shed his confining cocoon. He whistled and placed an arm around her, turned them to face the wind, and kissed her.

He felt alive for the first time since . . . Meggie's death.

Destiny must have sensed the change in him. "Your satisfaction did a quick backpedal," she said as he helped her from the boat. "Did you forget something?"

He paid the driver and added a tip big enough to remove her bad impression of him, then he turned to the source of his former high spirits. "A wildcat with the instincts of a fortune-teller. You freak me out sometimes."

"Then I'm right."

"You've been right too scary often. I just hope your roll comes to a quick stop, short of the tower collapsing."

She caught his arm, leaned into him, and regarded him earnestly. "So do I."

Arm in arm, they walked to his car, which he paid to park on the dock.

"I never pegged you for the toy car type. It's a nice old Mustang."

"Nice! I refurbished it myself. It's a king of the road Cobra, a '68 Shelby Mustang Convertible, GT500 KR, 428 Jet V-8 engine, one of only five hundred and thirty produced. Note the racing stripes. I'm talking *deep* rebellion."

"Lucky for me." Her grin made him want to make love to her in his car, convertible top down, in broad daylight.

He resisted and drove the short distance to Destiny's house, a Victorian that also housed the family business, painted in colors he couldn't have chosen better: eggplant, sage, and buttercream, the colors he'd painted his latest birdhouse. Hmm. Something more in common? Or something else psychic on her part?

"Aunt Destiny!" Jake whooped as he came running down the porch steps to meet her.

Destiny got out for a hug, and to Morgan's surprise, after Jake embraced Destiny, the kid grabbed his legs in a tight bear hug. "Hey, Uncle Morgan."

Touched, Morgan took the boy up in his arms. "Hey there, buddy. How do you like helping your mom in the shop?"

"I'm no help. I'm a pest. She said so."

Morgan ruffled Jake's dark hair. Hard to believe Jake was King's grandson. "Bet your mom grins when she says it."

Jake rolled his eyes. "Not all the time."

Reggie, Jake's mom and King's daughter, followed a departing customer as she came out to greet them. Destiny's sister, Harmony, had married King, which made Reggie . . . no relation at all. But in Destiny's family, any connection made her a sister. Every sister—half, whole, identical, or in between—worked at the Immortal Classic, the Cartwright family business, at one time or another.

"Thanks again, Reggie," Destiny said, "for filling in for me here."

Reggie looked from one of them to the other. "What are you two doing together? Des, I thought you stayed home from Scotland to keep from being paired with Morgan. Oops, sorry." Reggie clapped a hand over her mouth, catching Destiny's wide-eyed warning later than he did.

"Let me," Morgan said. "I went to the lighthouse to keep from being paired with Destiny in Scotland."

"How's that workin' out for you?" Reggie asked, her gaze flitting between the two of them, her eyes growing wider by the minute, as if she'd discerned the inconspicuous fact that they were sleeping together. "What is it with the women in this family?" Reggie asked. "Do you all have some kind of skewed man radar that you *ignore*?"

Destiny nodded. "Exactly. That's why Morgan and I are ignoring each other."

Reggie chuckled. "Sure you are. And that invisible

fireball you're juggling between you is a figment of my imagination?"

"What fireball?" Jake asked.

Reggie looked them up and down. "The kind that flares fast and hot," she said, "and leaves a path of destruction behind."

Chapter Twenty-five

"I don't see no fireball," Jake said.

"Adults only," his mother said, which made the boy shrug.

Morgan chuckled. "Hey, we're doing our own thing, separately, except when we're doing it together, if it's convenient, like now. I needed to come to town and call my parents."

"And I needed fresh clothes."

Reggie chuckled. "You brought a shipload of clothes."

"I know, but they went down with the ship."

"You wanna run that by me again?" Reggie asked.

"Later," Destiny said.

"Okayyyy." Reggie cleared her throat. "Well, I'm glad you're here. I could use a business consultation."

Morgan was glad they were here, too.

"Perfect," he and Destiny said together, which caught them in Reggie's super radar. Slam.

"Uncle Morgan," Jake said. "Will you take me for a ride in your muscle car?"

Morgan looked at Reggie. "Where does he get these things?"

"Television. Books. He's a sponge."

"Can I take him for a ride? It's okay to say no."

Reggie looked at Destiny, who gave a nod of approval, then at Morgan. "Are you sure you want to put a car seat in that beauty?"

"What good is a car this rad if I can't take a connoisseur for a ride?"

Reggie knelt in front of her son. "Company manners. Bathroom before you leave, and don't ask Uncle Morgan for anything."

"Can I take a—"

"*One* toy. No food."

Jake ran. "I'm bringing my mustang!" He returned with a mini Mustang, over which he and Morgan totally bonded.

"Are you sure this is okay with you, Reggie?" Morgan asked again as he strapped Jake into his seat.

"This is a blessing." She leaned in and kissed her son's cheek, before she shut his door. "Thanks, Morgan, Jake needs the occasional distraction, especially with a male influence. He's too smart and gets bored easily."

Morgan got into the driver's seat. "Let's go, Baby Einstein, I'll let you teach me about Salem. I've never taken the tour."

"Can you drop the baby part of my nickname?" Jake asked. "Einstein is fine."

Once again, Morgan bit off a smile. "Einstein it is. I'll follow the trolley but *you* can tell me about Salem."

Turned out that the Parker Brothers invented Monopoly in Salem. Who knew? Jake made fun of the touristy haunts, but he knew a lot about the history of the city, the witch trials—big surprise—the Counting House, and the House of the Seven Gables. Jake gave an enchanting tour with his small voice and big words. Morgan grinned with pride and amusement the whole way.

When he spotted a pet store, Morgan pulled into the parking lot. "Jake, I'm not buying a pet for either of us," he said unbuckling the boy. "I couldn't get you one without your mother's permission, anyway. You understand that, right?"

"Sure." Jake pulled on his hand, too curious and eager to let his caution stop him from exploring.

"As long as you know that we're here to bark at the pooches and yowl at the cats."

"Cats don't yowl. They meow."

"Have you met Caramello?"

"That's one strange cat," Jake said. "Are you here to buy a dog?"

Morgan ruffled his hair. "Someday, I wanna buy a schnoodle, but not today."

Jake giggled. "Schnoodle, noodle, doodle."

Once upon a time, Morgan had been trying to earn enough money to buy a schnoodle for his sister's thirteenth birthday, which she never celebrated. Meggie had passed too soon. Way too soon.

After checking out the guinea pigs, cats, and gerbils, with Jake wide-eyed and happy, they found a pen of take-me-home adorable teddy bear schnoodles. Jake fell for a black and brown male, but Morgan preferred the silver, curly haired girl pup with white eyebrows. She seemed to go for him as much as he did for her. "Boy, I'd like to take this one home with me right now," Morgan said. He and Jake were being licked to within an inch of their lives.

Jake's giggles were contagious. "Buy her."

Morgan laughed. "What would I do with her on a construction site?"

"Can't you take him to work with you?"

"Her. This one's a her," Morgan said.

"Is mine a girl or a boy dog?"

"That one's a boy."

"How do you know?"

Holy crap. That'd teach him. And there was no fooling Einstein, here. Morgan picked up the black and brown so Jake could see beneath it. "Anything under there look familiar to you?"

"Ohhhh," Jake said. "He's got a peanut."

Whew, Morgan thought. Not as bad as he expected.

"Show me the girl dog, Uncle Morgan."

Okayyy. Morgan showed him, and Jake scrunched his brows. "Girls don't have peanuts, do they? People girls or doggie girls?"

"Right." Please let this be the end of it.

"When you work on a house, your puppy could play outside," Jake said, and Morgan released his breath.

"Maybe. C'mon, let's go. Your mom and Aunt Des are probably finished doing business by now."

"Bummer," Jake said, hands in his pockets, head down as they left.

It might have been a tactical error, taking the boy to a pet shop, Morgan thought. Hindsight is so clear.

Back at the Immortal Classic, Jake said he needed to talk to Destiny alone, so Morgan stayed in the bright vintage clothing shop with Reggie. He looked around at the shelves of antique curios and understood why Destiny could identify all the old junk at the lighthouse.

Then he faced Reggie and cupped his neck. "I, ah, took Jake to a pet shop, and he fell in love with a black teddy bear schnoodle with a brown mask."

"Morgan Jarvis! How could you?"

"That's not the half of it. He now knows what boy dogs have that girl dogs don't, and he made the connection to people."

"Of course he did," Reggie said. "I'm surprised it took

him this long. Then again, he's never had such a clear comparison. Thanks loads."

Morgan felt his ears warm, but Reggie waved away his embarrassment.

"I thought he'd like the pet store. I'm thinking about getting myself a schnoodle when I buy the lighthouse."

"Did you find a pup you liked?"

"I did, a bit precipitously, a silver, curly haired girl dog. A real sweetie."

"Are you going to get her?"

"I'm seriously considering it. Have you heard from your dad?"

"They're having a good time in Scotland. I miss him. I didn't know him when I was growing up, but now I can't wait for him to come home."

"Why didn't you go to Scotland?" Morgan asked. "You were invited."

"A little matter of proving to my dad that I'm ready for the work force."

"Instead of college?"

"Yeah."

"That's gonna be a tough sell. King's big on education."

"I've been thinking about a compromise. My dad would like to see me in Harvard, of course, but I was thinking maybe I could do like Harmony, Destiny, and Storm, and go to Salem State while I work and live here. That way, Jake and I could spend weekends on the island with Dad and Harmony, and I wouldn't be leaving Jake behind for school. I'm not free to go just anywhere. I grew up without a parent; I don't want Jake to, even for a few years when I'd see him on weekends."

Morgan nodded. "Makes sense, and compromise is good."

"Tell my dad that, will you?"

"Sure thing, but Regg, you might make your father a counteroffer."

"What's that?"

"Tell him what you want to do, then tell him that he can send Jake to Harvard."

Reggie fell against the counter. "You're a genius."

"Who's a genius?" Destiny came into the shop through the house. "Morgan, I've got a few suitcases on my bed. Can you bring them down to your car? They're a bit heavy."

"I'll bet." At the top of the stairs, he stopped in front of a framed painting of the abbey Meggie had attended as a boarder, the painting's main focus, the tower where she slept.

He wondered, hoped, that Destiny's young mind had psychically confused the collapsing towers.

"Hey, what's taking you so long?" she asked from behind him.

He pointed to the picture.

"I painted that fifteen, maybe twenty years ago. Does it look familiar?"

"Meggie went to school there."

"Eerie."

"Everything you paint is eerie." He took a deep breath and tried not to growl. "Have you always painted only what you see in your mind? You couldn't have been there one day and painted it later?"

"Where is it?"

Where was *it,* he corrected in his mind, because her question had given away her lack of knowledge. "Gorham, New Hampshire," he said.

She shook her head. "Never been there, but what does it matter that I painted Meggie's school?"

"She died there."

Destiny's unexpected sob surprised him. He pulled her close.

"Now I know that I was truly meant to be at the Paxton

Island Lighthouse with you and Meggie," she said. "I'm more certain of it than ever. Meggie's been gone for how long, now?"

"Too long. Let's get out of here."

Chapter Twenty-six

"THINK you've got enough luggage?" Morgan asked, packing Destiny's suitcases into the trunk of his pride and joy, though she, herself, was quickly taking the Mustang's place in his heart.

He figured it was okay to like a woman more than he liked his car. No commitment involved. Just a matter of like, right? Sure, right.

"This trunk is getting full. I might have to put some of your luggage in the backseat. You brought another portfolio? Why?"

"The way you recognize my pictures is starting to creep me out, so I thought we could look at these together."

"I'm not sure I'm up for that."

"To balance the scales, and take our minds off more serious matters, I filled a suitcase with toys."

"Don't you think we're a bit old for toys?"

"Sex toys."

Morgan's head came up so fast, he hit it on the trunk lid. "You have my attention."

"Nothing like the way I will when I take them out to play."

"As a freshly deflowered virgin," he whispered, "I feel compelled to point out that anything you say could put you in an awkward position, like up against the car."

"Words are powerful," she said, "on any sexual journey, but since Jake is watching through the window, I think I'm safe."

Destiny went back in the shop to say good-bye to Reggie and Jake, but she took her time. He used it to call his parents in Rockport. Not that his dad was likely to answer. His mother wouldn't allow it, so basically, he was calling his mother. He'd rather stick a fork in his eye.

"Hi, Ma, it's me. How are you? Besides, being disappointed in me, I mean."

Her list of random complaints didn't surprise him, but she ticked him off, as usual, because he was sick of hearing them.

"No, I can't make it in time for lunch. It's too far away. I wouldn't have time to drive up there.

"What do you mean, Dad's sick? He's never sick. Does he have a temperature? Does he need to see a doctor?" Morgan listened to his mother and smacked his head on the headrest three times before responding. "Yesss, if you make it a late lunch, I could make it in time and see Dad for myself."

He held in his impatient sigh while he listened to her personal health grievances, a long diatribe, all in her head, because she was healthy as a horse, according to her doctor.

When had she grown so negative? So bitter? He barely remembered her any other way. Made him wonder, not for the first time, why his father had married her.

Destiny saw him on the phone when she opened the car door, so she got in quietly and left the door ajar so as not to slam it.

"I have to go, Mother. See you in a few hours. Right." He hung up and looked at Destiny. "Calling them backfired. They, no, my *mother* wants me to come for a late lunch, which she'll try to stretch into staying for supper."

"No problem. I'll be happy to spend the day with Reggie and Jake while you're with them."

Morgan knew, like he knew his nightmares, that his mother would try to talk him into staying for a few days, so she could try and talk him into going back to the priesthood. "Come with me and meet my parents. Not that it'll be a pleasant experience, but there'll be a lot less pressure on me with you there."

"So you want me as a buffer between you and your parents?"

"My dad's pretty great, except for the fact that he lets my mother call the shots. It didn't take me long to figure out why he spends so much time in the garage refurbishing old cars."

"So that's where you got it."

"Absolutely. I learned to hide at a young age. Meggie could get under the hood with a wrench, too." He covered Destiny's hand. "I'd like your company, Kismet, honestly, but it would help that my mother would *never* ask me to spend the night if I had a woman with me."

"Okay, I'll go, but I have to go back into the house to change my clothes."

"Why?"

"To make a good impression on your mother." Destiny got out of the car and disappeared into the house.

No woman *he* brought home could possibly make a good impression on Olive Jarvis, but there was no point in telling Destiny and spoiling the ocean view on the drive up there.

Morgan only hoped that his mother's heart could stand the shock of him bringing a woman home.

He was just thinking that he should have given Destiny some clothing guidelines when she came back, and he got an instant wishbone.

He went around to her side to open the door for her. "Is that what you're wearing?" On any other woman, a white dress covered by a lacy white sweater tied at the waist, and ending in a row of lace vees at her hips, would exude innocence, not sex. But Destiny would look smokin' in a sack.

She'd further buried any semblance of innocence with the length of her dress. It had none. Her miniskirt revealed legs that went on forever and ended in a pair of beaded strappy spikes. She exuded pure hot sex. At least sex is what he thought about when *he* looked at her.

She had pulled her hair back on one side with a white feathered clip, her curls flowing down her other side to cover one breast, like a mermaid. Hotter than shower sex.

She frowned at the way he looked at her and reexamined her outfit. "I wore white. Virginal. Pure. To make a good impression."

"Sorry, Kismet. Didn't work."

"How should I have dressed?"

"To make my mother like you?"

"Of course."

"Like a nun."

"You're not kidding, are you?"

"Nope."

"I fixed my hair so it wouldn't *look* like we just had sex in the shower."

"But we did." And somehow, his mother would sense it. He opened the car door for Destiny to get in, blaming himself for her outfit, but his lust-mushed brain forgot why blame was necessary when she looked so hot.

"Your parents don't have to know we did." She pulled in her long legs, and he wanted to hump them. Great.

"Kismet, the last time they saw me, I was a celibate. I'm bringing home a sex goddess, and I can't stop smiling. I think they're gonna figure it out."

"So what if they do?"

"Pestilence, flood, famine, even locusts, or so my mother will predict, only because it would be a sin for her to throw herself off the roof."

Chapter Twenty-seven

DESTINY scowled. "Hey, I came out here all excited about meeting your parents."

"That's what worries me. I like you, Kismet. I shouldn't have asked you to come."

"They can't be that bad."

He got into the driver's seat. "You'd think so, wouldn't you?"

"I hope she's at least a good cook. We never did have breakfast."

He pulled into traffic. "I ate an ice cream cone with Jake."

"Before lunch? Reggie's gonna *love* you."

"Oh, she already does. I took him to a pet store."

"Jake told me. He also told me the difference between girl dogs and boy dogs then he asked me if I wished I had a peanut. Speaking of which, I'm starved."

Morgan did a double take. "For peanuts, or my peanut?"

"Both."

He shook his head. "Do you want to find a light bite to hold you over?"

"Nah, I raided my candy stash and ate a few gummy penises."

Morgan swerved and nearly drove off the road. "Pardon?"

"What? You never ate a candy tit?"

"Oh sure, we ate them all the time at the seminary and rectory."

She fished in her purse and pulled out her candy bag. "Here, want a couple of penises to hold you over?"

He shuddered. "My balls are shrinking just hearing about them. Geez, don't show them to me."

She made sure he watched as she bit one in half.

"Cannibal!" he snapped. "Such a beautiful sense of humor, Kismet. Too bad it's about to be extracted, without Novocain."

"I doubt it." For fun, she showed him the pink penis lollipop she planned to torture him with, later. "Maybe if I suck on this along the way," she suggested, "you'll calm down?"

Morgan did a double take. "You're enjoying this."

Destiny scooted over and rubbed his thigh, higher and higher. "It's called seduction by association."

"I never heard the term, but I can tell you that it works."

"I made it up."

"No, Kismet, you stood it up. But it damned well better behave at my parents' house, and that goes for you, too."

"What could go wrong?"

He nearly missed a right turn. "You cannot bring phallic candy into my mother's house. Empty your purse into the glove compartment."

"What, you think she's gonna smell sin in my purse? She can't be that strict."

"My mother is certifiably devout. I come from the 'buried bathtub shrine in the front yard' persuasion. She calls it a grotto. My father isn't as kind. He adds 'plucking' to the shrine with the original spelling."

"I've seen those. They're not so bad."

"My mother has worn black since the day I left the priesthood. She's in mourning for my vocation."

"Sounds like she needs to get a shrink and a life."

"She needs my father to—"

"What?"

"Grow a pair. I'd think they never had sex, but I know they had it at least once, about thirty-one years ago, or I wouldn't be here, unless Meggie and I were adopted?"

Morgan and Meghan. The babies from her nightmare being christened together. "The priest uncle who baptized you. He was your *mother's* brother, wasn't he?"

Morgan said nothing as they drove through the Endicott College campus, and she caught peeks of the ocean on the right. "I love New England in the fall. So, he was scary, that uncle, right?"

Morgan shook his head. "So, you came to the lighthouse to keep from spending time with me in Scotland. Why?"

"Change of subject noted. How about that? We went to the same place to escape being paired with each other socially, and we ended up paired sexually, instead. You think maybe we would have ended up having sex in Scotland?"

"I don't think so. Not with all our relatives around to watch and comment."

Destiny sifted through her purse. "You're right. I'm convinced that our being at the lighthouse together was meant to be, in more ways than one, especially with Meggie there. You were furious the night I got there. Are you still?"

"Hades, no. I got laid. I've been waiting all my life for y—for sex."

"You're such a romantic." Destiny stuffed her X-rated candy into his glove compartment. "You're right, though. In Scotland, we'd still be looking daggers at each other, with our family shaking their heads in disappointment."

"They can't know. We'd never live it down if they knew. Swear you won't tell your sisters."

"None of our family can know, except for Reggie and Jake, who already know."

"Slam it." Morgan made another turn along the coastline. "Technically, they're your family, not mine, I realize, but when you meet my parents, you'll see *why* I joined yours, and made the lighthouse my getaway."

They passed a cemetery that made Destiny's heart pound. The way Morgan glanced at it, out of the corner of his eye, confirmed her suspicion. "A family is never the same after the loss of a child," she said.

"Mine wasn't normal *before* Meggie passed."

"Died is difficult to say, but that's all right, because passed is a truer description anyway. Her body is gone, but her spirit isn't, and though she's passed to another realm, she's with us still—"

Destiny placed her palm on Morgan's heart. "Meggie's right here. Losing her must have been like losing half of yourself. I'm a triplet, and I can't imagine losing one of my sisters; I just can't."

"You and I *do* have the multiple birth thing in common," Morgan said.

"Did you and Meggie ever, like, talk to each other without using words?"

"I hate to admit it, but yes, we read each other's thoughts, it seemed. I still talk to her in my mind, but she doesn't answer anymore."

Destiny took his hand and squeezed. "Meggie answers, Morgan, but you've stopped listening."

Chapter Twenty-eight

"THIS is my parents' house," Morgan said, which she instinctively knew. She turned his chin with her hand so he
could see the house across the street. "Don't look now, but
do, because that's the purple house I painted the other day
with the It's a Boy flag out front."

Morgan blinked but showed little surprise. "Of course
it is."

"Morgan Jarvis, are you mocking me? What will it take
to prove to you that I'm psychic?"

"Please don't use the word *psychic* within hearing range
of my parents."

"Why? Are they as hardheaded as you are about it?"

"Worse, and much worse. You may as well keep apply-
ing the word *worse*, whatever happens." He squeezed her
hand and kissed her knuckles. "For the record, I'm sorry."

"For what?"

He put his hand on the back of the seat and leaned toward

her. "For being so selfish as to bring you here. You'll understand soon enough."

She unbuttoned the top three buttons on his shirt. "I find it hard to believe that you haven't been exaggerating."

"You'll unfortunately find out." He came to open her door, and when she got out, he pulled her close, there in the open car door, for a long, hungry, openmouthed kiss.

"Why Mr. Jarvis, you're better at kissing today than you were yesterday. Such a fast learner."

"I intend to get better."

"Morgan!" a woman sniped—yep, snipe said it all. "You're making a spectacle of yourself in broad daylight!"

"And it starts," Morgan whispered, kissing her once more but quickly. "Mother," he said taking Destiny's hand and squeezing it, as if for her safety, as he led her toward the rigid-backed woman who looked as if she'd rather chew glass than look at her.

As stern as an army sergeant on the stoop of her white, New England Cape Cod, Morgan's mother stood about four foot nine, and she couldn't look less welcoming if she were about to meet a cobra.

Destiny stifled an urge to hiss.

Though the woman couldn't be more than fifty, she looked seventy. White hair, no makeup, lips so pursed, an onion would seem sweet by comparison. Even when Morgan kissed his mother's dry cheek, and her mouth relaxed for a beat, her lips held their deeply carved lines, probably from a lifetime of sucking lemons.

"Mother, this is Destiny Cartwright. We were spending the day together when I called you, so I invited her to come along."

"Thank you for having me, Mrs. Jarvis. You have a wonderful son, er, home, *and* son." Flipping frangipani, she was shaking in her bargain vintage Manolos.

Morgan's mother stepped aside, nearly knocking her off the stoop while blocking her entrance to the house. Uh-oh.

Morgan caught her around the waist, clearly ready for a fight. He pulled her tightly against him—each of their body parts met, even the most intimate—and the look he gave his mother offered a counter challenge.

Escorting her around his mother, Morgan let her precede him into the house. Maybe he *hadn't* been exaggerating.

"Behave yourself," Morgan snapped, and Destiny realized he'd been speaking to his mother. Had the woman called her a trollop?

"Aren't you the pretty one?" an ageless, white-haired man said as he ruffled his newspaper to fold it. He jumped to attention, a move he'd probably learned the hard way over the years.

"Hello, Mr. Jarvis," Destiny said extending her hand, while mother and son continued to bicker on the stoop. "I'm Destiny Cartwright, Morgan's friend."

Morgan hooked his left arm around her waist as he stepped up to shake his father's hand. "I see you've met my girl."

His mother hissed, but his father winked. "Good for you, son. I didn't know you had it in you."

"I'll take that as a compliment, Dad."

Hmm. He called them Mother and Dad. Formal and informal.

Either Morgan's father was twenty years younger than his mother, or the woman was not as old as she looked. Maybe she'd married a younger man late in life. "Oh, is this your wedding picture? It's beautiful." Nope, she'd married young and started out looking the same age as her husband. Life had been tough on her, or she'd been tough on herself.

Destiny examined the entire wall of pictures. Most of them were of Morgan in his priestly garb beside his mother. "Wow, there's actually an active association for mothers of priests, and you were the president, Mrs. Jarvis?" Yikes, talk about your own agenda. "But where's

Meggie? There are no pictures of Meggie here? I wanted to see what she looked like when she was small."

A nut dish hit the floor and barfed cashews all over the rug. Mrs. Jarvis got on her knees to snap them up. Destiny tried to help and got her hand shoved aside so hard, the woman scratched her.

Destiny stood, patted the bloody scratch with a tissue, and thought about getting a tetanus shot. This was like Ward and June Cleaver's before the exorcist arrived. Either that or a reality show, *Psycho Mothers of Suburbia*, and she hadn't yet spotted the cameras.

Destiny took in the room: rust colored sofa, orange burlap lampshades on teak lamps on crocheted doilies, white milk glass hobnail vases and basket, kidney-shaped coffee table.

Destiny sought Morgan with her gaze, but he stood in the far corner of the dining room, adjacent to the parlor, asking his father how he was feeling. How could she interrupt them?

She swallowed and tried to calm herself. "Mrs. Jarvis," she said when the woman rose from the oval, fringed persimmon area rug. "Is there anything I can do to help you in the kitchen?"

How stupid. This wasn't Sunday dinner in the seventies. And she didn't need anyone's approval.

So an ex-priest brought a witch home to meet the parents. So what? Normal new millennium stuff, though somebody forgot to tell the mother from hell—positively appropriate in this case—who hadn't responded to her offer of help, anyway.

Olive, as her husband called her, had ignored her offer and marched into the kitchen, letting the swinging door shut in her face. Charming hostess.

Destiny had at first pictured Morgan's mother as a green Olive. Now the woman appeared more in her mind's eye like a black one, though she didn't want to be unfair. She liked black olives.

Destiny girded her loins and confronted the fighter in her kitchen. While being ignored, she noticed the statue of one of their saints facing the wall. To keep busy and useful, she turned it right side out to face the kitchen.

Morgan's mother rushed over to turn the statue back to the wall. "When the Blessed Mother doesn't do as I ask, I can't look at her," Olive snapped.

Whoa. Destiny backed up a step. "Do you turn the statue in the bathtub, too?"

"Brazen thing."

This must be how Morgan felt that first night at the lighthouse, *after* she gave him a concussion, the cart fell on his balls, and Caramello clawed him.

Olive Jarvis opened a linen drawer, took out a black cloth, and draped it over the statue. "The wall's too good for her now that Father Morgan's brought home a hussy!"

Shock caught Destiny by the throat. She stepped back as if struck, faced the venom in the woman's expression, and raised her chin. "That would be the Whore of Babylon, thank you."

Chapter Twenty-nine

MORGAN ran when he heard Destiny's scream.

He found her doubled over in the kitchen, trying to catch her breath, except she wasn't crying, thank God. She was laughing.

Judging by his mother's mottled burgundy face, she looked like her head might explode.

Morgan took Destiny's arm. "Kismet, are you okay?" He caught his mother's evil eye and changed tack. "Destiny, what's wrong?"

"Her expression when I—because she—" Destiny pointed his mother's way but couldn't seem to catch her breath enough to talk, because she was laughing too hard. She fell against him, tears streaming down her face. "Not important." Destiny shook her head. "House?" she whispered in his ear, her hand in his hair as she tried to subdue her breath-stealing, hiccupping laughter. "Show me the house."

Translation: "Get me the holy Hades out of here." He knew the feeling well.

"Mother, I'm giving Destiny a tour of the house to calm her down." He led Destiny through the dining room, and she started laughing again as she maneuvered him toward the stairs. As they passed his father, his dad winked.

At the top of the stairs, Destiny stopped. "*Your* room," she said.

Morgan took Destiny to his old room, a boy's room with bunk beds and red and blue plaid curtains. Nevertheless, the laughing charmer closed the door and went for his zipper.

"What are you—?"

"I'm a hussy, I know." She unzipped him and pulled out his enthusiastic pecker, pushed him back against the mattress of the bottom bunk, where he'd slept as a kid, followed him down, and impaled herself.

"This bed never felt so good," he said, raising his hips to meet her.

"Morgan?" his mother called from a distance. "Morgan, are you up there?"

"Bathroom!" he whispered, helping Destiny off him, both of them groaning, hitting their heads on the top bunk, and making for the bathroom, him hobbling like an ass with his pants around his knees.

Destiny started laughing all over again, at him, at them. "I like being a hussy."

He locked them in, leaned Destiny against the pale blue tiles edged in black, and slipped inside her warm and welcoming center.

It was wild, taking the woman you lo—lusted after, under dangerous circumstances, with the threat of getting caught.

Faster and faster he surged, kissing Destiny, devouring her, as greedy and insatiable as him, cupping his ass, fondling his balls, and generally making him hotter. "This is the most fun I ever had at my parents' house," he whispered.

A knock at the bathroom door nearly gave him a heart attack.

They stilled. Destiny's eyes got so wide, he kissed her.

"Morgan?" his mother called from the other side of the door. "Are you in there?" She jiggled the knob, and his heart actually stopped.

Des saw the fear on his face and looked as if she was about to crack up again. Who wouldn't? How absurd was this? His mother trying to break in on them.

What was she gonna do if she caught them? Ground him?

He placed his hand gently over Destiny's mouth, and she placed her hand over his, her eyes dancing merrily, her hips beginning a slow torture that he couldn't stop or deny. Damn it, at thirty years old, he could damn well do what he wanted and who he wanted wherever he wanted.

They moved in sync, slow and silent—sex, sex, sex—in his old room, his little old bathroom, but who cared, because Destiny was here milking him, until he lost control, they both did, and they exploded together, fast and bright as the sun, there in his parents' house, no sin allowed.

Morgan stayed inside Destiny, his palms on the wall on either side of her head, his breath coming hard and fast.

He kissed the perspiration on her brow, her cheek, her nose, and then her lips again, hungry and sated at the same time. He brought her head against his heartbeat. She kissed his knuckles. A perfect moment, if he didn't have to figure out what to say when they got downstairs.

He heard the back door slam, which brought him to action. "Quick, we have to clean up. Sex is sticky," he noted, bringing the amusement back into Destiny's eyes.

They washed each other, the most intimate experience of all. He wanted to kiss her again. He liked her, sincerely. So much so that he wanted to show her every silly pebble and seashell in his childhood collection box.

After they washed and got their underwear in place, they

faced the mirror, him standing behind her. He straightened his collar while Destiny, a head shorter, brushed her hair. She turned, and he patted the moisture on her brow, cheeks, and neck, while she stood on tiptoes and rearranged his hair.

Finally, he fished her strappy high-heeled sandals from behind the toilet, and she put them on, which raised her up and brought her head to his chin.

"Lipstick," she said.

"No thanks."

"Too late," she said. "You're wearing it instead of me."

"Oh, good God." One more shot at the mirror with a facecloth for him and a tube of lipstick for her.

He looked for a place to put the lipstick-covered face-cloth, and decided it was time his mother grew up. He folded it over the towel rack, lipstick side out.

At the top of the stairs, he took Destiny's hand. "Chin up," he said, as they went downstairs side by side. "I'll take care of this."

His father rattled his newspaper and jumped from his easy chair. "Quick, sit on the couch and grab a crab puff. I told her you went to see the neighbors' prizewinning garden." He winked. "She'll be back any—*there's* my bride." His father turned back to them. "The neighbors have a new baby, a boy. She miscarried four times in the last six years, and they're so excited. He's such a blessing."

"Gordon, mind your talk in company."

"Olive, we're all family here."

"It's me, Mr. Jarvis. I don't think Mrs. Jarvis considers me family."

His mother gave a tight-lipped nod. "If the miniskirt fits."

Chapter Thirty

MORGAN coughed. What was he supposed to say to that? To the devil with being careful; his mother could stand the truth for once. "I like Destiny's skirt. I especially like looking at her legs in it."

His mother regarded Destiny with deep dislike then— an understatement. "I won't let you destroy him," she snapped.

"Did you just threaten my friend? It sounded like you threatened her," he said. "Mother, Destiny is our guest. You taught me to be gracious to guests in this house."

Destiny elbowed him. "It's okay, Morgan. Your mother has a right to her own opinion. I'm a big girl. I can take care of myself."

He pulled Destiny down to the sofa and slipped his arm around her, brought her close, lifted his legs, and crossed his ankles on the coffee table, a rebellious act that he wouldn't get called on, because *he* was the chosen child. "I'm playing your knight in shining armor, Kismet."

"I'll let you," Destiny said. "*If and when* I ever have an enemy who needs vanquishing."

Saints alive, he couldn't fight them both. "Mother?" Morgan sat forward. "Is lunch ready yet? We've got a long ride back."

Conversation at the table became stilted when all avenues, also known as "the third degree," led to the undeniable and unspoken conclusion that he and Destiny were both staying at the lighthouse.

"I thought the lighthouse had only one bedroom," his father said.

Destiny rubbed her nose. "It has four bedrooms, Mr. Jarvis."

Morgan cleared his throat. "But only one bed. That's why I'm glad that you taught me to share, Mother."

His father coughed into his napkin, his mother sucked lemons, and Destiny kicked him under the table. "Quit poking the tiger," she whispered. "Seriously, Mrs. Jarvis," Destiny said. "Why *aren't* there any pictures of Meggie in the house?"

His father now choked on the coffee he'd sipped to stop coughing.

Destiny stood and poured Morgan's father a glass of water from the pitcher on the table. "Should you be having coffee, Mr. Jarvis," she asked, "if you're not feeling well?"

"I feel wonderful. Never better. Why would you think—"

Morgan's mother coughed, rearranged the napkin in her lap, and Morgan's father shut up.

"Mother, Dad," Morgan said, standing and pulling Destiny up with him. "We have to go now. Thanks for lunch." He took Destiny's purse from the floor and set it on the table. It fell over, and her huge pink penis pop rolled into the center of the table.

His mother screamed as if a rat sat there.

His father's rolling belly laugh about knocked him over. He'd never heard Gordon Jarvis laugh like that in his life.

"Well, Dad, you do sound healthy. Thanks for the talk. The hussy thanks you, too." Morgan railroaded Destiny to the door. When he'd nearly got her over the threshold, she stopped and tugged him to a halt.

She stood her stubborn ground, and he got a really bad feeling about that. "By the way, Mrs. Jarvis," Destiny said, "I'm a wit—"

Morgan yanked her into his arms and shut her up the only way he knew how. He kissed her, and kissed her again, after which, he picked her up, still dazed from the kiss—both of them—and carried her down the walk. He deposited her in the passenger seat of his rebellious Mustang and walked around to the driver's side.

He would have gotten away, if his father hadn't come ambling out to the car, hands in his pockets. Morgan rolled down his window, but his dad went around to the passenger side.

Destiny rolled down her window, and as if she and his dad were on the same wavelength, she raised her face for his father's kiss.

"You're good for my boy," his father said. "I like you."

Then his father came to his side and strangled on his words, as usual.

"Say it, Dad. You're allowed to say any damned thing you please."

The poor man, who'd rarely been allowed to talk around his wife, blustered, but for maybe the first time in Morgan's life, he unstuck his tongue from the roof of his mouth. "I love you, son. Be happy." He squeezed Morgan's shoulder. "You have good taste in women." Then his father turned and went back into the house to face the wrath of Olive the Ornery.

If Morgan didn't know better, he'd think his father had just congratulated him for getting laid.

"Quick," Destiny said. "Drive, before your mother comes after me with a broom."

"It would serve you right if she tried, after nearly telling her you're a witch."

"Sorry, I got carried away."

"Ya think?"

She broke into laughter all over again.

Charmed the holy frustration out of him. Scared the swell out of him, too.

Chapter Thirty-one

"STOP here," Destiny said a few minutes later, raising the hair on the back of Morgan's neck, though he shouldn't be surprised.

"Where?"

"The cemetery, of course. I wanna see Meggie's grave and say a prayer."

He didn't ask how she knew where to stop, but he did need to know why. "Des, what are you looking for?"

"Buffy. She's the tallest gravestone in here. She looks out above all the rest, but you know that." Destiny stopped to shield her eyes from the Indian summer sun. "There she is."

Meggie had named their guardian angel Buffy when they were in kindergarten.

Morgan stopped to see if Destiny would actually go to Meggie's grave, but he shouldn't have doubted her. By the time he joined her, she had knelt to run her fingers over the carving of Meggie's name.

Butterflies appeared as if from nowhere, different species in varying colors, fluttering around them, landing on the carving of Meggie in her grotto of angel wings. No butterflies on the other gravestones. They looked forlorn and barren.

The butterflies reminded him of the ladybug infestation, and he wondered if he'd find a butterfly painting in Destiny's new portfolio, though she did have a butterfly tattoo.

Destiny began to weep, softly, shocking him, releasing the emotional lock on his heart as if from a cage. She was mourning with him.

He could feel again. And it hurt. It hurt like a thousand bee stings.

He knelt beside Destiny, put an arm around her to console them both, and he mourned like he had as a boy—the first time in nearly twenty years.

He missed his twin. Yet his heart also recognized that this woman beside him moved him—Morgan the man—in ways he couldn't rationalize.

"One of us is crazy," he said, taking out his handkerchief to dry her eyes.

"No, both of us are psychic, but I'm not looking for an argument, so don't answer." She crossed his lips with a finger. He covered it with his own. And when their gazes met, something else shifted in him, something monumental but as basic as the need to breathe, the need to be with this woman for a scary long time. Maybe, for the rest of his days.

The knowledge came softly, like getting hit upside the head with . . . Meggie's stuffed dog? He looked to see if his sister was there and thought he saw a shadow run behind the headstone. An old familiar giggle floated on the wind. He doubted hearing it, and yet, there was no mistaking that giggle, that joy.

A butterfly landed in Destiny's hair.

She saw it from the corner of her eye. "In the Celtic tradition," she said, "the butterfly signifies transformation and rebirth, a spiritual and physical recycling. Butterflies leave their chrysalis and remind us that after pain, life is beautiful. I'll bet Meggie's angel is using the butterflies to help you understand."

"Meggie and I shared a guardian angel, or so Megs said."

"I know. She told me. She thinks you stopped talking to Buffy when she passed."

He shrugged. "Maybe I did."

"Celtic women used butterflies to adorn gowns, blankets, and cradle sheets for expected babies. Did Meggie chase butterflies?"

"Incessantly, giggling the whole time."

"Or did the butterflies chase her?"

Morgan thought about that. "You know, thinking back, it would be difficult to say."

Destiny indicated the pink granite angel. "See the way Buffy is making a grotto of wings to protect Meggie? That's how the two of them often appear to me, except that Meggie's hair is in braids. She's wearing the red plaid school uniform, and clutching a curly haired stuffed dog."

"You're kidding? She has the dog?" Morgan looked around again and resisted an urge to call his sister. Had she hit him with her stuffed dog just now? Like the old days? Nah.

"The angel's gown is blue," Destiny said, standing. "Blue here, and red there, with a gold sash, and her wings are a bright, glittery white. Now that may be *my* perception of an angel, but that's what I see. Buffy's face is different from this angel's, though. Buffy doesn't smile, but she looks at Meggie with a great deal of love. Meggie didn't catch that in her drawing so it's not on your tattoo, either,

but I don't think that kind of love can be captured on canvas."

That kind of love. Buffy. Meggie. All the right words.
As if this beautiful, loving Destiny was his.

Chapter Thirty-two

HIS destiny? Morgan thought his head might explode. He searched for the meaning in his life, but found none, until Destiny took his arm.

"Let's go," she said. "I want to stop at a nursery to buy some plants. Meggie wants a healing garden for you, and I also want it to be a memory garden for her."

Morgan went along with plans so ludicrous, they made a strange sort of sense, because he didn't want to be left in Oz without Destiny. Down the road at the nursery, she pulled a list from her purse. "I want Frikart's asters, joe-pye weed, plumbago, sneezeweed, snakeroot, tickseed, turtle-head, and tree mallow."

Morgan's heart about stopped.

"Yep, you guessed it," Destiny said. "Meggie chose the plants, and I made the list."

"I recognized her sense of humor right away. It's a lot like yours, actually."

The clerk filling her order kept shaking his head.

Hands on hips, Destiny circled the guy, who should be very afraid. "What's wrong?" she asked him.

The clerk wiped his hands on his gray apron, as if his palms were sweaty, then he looked around and lowered his voice. "Most of these plants won't come up next year because you're planting them so late, but I could get fired for telling you so."

Destiny leaned close. "I won't give you away. I don't care. I need to plant them. I also want that garden statue of the angel."

Morgan smiled as she linked arms with him. "For Meggie," Destiny said.

He fought the urge to kiss her in public. Destiny spelled trouble with a capital *T*.

"Look, Morgan, a lighthouse," she said. "We'll take that, too," she told the clerk.

Morgan chose an engraved stone and put it on the counter with the rest of their purchases. "A garden stone that says Destiny," he added. "Meggie needs that, too."

Later than they expected, it took two water taxis to get the two of them, Destiny's luggage, and their plants and statues back to the island.

"I wonder if the ladybugs are gone," Morgan said picking up as many suitcases from the dock as he could carry. "I hope they didn't migrate upstairs. I planned to take the tattoo tour tonight. I've had glimpses, but I'm talking spotlight on talent, here."

Destiny shivered. "I don't have the only tattoos in the neighborhood."

He shook his head. "You first saw mine when you were spying on me in the shower, didn't you?"

"Never mind that. How does a priest get tattooed?"

"He goes sailing to the islands with his crazy friends, where they all get hammered and tattooed."

"Aiden and King?"

"I can't believe your sisters haven't shared, though we

vowed on penalty of death not to rat each other out. They must have sworn their wives to secrecy."

"Screw that," Destiny said, leaving her newest portfolio outside the kitchen door and going back for the plants. "Their wives are my sisters. I should know what Harmony and Storm know."

"I don't think the sister thing counts after you're married. Besides, each might only know about her own husband. I think husbands trump sisters."

"Figures. I'm such a late bloomer. The middle child but the only one with no psychic mandate or prospects."

Morgan dropped one of her suitcases. "You mean marital prospects?"

"Get real, and be careful with my things. I don't want a man gumming up my life. I'm only toying with you."

He sighed inwardly with relief and slapped her on the ass on his way back to the dock a while later for the statues. "You weren't talking like that in the shower this morning."

"We weren't talking at all in the shower this morning. Screw you, Morgan."

He stopped and raised his hands. "*That's* all I'm saying."

As he opened the kitchen door, a racket greeted them, cupboard doors opening and slamming, plates flying from the cabinets, hitting the floor and each other.

"Meggie," Destiny said, "What's wrong with you?"

Everything calmed. Cupboard doors stopped, some open, some closed. Plates lay in pieces on the floor.

"Why are you crying?" Destiny asked, but nobody was there.

Morgan hurt as if Meggie did—an old familiar ache. "Well?" he snapped, in over his head, and going down for the count. "What's wrong with her?"

"She's upset. She couldn't find us last night, and she's angry that we went away today."

Good thing Destiny cast the spell so Meggie *couldn't* find them last night. "But she was at the cemetery today. She knew where we were." Morgan heard himself and shut his mouth for half a beat. "I said that out loud, didn't I?"

"Yes. Congratulations." Destiny started picking up plate shards. "That's why she *knows* we went to see your parents today."

Morgan rubbed the back of his neck. "Meggie always did have a temper, but if she knows where we were, she knows how lucky she is that she wasn't there."

"Ah, you made her smile."

"That's something—no!" he snapped. "It's not, because Meggie isn't here!"

Chapter Thirty-three

SADDENED by his response, tired of arguing, Destiny almost folded. But some things were worth fighting for. "Your sister is here, slam it."

More than anything, Destiny wanted Morgan to open up about his past, to believe in Meggie's spirit. Half the time, he seemed to believe that Meggie could exist on the spiritual plane, and the other half, he argued against it and his own instincts. An understandable reaction, but frustrating, nonetheless.

"Destiny," Meggie said. "Tell Morgan to go into the parlor and wait for you. I want to show you something."

Destiny translated his sister's wishes to Morgan.

"Fine," he said, shaking his head, as if one of them needed a shrink.

"Try to show some enthusiasm," Destiny whispered. "She can see you."

"Try to show some sanity," Morgan snapped. "I can't see her."

Meggie shrugged and led the way to the captain's chest in the closet beneath the stairs.

Destiny stopped short of picking it up. "I know about this chest, Meggie."

"Morgan needs to look inside at the things he put in there," Meggie said. "It's time."

"Ah." Destiny dragged the heavy chest into the parlor.

Morgan jumped up to help her. "Destiny, what are you doing with this? Put it back."

"No. Meggie wants you to look through it. Now. With me here. She said it's time."

"I could almost believe it's her, she's such a pest."

Meggie gave a thumbs-up.

Morgan carried the chest to the center of the Persian rug and knelt beside it.

"Go ahead," Destiny said, reaching for the latch. "Open, open, open."

Morgan sat on his heels. "I know what's inside."

"Meggie says you have to look and remember."

"Can't I do it alone?"

"No. She's shaking her head no. You have to share your memories with both of us."

"Both?"

"Me and Meggie."

"Of course. Anybody ever tell you that you're as bossy as my mother?"

"Whoa. Anybody ever tell you that witches are rumored to be capable of turning princes into toads?"

"You think I'm a prince?"

"I think you're a pain in the—"

"Buttkuss," Meggie said. "Tell him."

"Meggie says you're a pain in the buttkuss."

He looked around. "Buttkuss? I'm starting to believe you might be psychic, Kismet."

"Good one." Destiny wrinkled her nose at him. "Show me what's in there."

He opened the chest, lost the twinkle in his eyes, and took out a ratty old rag doll, scorched around the edges. "This is Samantha. Meggie loved this doll. The authorities found it in the tower. My mother threw it away, but I fished it out of the trash. I—" He shook his head as if he couldn't go on.

Destiny touched his hand. "It's okay."

"I took Samantha with me to the seminary. A doll. Imagine. No wonder I kept it under lock and key. I'd take it out when I missed Meggie. Eventually, I left it here. Meggie told me to take care of Samantha, if she couldn't. She said there'd be a fire, and Samantha would be in danger."

Destiny's head came up with her radar. "Wait. *Meggie* was psychic?"

"She made my parents—well, mostly my mother— furious when she predicted the future."

"Didn't they understand when the things she predicted happened?"

"No, that just made them madder." Morgan held the doll up to his face. "She doesn't smell like Meggie anymore." He set it on his lap, took out a metal flute and played it. "She warned me to be careful with this, that her throat hurt when she looked at it. She was right."

"What happened?"

"I was playing it on my way into the house, and the flute got to the door before I did. It cut my throat up. Lots of blood. Fast ride to the emergency room."

Destiny knuckled his throat; she needed that badly to touch him right then. "Why did you keep the flute?"

"To remind me that Meggie was right, and I was wrong." Morgan shook his head with regret. "So very wrong." He looked up. "Meggie talked and laughed all the time. Mother spent half of Meggie's life shushing her. Meggie would have reacted the way you did today. She would have laughed at my mother's nonsense. Mother said that Meggie's predictions were insane, and she meant that literally."

Destiny gasped at the cruelty, and she felt hurt radiating from Meggie even now.

Morgan looked around. "You weren't insane, Meggie," he called. "See?" he said to Destiny. "Now I feel a little insane. Why would she be here, anyway? Why not at my parents'? Never mind. Dumb question. Who'd go there if they didn't have to?"

"Meggie attached herself to you, Morgan, and when you started coming here, she stayed, knowing you'd return."

"But why? Why didn't she just move on? Aren't ghosts supposed to do that?"

"Not if they have unfinished business."

"What's Meggie's?"

"You, apparently."

"This is crap. I've had enough." Morgan shut the chest.

Destiny opened it on command. "She says you have to remember."

"Look, Kismet. Part of me wants to believe you, but—"

"You're frustrated and falling into your old habits of disbelief. It doesn't help that you went home today."

"Are you implying that I let my mother influence me?"

"She's a powerful woman who influenced your entire life. Old habits, as they say. I dare you to take out your electronic debunking equipment to prove there are spirits here. Meggie says you never turn down a dare."

"The brat," he muttered, as he went upstairs. "No, scratch that," he said, stopping in the middle of the stairway, recognizing his turn toward belief. "Tomorrow I'll take out my debunking equipment and put this ghost talk to rest."

"Tonight," Destiny said, ready to do cartwheels, she was so close to proving to him that ghosts, psychics, and magick did, indeed, exist. Close, but no cigar. Yet.

She passed him on the stairs and turned to look him in the eye. "You believe, but you don't. I understand. It takes time to go against a lifetime of disbelief."

"Tomorrow, I'll prove I'm an idiot for this belief creeping into my good sense, without my permission. *Tonight*, I plan to practice my new skills."

She took his hand to lead him the rest of the way up the stairs.

"I want more lessons," he said. "I want to see what you have in your toy box—great pun, eh?"

"Shh. Meggie can hear you."

"Shh," he whispered. "I want to bury my memories in your—"

Destiny stopped, and he walked into her. "You have memories?" she asked.

"None that I want to keep or acknowledge. Subject closed."

Chapter Thirty-four

SUBJECT closed, until she opened it again, but Destiny knew how to bide her time and choose it wisely. "I want to see your angel tattoo," she said as they got to the bedroom. "Is it Buffy?"

"It's Meggie's drawing of Buffy. I've kept it for years." He emptied his pockets and took the folded paper from his wallet to show her. "The tattoo artist used it as a model."

"Good thing you didn't put it on your butt."

"Sacrilege."

"Even I know that." She took the drawing. "Wow, Meggie is a good little artist. It's Buffy to a T. See the colors? I told you, red and blue gown, and a gold sash."

"Yeah, yeah, Sassy Ass. Let's play with the toys."

"Shh. Not yet. Let me lull Meggie in a way that won't hurt her like we did last night."

Morgan's stricken expression said he believed more than he wanted to. "I'd never knowingly hurt her."

"She's aware of that. But she died an innocent, and she'll always be one. While *you* are anything but."

"About time." He sat at the foot of the bed. "Go ahead and protect Meggie, nutcase that I am for saying so."

Destiny went to the top of the stairs where she could see Meggie, protected in her angel-wing cocoon.

> *"Meggie, sweet, float in sleep.*
> *A sphere of light so white,*
> *Soft with wings, angel bright*
> *To protect you from sight.*

> *"Private here, private now.*
> *To keep your innocence, I vow.*
> *Come the dawn you will be*
> *On the camera; he will see.*

> *"Happy our forever child.*
> *Your fate to ever run wild.*
> *My will for you be done.*
> *And it harm you none."*

When she got back to the bedroom, Morgan caught her around the waist with a growl. "Low blow on the camera thing."

"I speak only truth in prayer."

He grabbed her by the buns and pulled her up to his knees at the edge of the bed. "You speak a different language."

"Different from you." She began to unbutton his shirt. "Your mother thinks that you and she speak the same language. Is that true?"

"Ouch! Another low blow. Your wit is as sharp as your wand tonight. Want to see mine?"

"With whom would you rather align yourself? Your sweet-spirited sister or your narrow-minded, mean-spirited mother?"

He kissed her. "You know the answer to that, but you'll look like a fool tomorrow, if I take out my debunking equipment."

"I beg to differ, and you *will* take it out. I'll dare you again and again until you do." She straddled him.

"If Meggie *is* goading you, she's still a brat. What else did she tell you about me?"

"Meggie is at rest for tonight. You and I are wasting time."

"You had to mention my mother. I'm not turned on anymore."

"This afternoon, in your parents' house, your mother was calling your name while we plucked our brains out."

"Rebellion!" he said, snapping his fingers. "Rebelling with you, Kismet, makes me hot."

"So let's rebel." She got off his lap, placed her red suitcase on the bed, and opened it.

Morgan looked closer. "What are they?"

"Surely your sex books mentioned how women manage on their own. There were enough chapters about how men do, which turned me on like crazy, by the way." She raised the first object. "This is a dual-action, multispeed kangaroo vibrator."

"Okay. Let's use it."

"That's only half the fun."

"Tell my pecker that."

She placed a second suitcase on the bed, a smaller one, and when she opened it, Morgan grabbed his heart, and his eyes glazed over. He fingered a red bustier and held it in front of her. "Put it on. Put it on."

"Not without the scarlet panties and spikes that go with it. What are you, a heathen? Do you want me to put it on in front of you, or do you want me to go in the other room to put it on, so you can get the full effect all at once?"

"Oh, I want the full effect. Not sure my heart can take it, but I'm game. Besides, I'll get the effect coming and going—pun intended—when I remove it to reveal every delicious inch of your flesh and when I come my brains out. Before you go, name some of the rest of these man toys for me, will you?"

"Yellow garter belt," she said, dangling it in front of him. "Sheer fuchsia bikinis with a slit-crotch entry system."

Morgan groaned.

"Purple camisole with matching V-string bikinis. I brought high heels to go with each set."

"No more. I can't take the heat. Neither can the studly spire. He's doing an Irish step dance."

"Your aura has been growing and getting brighter by the day, but right now, if I didn't know you better, I'd think you were happy."

Morgan gave her a wicked grin. "Hey, if the big guy is happy, *I'm* happy."

"Man brain doing your thinking?"

"Who cares? Man brain just learned how. Cut him some slack. He's in practice mode."

Destiny knuckled his studly spire to get a wild rise out of him before she turned on her heel and left the room.

"Oh, wicked girl," Morgan shouted after her. "Naughty, teasing, wicked playmate, you will *so* get what you deserve."

When she got back, Destiny stopped short. Morgan the grumblestiltskin, ex-virgin, ex-priest, naked on his bed—their bed—beneath her scattered underwear, a pair of yellow V-string panties swinging from his boner like a flag run up the flagpole in a high wind.

His aura had turned blue with white edges, which meant pure and *loving*, which she would never tell him.

"It's raining bras," he sang to the tune of "It's Raining Men," while wiggling a foot to wave her fuchsia underwire. He sat up and lost half his rain. "Sex on a hot tin roof," he said, licking his lips as he looked her up and down. "You

look good enough to eat, and I'm starved. How do you prefer your foreplay?" he asked, raising a vibrator in each
hand. "Bunny à la Mode or Pig in a Blanket?"

Oh, we got trouble, right here on Paxton Island. Morgan
the Magnificent could play. He could try new things and
make himself look like an ass to amuse her. *Begone, trip
wire to my heartstrings.*

She could so fall for this man, and it scared the blessed
thistle out of her.

Morgan rose on his knees and bowed. "I remain at your
command. A feast awaits."

She got into the bed, pushed him back, and climbed on
top of him to abrade his dick with the crotch of her scarlet
panties, and her breasts fell from her scarlet bustier into his
gleeful and expectant face. "I'll take the bunny," she said,
"for bunny ears are tidbits of orgasmic delight. And you,
my good man, shall get porked—which, by the way is a
gnome, not a pig—to within an inch of your man glue."

Destiny found herself riding the epicenter of an earth-
quake, a bucking bronco of rare man laughter, an eruption
so violent, she got thrown and landed on the bed, so Morgan could sit up and catch his breath.

Morgan Jarvis, carefree. Happy. Loud. Raucous.

The man who'd growled through the first four months
of their acquaintance. The man who talked her ear off
while necking on the night of Harmony's wedding, who'd
grumbled as he walked down the aisle at Storm and Aid-
en's wedding.

Something in Morgan Jarvis had snapped.

More than his dick but less than his sanity.

Chapter Thirty-five

SUDDENLY the laughter stopped, and something momentous and emotional took its place. Destiny didn't dare try to name it; she knew only that it existed.

As one, they swooped, and fell on the lingerie-strewn bed together, both aggressive and starving, giving and taking, coming and coming, slick with sweat, sticky with sex, each shouting or screaming, satisfaction guaranteed, sometimes together, sometimes in turn.

After the first formidable flash of lust, Morgan found Bunny à la Mode, turned it on, examined it, placed his thumb at the tip of its jackhammer ears, and grinned. "Hunh, hunh, hunh," he said, imitating a Frenchman by twisting his nonexistent handlebar mustache, "Thee bunny ears, they are deelicious for thee happee clit?"

Destiny rolled into him to hide her face, while he lowered her scarlet panties and rubbed his five o'clock shadow against her butt cheek, tickling her and staking his claim.

Then he put the bunny where it belonged and played her like a French horn.

At one point, she was certain she'd passed out.

The following morning, Destiny woke to Morgan tickling her nose with a feather from her sex toy bag. She wiggled her nose, scratched it, and tried to go back to sleep.

"What have you done to me?" Morgan whispered rather earnestly.

"Witchcraft, that crazy witchcraft," she sang, keeping her eyes closed so she wouldn't wake up entirely.

He chuckled. "I don't think so."

"I planned to use that feather on your most prized possession," she said, rolling over and trying to go back to sleep.

"Please do." He feathered her ear.

"Mmm," she sighed.

"Come on, Kismet, get up. I feel like a new man today. Let's play. Tell me what you want to do, and we'll do it."

She rose up and leaned on an elbow. "I wanna play with your debunking equipment."

"No, that's crazy. We can't; I mean we don't need—"

"Yes, we do. A belly laugh and a good pluck do not a free man make. You *need* to talk to your sister."

"That again."

"You let me protect her, though you don't believe she's here?"

"I let you protect her, in case I'm wrong to disbelieve, because I *was* wrong once."

Destiny swatted him and got up, hoping to gain his cooperation by manipulating him with her nakedness. "Get your debunking equipment and *prove* me wrong, or yon rising sex slayer will rust from disuse."

"Now don't go off half-timbered," he said following her to the shower. "Letting the big guy rust sure trumps a headache."

After separate showers and breakfast, Morgan reluctantly set up his debunking equipment.

Deep inside, Destiny was doing a happy dance. She planned to *make* him see his sister, come hail or high priestess, which called for a couple of silent spells, the first to wake Meggie, the next to wake Morgan.

> *Angel wings unfold*
> *Allow Meggie sight.*
> *Meggie, my sweet,*
> *Come into the light.*

Horace, Meggie, and her angel appeared in the center of the rug, almost like the first time she'd seen them, except that this morning, they were watching Morgan set up his equipment.

> *Memories unfold*
> *Give Morgan sight*
> *Morgan, my dear,*
> *Come into the light.*

His debunking equipment with all those wires and dials and recording devices looked complicated. He brought the recording stuff into the kitchen, where Meggie had had her tantrum, and it took him a while to set it up.

"It's plugged in and running," he said returning to the parlor.

Meggie shrugged. "I could have a tantrum in here, too."

"What?" Morgan asked.

"You're sister's being flip."

"Quiet, brat."

"She's sticking her tongue out at you."

"Guess I don't need to replace the batteries in this electric and magnetic field meter, because I'm already getting an off-the-charts reading, and we're nowhere near a power plant."

Destiny combed Morgan's burnished hair back from his brow. "Gee, what a surprise."

"Now *you're* being flip. Are you sure you're not manifesting your sarcasm on Meggie?"

"Are you sure you're not locking that meter on high?"

"Touché." He took a block of batteries from a leather camera bag and ejected the old ones from a small piece of equipment. "This is a kind of camera that senses heat or energy and projects it onto the screen in different colors. Different energy levels equal different colors. A spirit would register energy, *if* spirits existed. You should know that it's never measured anything but living energy."

"I'm sure it's hasn't. I'm also sure it's about to be tested. What *is* living energy?"

"An actual person. Body heat left on a chair or bed after somebody gets up, that kind of thing."

"I understand." She watched him turn the camera on and dial it to daytime, indoors settings.

At Meggie's urging, Horace and Buffy moved away from her, as if the little imp understood that Morgan needed to discern them each as separate entities, her especially.

"Your sister's a smart girl."

He sighed. "Like I never heard that before."

"Your grades weren't as good?"

"My grades sucked. Meggie was a straight A student. Our teachers were always telling me to be more like her. Camera's ready," he said, changing the subject.

Said camera looked something like a cell phone with a screen. Destiny stood beside him and let him aim on his own. She didn't want to guide him at all. Her heart quickened as he got closer and closer to any one of the trilogy of spirits in the middle of the parlor.

"Whoa," he said. "What is that?"

Destiny checked the aim against the subject. "That's Horace the lighthouse keeper. Wave at Morgan, Horace."

The colorful shadow of an arm came up in a naval salute.

Morgan looked at her and back at the shadow. "Meggie? Where's Meggie, Des?"

"You'll have to find her yourself, or you'll never believe me."

He caught a huge white shadow, so blinding that Destiny looked away. "That's your guardian angel, in case you haven't guessed."

"Holy sh—Buffy? That's Buffy? She's bigger than I expected."

"Buffy?" Destiny asked. "Care to wave a wing? She doesn't say much, but I believe she's abstaining."

Meggie took to running around the room, giggling, dodging the camera, and frustrating Destiny. "Meggie, will you cut that out!"

"Morgan *likes* to play tag," she said.

Destiny shook her head at Morgan. "If you want to see her, you'll have to chase her."

"Cut it out, Megs," Morgan said. "This is no time for tag."

Destiny saw something amazing, and a bolt of wild elation shot through her.

She held her hand to her fast-beating heart while Morgan followed his sister around with the camera, as if he *could* see her, but he hadn't caught up with her yet.

Hot damn. Could it be that Meggie wasn't the only psychic twin? That could be the key to what Morgan was blocking. True, he was letting down his guard in a big way, but Destiny wasn't about to tell him so. "You're getting warmer," she said, getting as close to an acknowledgment of his possible gift as she dared.

At that moment, he caught Meggie in his sights.

She and Meggie knew it. Did he?

He shook his head, as if in denial, but gasped when his sister held up her stuffed dog and waved its furry arm at him. He fumbled the camera, nearly dropped it, but his need to see his sister overrode all else, and he caught and refocused it immediately. "What the pluck?"

Meggie giggled, but Destiny remained silent, because she didn't want to break Morgan's focus.

"This isn't possible." He looked around the room. "It's the windows, the sun and its shadows. Shut the curtains."

"That's what you think, big brother," Meggie said while Destiny did as she was told. "Tell me the light can do this," Meggie added, challenging the brother who couldn't hear her, as she separated her ring finger from her middle finger in the "Live long and prosper" salute made famous by Spock on *Star Trek*. "Morgan will know *this* is me," Meggie said raising her saluting hand away from her body.

"Jesus!" Morgan whispered, beads of perspiration forming on his brow, as if he might pass out.

He shook his head. Stepped back, then closer, and closer. "Meggie?"

Chapter Thirty-six

MORGAN'S heart beat out of his chest. Lights flickered in his vision. A straight chair hit him in the back of his legs, and he sat. "Thanks, Des.

"Impossible," he said, but he couldn't take his gaze from the camera's viewer. "So much energy after seventeen years?" he whispered. "It can't be."

Destiny touched his arm. "It can be. It is. Do you want a glass of water?"

"No. I want to watch the sweet clown dance," he said, speaking over the emotion rising in his throat but trying not to let it show. Dancing is exactly what Meggie, or whatever, *whoever* he'd caught in his sight, seemed to be doing.

Morgan covered Destiny's hand on his arm; he needed her strength.

"Your sister is clowning it up for you. You *do* believe she's here?"

How could he not? "What kind of shadow makes that

precise a salute?" he asked. "We used the salute when our mother was being her strict, controlling, complaining self. Momzilla is what Meggie called her, by the way, not to her face, of course. To us, back then, the sign meant, 'I feel for you.' It ticked my mother off, because *she* didn't know what we were saying to each other."

"I'll bet it did."

"What kills me, here—pardon the pun, Meggie—is the real meaning. My dead sister just told me to live long and prosper."

"Yes!" Destiny said. "That's exactly what Meggie wants for you. That's why you need to remember. What are you blocking?"

"How should I know? I'm blocking it."

"Meggie says to tell you that you're blocking something important."

A sick feeling rose up in him, telling him that he *didn't* want to know what. "Well, it can't be very important," he said.

Destiny chuckled. "Your sister just called you 'Meatball.' She dares you to remember."

Another reminder of their childhood. He took a deep breath and glanced up at Destiny. "Look at me. I don't have the legs to stand, and I can't hold the camera steady anymore. How the Hades am I supposed to remember what I've been blocking for nearly twenty years?"

Destiny leaned into him, slid an arm around his neck. He drew strength from her.

"Tell me about Meggie and your childhood together," she said. "You might hit on something."

Morgan shook his head against a return of the sick miasma that was coming with every request for him to remember. "Ask *her* what I'm supposed to remember."

"She says you have to remember it yourself. Talk to me."

"I don't want to talk. My head aches." His insides trembled, too, but he didn't want Destiny to know that.

He unobtrusively rubbed his palm on his jeans, switched the camera to his dry hand, and repeated the action. He didn't want to *think*, either. He wanted to *see* his sister without an infrared camera—a real problem, since he was probably losing his mind. A thirty-year-old with a twin, aged twelve. Right. Here, but not. Yet the pull was killing him. "I saw Mother the other day, Meggie. She hasn't changed at all."

Destiny cleared her throat. "Meggie says she never will."

"There go my hopes for family peace."

"How did Meggie die?" Destiny asked.

"Stick a knife in my heart, why don't you?" That damned sob he'd been holding back escaped without his permission. "Sorry." He cleared his throat. "My mother thought Meggie's predictions were a form of mental illness, or that Meggie might be possessed—sorry Megs—by the devil, so my parents put her in a convent boarding school where the nuns could look after her."

Morgan hated the way the speck in his eye clouded his view through the lens. Slam. He noticed that his sister had stopped dancing. "Meggie, I won't tell her what happened, if it hurts you."

Destiny knelt in front of him and laid her head on his lap. God, he needed her in his life.

"Meggie's glad you're remembering," Destiny said. "She's only sad because you're sad."

Morgan touched Destiny's hair, wove his fingers through it, and absorbed her comforting and reassuring presence. "Okay. Meggie, I won't be sad anymore. I'll just say it like it was. The nuns put Meggie in a tower bedroom, away from the other kids, to keep them safe from the lunatic—again, sorry Megs. The tower got hit by lightning and caught fire. Meggie couldn't get out."

"Whoa. Your mother's scarier than I thought." Destiny raised her head as if listening to something important.

"You're a better girl than I am," Des said. "Morgan, Meggie says that she forgave your mother a long time ago."

"I thought I did, too, until now. The thing is, after Meggie passed, my mother didn't want me talking about her, my own sister, but I couldn't help myself, so that's when they sent me to the seminary to shut *me* up. They thought the priests could straighten me out."

Destiny raised her head, her expression puzzled. "So you became one of them? That doesn't make much sense."

"I buried my memories in my studies. In a way, I think I brainwashed myself. The happiest day of my mother's life was the day I was ordained. It was also the first time I'd *ever* pleased her." Hearing it in his own words, Morgan knew he *had* been running from memories, some of which were resurfacing.

Some, he wasn't ready to face.

"Why did you leave the priesthood?" Destiny asked him.

"A little girl in my parish asked me if I was happy. Here's the kicker; her name was Meggie. I sat down that afternoon and tried to define *happy*. However I defined it, *happy* didn't apply to me. That night, I came here, hung my cassock beneath the stairs, and went to work for King."

"And that made you happy?"

"Not as unhappy as I'd been as a priest. Happy didn't seem possible. I'd lost my focus. It's hard to explain."

Destiny rubbed his arm. "Maybe you're psychic like your twin. You *did* have another career waiting in the wings."

"When I worked toward my architectural degree, I told myself I'd maybe help restore the Vatican someday—lofty goals, hey—but eventually I realized that I'd always been looking for an out. My mother will never stop trying to get me to go back." He checked his camera. "Where's Meggie?"

"They're gone for now. Probably because we were talking. They pop in and out."

"That doesn't freak you out?"

"It sure did the first time. The night I arrived. Scared me enough to give *you* a concussion."

"Right." He touched his brow to hers. "I can't believe my sister's here but she's not. I want to see her face. Why can't I see her like you can?"

"You're not open to it. You have to believe without question. You didn't believe until she gave you the sign, plus you failed to remember what she believes you should. Maybe if you did believe, and you remembered what she needs you to, she'd show herself to you."

"Let's plant her memory garden now. Maybe she'll chase butterflies here."

"I wish I'd thought to get butterfly garden plants to attract them," Destiny said. "Isn't it late in the year for butterflies?"

"Meggie did a science project on butterflies once, so I happen to know that in warm years, like this one, some species have more generations, so you'll see them longer. Some butterfly species prefer the cold, some prefer the sea. So next trip into town, let's get some butterfly garden plants." Morgan grabbed the tray of crazy-named plants. "Where do you want to plant her garden?"

"Anywhere that won't interfere with construction equipment when you remodel the place. We want it to be permanent, right? Too bad we don't know where the cemetery is."

"Kismet, we went to the cemetery yesterday."

"No, Horace's wife is buried *here*. I think that's why he's hanging around. I'd like to clean it up, plant mums for the fall, daffodils for the spring, and a holly bush for the Holly King. I mean, we already have oaks for the Oak King."

Morgan scratched his head. "That's a witch thing, right?"

"Yep. This is a nice spot. Far enough from the house to

be safe, and we can still see it from there. It needs weeding. We should have brought a spade."

Morgan took his work gloves from the tray. "I brought one." He got on his knees, pulled weeds and turned the earth.

When Destiny dug a hole for a plant, she hit something. "A headstone. Oh, and it's broken." She dusted it off. "Morgan, it's Ida and her baby. They died the same day. Poor Horace. No wonder he wants to be here. He never told me about the baby."

Morgan rubbed the perspiration from his brow and rested his hands on his knees. "Do you know how much it would cost to have a body exhumed and reburied?"

Destiny tilted her head his way, her eyes shining. "Are you the one being psychic now? I never said that's what I wanted."

"You implied it clearly enough. Except that I don't quite believe in Horace."

"This stone doesn't prove his existence?"

"The way you see the future? No."

"Oh, so you believe in my psychic ability, now, but not in your sister or Horace?"

"I'll always believe in Meggie. Not so sure about—"

"You're a doubting Thomas, Morgan, from one end of the spectrum to the other. You have to believe in something."

"I walked out on the only belief system I ever knew, and, pluck it, I'm having a bit of trouble finding a new one. Get off my back."

Chapter Thirty-seven

DESTINY didn't like this peek at the old Morgan. She wanted the new fun-loving, belief-filled Morgan back, but he seemed as lost as her. More lost. He didn't even have a family to fall back on. "You have your dad to believe in. You have King and Aiden's friendship, and mine."

"Not quite the same as having a purpose," Morgan said, "but thanks."

"You'll find your purpose. You've made great strides this week. You had sex *and* you believe in psychics."

"Extraordinary strides," he said. "I can't wait to tell my mother."

"Hah! You got a death wish, Boy Scout? But seriously, you do believe I'm psychic, don't you?"

"I guess I do. There's no other explanation for the canvas ladybug prediction, the design for my lighthouse, and the painting of Buffy dated the day Meggie died."

"Damn you. You only believe because you've seen proof? It's always proof with you."

"I'm sorry. Forget the proof. I do have to believe in something, and it may as well be you. You're the most tangible, fascinating, and entertaining lunatic I ever took to bed."

"My cup runneth over with gratitude. Such compliments. And only yesterday you were a grumblestiltskin."

He pulled her cowboy hat down over her eyes. "C'mon, Kismet. Let's plant Meggie's garden to the left, closer to the lighthouse, and leave Ida's resting place alone. When we're done, there'll be flowers for all of them."

They worked silently together as they planted Meggie's flowers around the angel statue, the lighthouse statue, and the garden stone with Destiny engraved on it. When they finished planting, they outlined the tiny garden with beach rocks and shells.

Together they sat back on their heels to admire their work, the bees buzzing, the air sweet.

Morgan nodded. "Ask Horace where he's buried—there's a sentence you don't hear often enough—so we can move his body. Do you think lunacy is catching?"

"Morgan Jarvis, you're hiding a heart." Destiny bit her lip. "I think I might be crushing on you."

"In that case, you're heading for a fall. Crush is the right word. Hit your head on me, and you'll crack it open. I'm made of stone. You don't crush on a man because he's going to spend a fortune to move the body of the hundred-year-old stranger haunting his home. Besides, what's the big deal?"

"You're acting on faith."

"Faith in you. Not in general; believe me." Morgan's denial brought out the grumblestiltskin in him. "All these years," he said, almost to himself, "I thought I *was* acting on faith, but I was trying to make up to my mother for failing her. Did you ever feel as if you'd lost your center? Like you were wandering aimlessly?"

"Yes!" Destiny's heart skipped a beat. She touched his

arm. "*That's* why I'm searching for my psychic goal. Without it, *I'm* wandering aimlessly. You and I both need something to ground us," she said, figuring it out as she spoke. "Want to buddy up and be there for each other until we find our paths?"

Morgan tilted his head thoughtfully. "Friends who are lovers? Sounds risky to me."

"Don't look now, but we're already there. Call it safety in numbers?"

"I guess we are." Morgan looked out beyond the sea. "Two against the world? You and me, babe? That kind of thing?"

He was mocking her. Her frustration came out in a sigh. "You know what I mean. For *emotional* support."

"Oh, Kismet, that's the most dangerous kind." Morgan pulled off a work glove, dropped it in the dirt, and cupped her cheek, as if she might be made of porcelain, but a fire raged in the depths of his tiger eyes. "The longer you look at me like that," he said, melting her to her core, "the more I want to take you to bed."

She covered his hand as their lips touched.

"Take me to bed," she whispered, combing a hand through his burnished hair. She could love this man. Maybe she already did. She knew only that she'd never wanted a lover so badly that she trembled with need and longing for him, and for more.

In this man, she recognized the possibility of a soul mate.

A soul mate. What an amazing thought. Frightening. Grumblestiltskin and Kismet Witch?

No way. She couldn't believe it, couldn't admit it. Didn't dare. Not to herself. Not to him. Lightning did not strike thrice.

She shivered. Pulled away. Wanted to run but stood her ground.

Morgan took her hand, brought her to her feet, slipped

an arm around her waist, and led her to the house. When he shut the front door, he pinned her against it in one move.

He cupped her waist, his thumb beneath her shirt.

Destiny squeaked and stopped him. "Morgan, wait. They're back. Meggie's smiling at us, but give me a minute before we go any further."

Morgan nodded silently and stepped away from her, so she could spell them gently away.

> *"Company, all three*
> *An audience not to be*
> *Ease away; let me pray*
> *Bide your time as I rhyme,*
> *And spell a prime*
> *Quest of the sublime.*
>
> *"Meggie Bee, run to see*
> *A brand-new garden*
> *Of silly-name flowers*
> *Beside the oak tree.*
> *Where Ida and baby,*
> *And Horace will be.*
>
> *"Play in white light.*
> *Let flowers delight*
> *Keep you from sight*
> *For a day and a night.*
> *I can heal your brother,*
> *But not your mother."*

Destiny went limp and fell into Morgan's embrace. "Your heart is racing as fast as mine," she said.

"That was scary," he said. "I love her so much. She won't be hurt by what she saw, or by us sending her away?"

"She'll be fine. She knows we love her, and she knows that we care about each other. Buffy and Horace helped and enveloped her in their love."

"We seem to have lost our momentum," he said.

"Let's heat some water in those big old copper kettles and fill that gorgeous old claw-foot tub."

"That'll take time, but"— Morgan raised a brow—"I brought a deck of cards. Care for a game of strip poker while we're waiting for—dare I say it—the pots to boil?"

"And you thought you were gonna play solitaire, in more ways than one."

He handled the stove's firebox while she filled a copper kettle at the big old copper sink. "Morgan, this boiler says it holds thirteen gallons. Is it too heavy for you to carry to the bathroom?"

He hefted a full boiler and approved its weight, so she filled them all. Three copper boilers nestled on the six-burner stove, while Morgan dealt the cards. "We'll have water before we get down to our underwear."

Destiny winked to raise his blood pressure. "If we're wearing any."

Fifteen minutes later she laid down her second winning hand, a full house.

"You're a cardsharp, Kismet." Morgan stood to take off his jeans.

"You could have taken off a sock. In a hurry, Boy Scout? You have great taste in boxers, by the way. Black. Yum. And so nicely filled at this moment."

"I came preboiled. If you don't know how to lose, just be a sport and take off that Any Witch Way T-shirt."

She pulled it off over her head, and he nearly swallowed his tongue.

"Don't tell me you didn't know I'd gone braless?"

"I was preoccupied."

"Sad man. You haven't felt up enough women. You need practice."

"Come, sit on my lap. I'll practice."

By the time the water boiled, they boiled, too.

Morgan started filling up the tub, and the doorbell rang.

"Slam it," he said, as he looked daggers at the door.

Disappointment filled Destiny. She looked down at the claw-foot tub promising an afternoon of hot sex.

"Let's pretend that nobody's home," Morgan suggested.

But Destiny suddenly remembered what day it was.

Morgan's day, and Meggie's, too.

Wonderful. She'd spelled Meggie away for a day and a night.

She began to chant, despite Morgan's frown:

> "White light, elliptical in flight,
> Dissolve and free Meggie Bee.
> Time limits counter clock, n'er to be
> Bring Megs and company back, all three.
> Back to where she'll be pleased to be."

"What are you doing?" Morgan snapped.

Destiny sighed. "Answering the door."

"Don't. No, wait," he said grabbing his pants. "Is Meggie back?"

"Don't you wish you knew the answer without having heard my spell?"

Chapter Thirty-eight

"HAPPY Birthday, Morgan," Reggie and Jake shouted as Destiny opened the door and then stepped aside.

Reggie came in carrying a birthday cake that must have had all thirty-one candles on it. Jake followed but stopped short. "Who's this?"

He circled Meggie, or Meggie circled him, hard to tell which.

Destiny gave Morgan an I-told-you-so elbow. Further proof Meggie was here. "She's Morgan's sister, Jake. Her name is Meggie, but she's like the lady you saw in the elevator at the castle a few months ago. Remember? Meggie's a ghost."

"Cool. But I can tell that she's not a mad ghost like that lady." Jake shrugged at Meggie. "Hi, Meggie. Do you wanna play?"

Reggie squeaked, but Destiny quieted her with a head-shake.

"Yes, please," Meggie said, and both children smiled.

Destiny didn't want Reggie to stifle her son's openness to new experiences. Okay, so he didn't understand death as a loss, yet, but he accepted the spirit world, and for now that was enough.

"Meggie does want to play," Destiny said, letting Morgan and Reggie in on the decision. "But today is Meggie's birthday, too, Jake, because she's Morgan's twin, so let's light those candles, Reggie, and we'll sing 'Happy Birthday' to Meggie and Morgan."

Reggie lit the candles, while Morgan shut the bathroom door on a cooling tub of delayed satisfaction.

Meggie slipped a finger into the flame of a birthday candle.

"Don't!" Jake snapped. "You're gonna burn yourself."

"It's okay, Jake," Destiny explained. "Ghosts can't get hurt."

"'Cause they're dead, you mean?"

So much for him not understanding.

"Did you cry, Uncle Morgan, when your little sister died?"

Morgan bent to Jake's level and squeezed one of Jake's shoulders. "I sure did, Jake. I miss my sister every day."

Jake stepped into Morgan's arms and got a crushing bear hug. "You can be sad, Uncle Morgan," Jake said patting his back. "It's okay to be sad when you miss someone."

Morgan swallowed hard as did Destiny and Reggie. Wow. They didn't call Jake Baby Einstein for nothing.

He started singing "Happy Birthday" first, not nearly as shaken as the adults. Horace joined in, while Buffy, the angel, watched. When they finished singing, Morgan and Meggie blew out the candles together, though Morgan didn't realize it.

Jake hopped up and down. "Boy, do we got a present for you, Uncle Morgan! Oh, but we don't have a present for Meggie."

"Playing with you can be Meggie's present, okay?"

Morgan said. "She hasn't had a chance to play in a long time."

"Okay! Can I get 'em now, Mom? Can I?"

Reggie pulled up the five-year-old's droopy shorts. "Go ahead."

When Jake went out to the porch, the barking that erupted raised Morgan's head, and his suspicions, by the looks of him.

Jake came back with two pups on leashes. He released them, and they ran in circles around Meggie, Horace, and Buffy. Like Caramello, the pups saw the ghosts, too.

Morgan bent to catch the ecstatic silver schnoodle in his arms, like they'd been reunited or something, and Meggie got close, petting the pup somewhere over her back, and winning the pup's wild, tail-wagging enthusiasm.

"I know you can't tell, Morgan," Destiny said, petting the pup as well, "but you're sharing your birthday present with your sister."

"I can't tell you how happy that makes me," he said, his voice breaking. "She wanted a schnoodle more than anything. I was saving to buy her one for her thirteenth birthday, but the day never came."

"She thanks you, Morgan," Destiny said. "She's touched."

Meggie kissed her brother on the cheek, or as close as she could get, and Morgan touched the very spot a moment later, whipping his head her way.

Destiny nodded.

"Really?" he said. "I felt her touch?"

"You felt her kiss."

Morgan blew out his breath and swallowed. "Thank you, Jake, Reggie, from me and my sister."

"Oh, it's not from us," Reggie said. "Thank Destiny. It was her idea and her money. On the other hand, I have a bone to pick with her. When we went to get your little girl teddy bear pooch, Jake wanted Einstein, and I fell in love with him, too, so now Jake has an *early* birthday present."

"Einstein?" Destiny and Morgan asked.

Jake was holding Einstein so Meggie could pet him. "I wanted a real nickname, so I decided to call him Einstein, so nobody could call me that anymore."

"Nothing gets by my boy," Reggie said.

Morgan took Destiny's hand and brought it to schnoodle licking level. "Thank you for my birthday puppy. I was trying to wait until after I bought the lighthouse, but I don't think King will mind if I move from my no-dogs Boston apartment before the paperwork is done."

"By the looks of the affection passing between you, I think she was meant to be yours. What are you going to call her?"

"I hadn't thought about it," Morgan said.

Destiny cupped the pup's sweet little face. "Meggie just suggested a name."

"This is the dog she always wanted, so what's her name, Meggie?"

Reggie leaned near Destiny, everyone on the floor with the pups. "Does he actually believe Meggie's here?"

"Sometimes," Destiny whispered.

"He seems less and less like the grouch I met at the castle."

Destiny chuckled. "Thank goodness."

"I can hear you," Morgan said.

"It's too bad you can't hear Meggie, because she suggested that we name the pup after her doll."

Morgan nodded. "Samantha, she is. Hear that, Samantha, girl? You're named after a doll, who was named after a sitcom character on *Bewitched*, of all programs." He looked at Destiny. "Don't tell me that Meggie believes in witches."

"Okay I won't, but cheer up," she said, winking at Meggie. "It's not a conspiracy."

"You're sure about that?" Morgan asked, but he didn't seem to expect an answer. "Nevertheless, Reggie, we need to hitch a ride to town in your boat to pick up some dog food and supplies."

"Nah," Jake said. "We got all that stuff in the boat already. Destiny thought of everything."

Destiny saw Caramello take a flying leap from the top of the stair rail. As she caught her cat, Samantha and Einstein barked, and Caramello gave them a *friendly* yowl, judging by her tone as she scrambled right to Morgan.

Empty-handed, Destiny shook her head at Morgan sitting there with Jake, Meggie, two pups, and a cat shawl crowding him. "I can't imagine why they find him so fascinating."

"Can't you?" Reggie asked.

She shrugged. "Everybody ready for cake?" She chose plates and cups from the weird assortment left to them.

"Me and Meggie want to take the pups out back to play," Jake said.

Reggie shook her head in the negative. "Wait until we're ready to take our cake out to watch you." She helped Destiny with the cake. "You're sure Jake isn't talking to thin air?"

"He's talking to Meggie, and Horace, the old lighthouse keeper. Meggie's angel's there, too, but I'm not sure Jake can see her, because I'd think he would have said something about such an imposing entity."

Reggie frowned. "Okayyyy. But he's not related to you. Why can my son see ghosts?"

"Children are open to every new experience, and Jake, especially, is so smart that even you said he sucks up knowledge like a sponge."

"Right."

Morgan rubbed his hands together. "This is my first party at the lighthouse. Between our guests, Destiny, and your generosity, our ghosts and our pets, this suddenly feels like a home."

"I'd say that's one big step for a debunking man." They kissed.

Reggie gave them a wolf whistle as she went outside.

The adults sat on wooden benches watching the children—one living, one not—a cat, and two pups, tumbling and laughing their way down a sandy hill, with butterflies chasing them.

The butterflies must look peculiar to Reggie, Destiny thought. "You can always tell where Meggie is when she's outside, because butterflies follow her."

"That's freaky," Reggie said, "but thanks for the heads-up. Jake, move closer to us and away from the dock!"

"Meggie, let's—Mom! Megs fell in the water!" Jake jumped off the far side of the dock and disappeared.

Chapter Thirty-nine

DESTINY and Reggie ran and screamed, while Morgan jumped into the water and swam beneath the dock.

Less than a second later, Jake was climbing on the dock. "An angel saved me!"

Reggie caught him up, wept, and clutched him. "You're gonna be punished big time, mister, but right this minute, I just need to hold you." She pulled away. "Why aren't you wet?"

"I told you. An angel saved me. She scooped me up with one huge wing"—Jake spread his hands as far apart as they could get to demonstrate—"*before* I hit the water. You couldn't see me because the dock was in the way."

"Oh God," Reggie said. "Have you ever *seen* an angel before?"

"Sure, she's Meggie's angel. Buffy. Why?"

"Never mind." Reggie pulled her son close again, while Destiny stepped out of her shoes, worried about how long Morgan had been under.

Jake squirmed. "Mom, you're hurting me."

"Morgan hasn't resurfaced," Destiny said, going in after him.

Destiny found him at the deep end of the dock. He looked dazed, but he was focused on Meggie holding his hand and bringing him up. Destiny took his other hand to get him out more quickly.

They surfaced to a circus of noisy animals and Reggie's helping hands. "Jake, you're okay," Morgan said, still trying to catch his breath as he gave the boy a bear hug. "Thank God. You know, I think I hit my head down there. I was having hallucinations."

Destiny rolled her eyes. He'd seen his sister, and still he called her a hallucination. "Here's where the dense don't believe what's right in front of them," Destiny told Reggie. "Morgan, go get some dry clothes on before you catch pneumonia."

He went, still looking dazed. Maybe his doubt was more like a last bid for sanity.

"Meggie's okay, too, Mom," Jake said. "She can walk on water. I wish I could. Hey," he said to Meggie as they met on the beach, "you're not wet, either. Why do butterflies like you? Do you see Meggie's butterflies, Mom?"

"I see them," Reggie said. "Come here. We need to have a talk."

Jake came, but he knew a scolding was in store.

Reggie took her son to the bench where she sat him down and knelt in front of him. "Don't try to save Meggie again. She can't die, if she's already dead. My point," Reggie said, "is that I can't see Meggie, and neither can Uncle Morgan. So, if *you* had fallen in that water, and drowned, I wouldn't be able to see you anymore, or hug you, and I sure wouldn't want that to happen. So you stay out of the water, unless I'm with you!"

Jake threw his arms around his mother's neck. "I love you so much, I could hug you forever."

"Same here, baby."

Jake held on. "I'm not a baby, anymore, remember?"

"Right, sorry. But you'll always be my baby, no matter how big you get."

Jake sighed as if he understood these things. "I know. How come Aunt Destiny and me can see Meggie, and you can't?"

"Let me answer that," Destiny said, taking Jake on her lap. "You and I have a gift, Jake. We can see ghosts. But not everybody will believe you, if you talk about seeing them, so let's keep your gift to ourselves for a while, until you get older and learn how to handle it better."

"I can do that. Me and my mom kept lots of secrets on our way here to find Grandpa." Jake jumped off her lap to follow his pup tugging at his pants with its teeth, and he went back to playing. Jake and Meggie with Samantha, Einstein, and Caramello—two kids rolling in the grass, three pets yipping, yowling, and rolling as well.

"We need to get back to Salem," Reggie said. "I closed the shop for a few hours, but it'll get busy tonight. Let's get Morgan's pup supplies out of the boat."

"Sure thing," Destiny said.

"You want to tell me what's going on with you two?"

"What? Nothing. We're sharing the place."

"I can see that. Playing cards with enough water on the stove to fill a bathtub. All very innocent, except for the fact that I saw Morgan zipping his jeans as the door opened. Strip poker, I take it?"

"Geez, Regg, you expect me to confess?"

"No, but the priest might."

"Where did you hear that bit of skewed and incorrect information?"

"From a crazy woman who came into the Immortal Classic this morning to tell me that my sister was seducing her son, the priest."

"When you go back to the shop, neutralize the negativity with a smudge stick the way we taught you. That woman's certifiable, and I'm not kidding. Plucking patchouli, I'm gonna smudge her son, too."

"Is smudging what they're calling it these days?"

Destiny raised a brow. "Morgan had a narrow escape from the asylum he was born into, but his sister didn't. It's a wonder he's almost normal."

"Des, you've been calling him crazy for months."

"I've revised my opinion, mostly."

"That good, is he?"

Destiny turned to lift a bag of doggie chow.

After Reggie and Jake left, Destiny and Morgan skipped the bath for a reunion shower, then they went to bed, where she spelled them some gentle privacy.

"Thank you for Samantha," Morgan said as they lay entwined afterward, their naked bodies slick with sweat, the sea stroking the shore outside their window lulling them further. With her head on his chest, his heartbeat matched the slowing cadence of hers. She traced the line of hair arrowing toward the sated, sleeping giant.

The doorknob turned on the closed door, and in fell Caramello and Samantha, who'd been standing on their hind legs. "Great," Morgan said. "Between them, they can turn doorknobs."

Their pets jumped onto the bed, curled up at their feet together, and went to sleep.

"Sweet sassafras tea," Destiny said. "I think Samantha has replaced you in Caramello's affections."

"Good. Now I won't be afraid to kiss you and piss her off."

As Destiny smiled and drifted toward sleep, Morgan's stroking touch went from soothing to agitated and chafing. "What's wrong?" she asked, looking up at him and covering the now tender skin of her arm.

"I'm sorry," he said. "I was thinking."

"About?"

"You're psychic. You should know."

"Stop being a smart-ass, and answer me."

"I got to thinking about Meggie and how my parents felt about her being psychic. I remembered something, but I'm not happy about it."

Destiny hit the light switch and sat up to face him. "Something about your childhood?"

"Meggie made predictions of the future, no matter how angry it made my parents. I, on the other hand, kept my mouth shut, unlike her, to protect myself from their anger."

Destiny settled herself against the headboard, ready for a long talk. "Let me get this straight. You're admitting that you're psychic?"

"I know you've suspected." He brought the blankets up to cover her shoulders. "I'm afraid I am, or was."

"There is no was. It isn't curable, and it isn't a disease or something to fear."

"When you screw it up, it is."

"How did you screw it up?"

"Before Meggie died, I got a vision of the school's tower falling—not of Meggie dying, just the tower—but I convinced myself that it was a dream, and by then I'd bought into the concept that no one would believe me if I told them what I saw anyway."

"Don't torture yourself like that." Destiny tried to pull him close, but he wouldn't let her, as if he'd break if he didn't finish.

"For months after Meggie died, I thought if I'd spoken up, my parents would have gotten her out in time, and she'd be alive today."

"Oh, Morgan, no."

He swallowed hard. "I blamed myself for her death, until I went to the seminary and buried my guilt in school-work. I studied hard, and my dark memories went into deep cold storage. I doubled up on my majors, took night courses in architecture at a local college, continued my day studies in theology at the seminary. Architecture, I enjoyed. Theology, I endured."

Destiny couldn't imagine what it cost him to reveal his guilty memories. "I've met your mother. She wouldn't have believed you. Meggie knows that. Time for you to realize it."

"You might need to keep telling me that." He went into her arms then, his eyes glistening.

Eventually, they made love again, gently at first, then almost savagely, and lastly with a burgeoning freedom, as if a damn had burst and Morgan had been set free.

As they drifted afterward, Destiny sat straight up. "Oh good Goddess. Just shoot me now. A falling tower, and I painted another. I must have gotten my psychic messages mixed. Was Meggie's tower made of brick, too?"

"It *was* brick. That's it then? The mistake I hoped for?"

"What made you hope for that?"

"The painting of the school tower in the upstairs hallway at your house."

Destiny had never been so relieved. "You're psychic, too. You must be right. I could have gotten the towers mixed up." She hoped. "When I think of what you went through, no wonder you were a grumblestiltskin."

"I thought you were a spoiled brat, but always the most gorgeous woman I'd ever seen."

"I look exactly like my sisters."

"No you don't. But your psychic energy is off the charts. I'm still worried about our tower. I hope the worry is *not* the psychic in me. Des, why didn't I tell somebody about Meggie's tower? Anybody."

"You'd been brainwashed, taught since birth to deny the existence of anything that couldn't be explained, psychics especially. All along, I thought it was the priest in you that couldn't accept my magick and psychic abilities, when in fact, it was your upbringing coupled with trying to deny your own psychic ability."

"You think I subconsciously denied my ability to keep my parents happy?"

"On some level, eventually. But wouldn't it make more sense if your determination to debunk psychics and paranormal activity was a deep-seated, unacknowledged need to prove that you *couldn't* see the future? Therefore, you couldn't have saved your sister, because you couldn't be a psychic, since they don't exist."

"You're pretty smart for a sex goddess."

"I grew up learning to pay attention to the signs. Having a sixth sense makes you a mighty powerful listener."

"Guess I buried plenty when I buried Meggie, because I stopped listening as well."

"We'll work on resurrecting your sixth sense the way we resurrected the big guy."

"He's always ready for a resurrection. My sixth sense, not so much."

Disappointment and frustration filled Destiny. But she figured there was more than one way to awaken Morgan's gifts.

Chapter Forty

"I'M hungry," Morgan said, recognizing the imminent arrival of dawn outside the window.

Destiny turned on her side, snuggled her bottom against his boner, closed her eyes, and sighed in contentment. "It's the middle of the night."

"It's still dark, but it's nearly dawn." He jumped from the bed and put on some sweats. "Wear warm clothes and meet me at the top of the lighthouse tower in fifteen minutes for a sunrise picnic. I'll teach you how to ring the fog bell."

Destiny moaned in frustration and tried to keep warm without him.

"Tower picnic," he coaxed, pulling her blanket slowly away from her and toward the foot of the bed.

She grabbed it to stop its defection, but she shivered anyway.

"Sex in the tower at sunrise. An experience to—" Tell their kids about? Was he nuts?

"To what?" she grumbled, as she got up. "And it better be good."

"An experience to make us come every time we remember it."

"I'm holding you to that."

"Now who's the grumblestiltskin?"

"Breakfast better be ready when I get there."

Morgan saluted and left.

AT the top of the tower, Destiny stole his breath when she arrived wearing makeup and a pair of purple sweats with a matching hair band, her blonde hair curling around it. What a stunner.

"I love it up here," she said, walking the birdcage around the Fresnel lens along the lantern room gallery, then going out onto the main gallery, the boxy deck surrounding the square tower, then a smaller gallery lower down that connected them to the fire escape.

Afterward, she came back inside, shivering. "What's for breakfast?"

"Champagne and birthday cake."

"Now that's something to wake up for."

"And sex, isn't?" he asked, making a bed for them on the main gallery around the caged lens, with enough blankets to throw over their shoulders while they watched the sunrise.

"Breakfast first, sex after," she said. "I worked up an appetite last night."

An unannounced and silent visitor startled them. A white owl landed on the gallery railing and stared right at them.

"Hello, Owl," Destiny said. "This is Morgan. Morgan, Owl."

"Kismet, you scare me sometimes."

"If an owl sits nearby, face your fears, for a great mystery is about to unfold. Grandmother Owl is the totem of psychics, a link between the seen and unseen. She encourages us to make peace with our pasts. She must understand your need, Morgan, or she wouldn't be here. Owls are night eagles, and since the owl is my totem, that makes us both eagles, Boy Scout."

"She could be here for you, Kismet."

"I embraced Owl a long time ago. She's here for you, believe me."

"I'm making peace with Meggie's presence."

"How about your parents?"

"I'm making peace with their presence, too."

"And how about your psychic ability?"

"It would be easier to make peace with that if I hadn't blown it first time out of the gate."

"You were twelve years old. You couldn't have saved Meggie's life, but you can still clear her memory. You can't let anyone continue to believe that your sister was crazy. You have the power to correct that misconception."

Morgan understood, and he was as appalled that he did as by what Destiny proposed. "You want me to tell my parents that Meggie was sane."

Destiny nodded. "As sane as you and me."

"They would debate that."

"Doesn't matter. We have to vindicate her, because she can't speak for herself."

The owl stayed, refused a bite of birthday cake, and watched the glorious sunrise with them. With Destiny, Morgan huddled in the blankets against the bite of the ocean breeze at dawn and began to make peace with his past.

A few hours later, he called his mother from town to tell her that they were coming.

Destiny had obviously decided not to dress to please his mother but to please herself. She wore her favorite cowboy boots and hat, a butterscotch leather straight skirt, a yellow

Western-stitched shirt, buttons open to the clasps on her yellow bra.

Morgan looked her up and down. "Thank you for not wearing your Save a Horse, Ride a Cowboy shirt, or the one that says Orgasm Donor."

"They're only words," she said, buttoning one more button on her yellow shirt, bless her.

As she got in the car on the dock, Morgan checked the backseat. "I can't believe we brought the cat and dog."

"Don't look now," Destiny said, "but they're not all we brought."

"Meggie? Are you kidding me?"

"No, and Buffy, too. Stop at the Immortal Classic. I need to pick up some picture frames. We have tons. Then we have to stop at a drugstore to make prints of these pictures of you and Meggie as kids that I found in the captain's chest."

Morgan did a double take. "I'm afraid to ask why."

"So you get to keep the originals? Speaking of asking, I'd like your permission to replace the priest pictures on your parents' wall with framed copies of you and Meggie."

"You're gonna piss off my mother."

"Either that, or she's gonna kill me."

"No, I won't let that happen. Changing those pictures needs to be done, and we're going to do it together."

"My hero." Their hands met and held. "You've just taken a big step in facing your past," Destiny added, which made him feel like he could do anything, even tell his mother the truth about his beautiful sister.

At the house, he didn't knock; he opened the door like he'd once done naturally and let Destiny and their pets precede him into this house where he grew up and learned to shut up. But no more.

Samantha the schnoodle jumped on his father's lap. His dad laughed and ate up the attention.

Caramello hissed at his mother, jumped on her coffee table, and a milk glass bowl went flying, though Morgan was sure that Caramello hadn't gone close enough to have knocked it over.

His mother screamed so loud, Caramello peed on her pineapple doily.

Meggie, the instigator, had surely come in with them. Morgan tried not to crack a smile as he went for a trash can, paper towels, and spray cleaner. This house needed some Meggie action, though Caramello's accident had been an unfortunate side effect.

"Mrs. Jarvis," Destiny said, on her knees picking up glass when he returned. "Go to my shop tomorrow—you know where it is—and Reggie will give you an identical replacement. I'll have it put aside for you on our way home."

Together, he and Destiny cleaned the mess while everyone sat in silence, Caramello on his mother's lap, despite her obvious dislike.

Dumb cat, unless she planned to pee again.

His mother wanted a fight. She looked hard. Purposefully older, a sympathy cane in her hand, granny shoes on her feet, hair pulled back so tight, her face was all severe angles.

She'd given him life. He'd been taught to appreciate that, but thinking about it, he couldn't imagine her taking joy in anything, ever. They heard a sudden racket upstairs. It reminded him of Meggie's tantrum in the lighthouse kitchen, minus the plates. Morgan ran, Destiny behind him, as they followed the sound to Meggie's room. Barren. Stark. Empty. White walls. Not a stick of furniture. Empty closets. "What the hell did you do?" Morgan snapped at his parents. "Erase Meggie from your lives?" No wonder his sister was upset.

Every door—closet, bathroom, hall—and every drawer and window opened and shut, slammed and crashed. Window glass broke.

His father shouted with alarm.

His mother screamed. "What's happening?"

"Maybe Meggie's haunting you. Maybe she's pissed off that you stripped her out of your lives. My room's the same as it was when I grew up. Why isn't hers? I'm ashamed of you both."

The tantrum stopped, another shock, and Morgan felt something lean against him, like maybe Meggie, grateful that he'd spoken up for her.

He swallowed the lump in his throat and stood straighter.

He loved her, and it was time somebody stood up for her. "Mom, Dad, I'd like to speak with you downstairs."

Chapter Forty-one

MORGAN waited until his parents were sitting. "Destiny," he said, "Give me a minute to do the first part myself, then you can help me."

She nodded and sat in a rocker, protecting the box of framed pictures in her lap.

He went to the stair wall and took down every picture where he was wearing his cassock or vestments or any form of priestly garb.

His mother shrieked once, as he began, and his father shushed her successfully. Very reassuring.

"I presume you came here for a reason," his mother said when he finished.

"I have a whole list," Morgan said, bringing Destiny up with him. "No, we," he said, keeping an arm around her. Because if he let his mother stare her down like that, Destiny would grow icicles.

His mother stood to face them head-on, firming her spine.

"Sit down, Olive," his father said.

"Gordon!"

"No. You had your turn at calling the shots, and now it's mine. Sit."

His mother sat.

"Son, Miss Cartwright, feel free to sit or stand. Whatever makes you comfortable." His father settled into his favorite chair, and Samantha and Caramello joined him. "We're listening."

"Give us a minute first to replace the pictures on the wall," he said.

Destiny opened the box, and they hung the ones she'd picked, great pictures of him and Meggie together as children.

His father got up, came closer, and gazed at each one, clearing his throat more than once. His mother remained ramrod straight on the sofa.

Morgan started a fire in the fireplace and threw in the pictures of him as a priest.

His mother rose, but he stood in her path while the fire behind him did its job. "You're harboring false memories," he told her. "The place should be full of Meggie and me together. That was real. That's the past to remember."

The fall board on the piano went up with a crash, revealing the keys, which started moving slowly, and individually, in a one-fingered version of "Chopsticks," the only thing Meggie had ever learned to play. His parents paled, but Morgan felt as if he could do anything with Meggie and Destiny beside him.

"Mother, Dad, I'm angry," he said. "I have been for a long time. Years. Nearly my entire life. I'm mad that you erased Meggie from our lives after she died, except for the pictures I stole from the trash along with Samantha, her doll, all of which I still have, though you now have copies of the pictures. You can thank Destiny for that, though she asked my permission, and I gave it wholeheartedly. I've been angry for years that you wouldn't let me talk about Meggie after she passed, and I hate that you sent her away to die."

His mother shot from her chair.

"Olive," his father warned.

His mother sat again.

"I'm mad/sad/furious that you made Meggie feel like a freak as a child." Morgan *hated* that his voice cracked as he tried to keep his finger in the dike on the dam he'd built to keep his emotions at bay. The only thing keeping him sane was the strength of Destiny's arm around his waist, her closed fist digging into his side with a kind of rhythm, a living reminder of her presence.

"Meghan loved life," he said. "She loved people, and she wanted to help anyone whose sad future she saw in her psychic visions, but you shut her up, called her crazy, and hid her away."

"Meghan was our punishment!" his mother snapped.

"No," Destiny said. "Children are gifts. No child, especially Meggie, should be considered a punishment."

His mother stiffened as she managed to look down her nose at Destiny even though she stood and his mother sat. "What do you know about Morgan's twin?" she whispered.

Morgan exchanged a glance with Destiny, and they decided, without words, against going there—a form of communication he'd only ever employed with Meggie. "Her name was Meggie, Mother."

The piano keys played the grand "Alleluia," used during high mass, which Meggie must have learned at the abbey school.

"Meggie. She lived for twelve years, and she made my life better because she did."

"Well, she made my life miserable!" His mother tore her handkerchief in half.

"No! Mother, take it back!" Morgan fisted his hands.

"Meggie was nothing but laughter and sunshine. Miserable? Where did you get such a horrible notion?"

His father sat forward. "Her brother, Jim, put it into her head, and she's never been the same since. That pompous old priest stole the bright lass I married and left a bitter woman in her place."

"Gordon!"

"Meggie was a treat, Olive. A blessing, like our boy here."

"What did you do to *deserve* punishment?" Destiny asked.

"She'll never tell," his father said. "But I will."

"No!"

"Morgan, you and your sister were conceived before your mother and I were married. She never got over the shame."

"I'll bet Father Jim never let her." He should have known.

His father nodded. "Twins come early, and you were small, so the secret stayed in the family."

"Gordon, stop talking about such things."

His crazy world started to make sense to Morgan, but the knowledge was breaking him.

Destiny caught his seeking hand, and he grasped it like a lifeline.

"That explains so much," Destiny said.

"I can't believe *that one's* here for this," his mother snapped.

"Who?" Morgan asked. "Destiny or Meggie?"

His father stood and looked around.

"Don't be foolish, Gordon," his mother said. "I mean the hussy hanging all over you, Morgan, of course."

But his father's eyes had widened as he looked toward the piano, up the stairs, and back at the piano, where "Chopsticks" played again. His father sat on the edge of the piano bench and watched every key.

His mother nodded toward Destiny. "I wish you'd put her in the car."

Destiny chuckled. "I'm not a dog."

"No, you look more like a country-western street-walker."

"That's better," Destiny said. "Thank you."

Morgan scratched his nose. Destiny was a light in the dark tunnel of his life. "Mother, I am no longer a priest, nor will I be one again, but this isn't about me. Meggie had a gift. A God-given talent. She was psychic."

"That's *her* kind of talk," his mother said, pointing at Destiny.

"No," Morgan said. "It's *my* kind. I'm psychic, too. I always have been, just like Meggie, but I hid it, even from myself, coward that I am. As a kid, Meggie was smarter than me in every way but one. I knew enough to keep my visions to myself, including the vision I got of Maggie's tower, the one where she slept in that boarding school, getting hit by lightning, burning, and falling to the ground. I wanted to tell you that Meggie was in danger. I made myself sick over it. But I knew you'd never believe me. It's *my* fault that my sister died." His voice cracked again, which he hated.

His father wiped his eyes. "Not your fault, Son." He touched Morgan's hand. "It's mine. All of it."

His mother pursed her lips in that way she had, only harder, her eyes cold and dark. Lost.

Destiny laid her head on his shoulder, a blessing, and Morgan raised her hand to kiss her knuckles.

"So," his mother said, standing. "Now I have two more heathen believers on my hands. You and your father both, not to mention this one."

Destiny shrugged. "I feel like what the cat dragged in."

For an instant, Morgan almost wanted to tell his mother that it was her fanatical fault Meggie died, but she wouldn't believe him. "Mother, I've been trapped all my life inside my head, filtering every word. Then I trapped myself at the seminary. Destiny," he said, turning to her. "I've remembered something else. Father Jim said that if I became a priest, I could atone for my parents' sins. I didn't know what sins, but he said that the parents of priests always get into heaven."

"That's not true!" His father looked at his mother and realized that she knew about her son's sacrifice for their sakes. He took out his handkerchief. "I swear, Son, that I thought you were happy as a priest."

"I don't blame you, Dad. I didn't know how to be happy until a little girl named Meggie set me straight. That night, I went to the lighthouse and took off my cassock. It didn't fit anymore."

Morgan brought Destiny kissing close. "I've known Destiny for four months, and now I'm no longer lost in the dark. She pulled me into the light, and we're taking it one beautiful day at a time."

He led Destiny to the door, his father behind them.

His mother got up and went to look at the new pictures on the wall, her shoulders a little less rigid than when they'd arrived.

His father hesitated then embraced him. "I loved you and your sister the same."

"Meggie knows that, Dad."

"Are you sure? Make certain she knows."

Morgan nodded. "Meggie and I, we still have that twin connection going. Take it from me, she does."

His father cleared his throat. "I think she might have been here tonight, hey? I think she might have kissed my cheek."

"I think you might be right, Dad."

"I won't see you anymore, will I?" his father asked, tears coursing down his face, sorrow lining his cheeks.

"I'll call next Wednesday as always."

"I'll be answering the phone myself. I'd like to see your lighthouse someday."

"Then see it you will." Morgan took Destiny's hand as they walked down the brick path. He felt drained yet elated.

A life door closing.

Another opening.

Maybe.

Chapter Forty-two

MORGAN leaned against his seat and closed his eyes. "What a relief to get that off my chest."

Destiny put an arm around his neck and rubbed his temple. "Your aura is always dim and red-hazed when we leave here."

He sighed and closed his eyes at the pleasure of her touch. "I'm not sure I ever want to come back." He turned to her, her head on the seat back, near his, facing him, kissing close. "You wouldn't mind if my dad came to visit, would you?"

"Over the next two weeks? Of course not."

Wake-up call. He'd meant over the course of their lives.

"What about your mother?" Destiny asked, distracting him.

"Oh, she'll never come."

"Don't bet on it."

Morgan groaned. "Tell me that is *not* your psychic knowledge talking."

"It's just a hunch."

"I can't believe Meggie heard what Mother said about her."

"Morgan, after your mother said it, Meggie kissed her cheek and whispered something in her ear, and your mother heard her. I could tell by her reaction."

"Good reaction or bad reaction?" Morgan asked.

"More like a revelation of a reaction."

"Is Meggie all right?"

Destiny looked in the backseat. "She's smiling. She thanks you for defending her. She says that you're her hero."

"Yeah, well the two of you are my heroes. I'm proud of her—of you, Sis," he added looking in the rearview mirror at an empty backseat. "For letting them know how you feel."

"I feel for them both," Destiny said. "Your father's filled with guilt, and your mother's a broken woman."

Morgan started the Mustang. "For a minute, I actually wanted to strike her," he said. "I don't think I love my own mother."

Destiny reached for his hand. "You might wish you didn't, but you do."

"The kicker is that she'll deny her guilt quickly enough. She's aces at that." He grasped Destiny's hand, and with his over hers, he shifted into second gear.

Her exclamation of delight washed over him like a healing mist.

"Will you teach me to drive this?" she asked.

His heart expanded. "You bet your flying buttress, I will." She'd become everything to him. He cared deeply for her. She'd become the focus of his life, for now, except that he didn't want that *now* to end.

He drove to the Rockport art colony, where they walked hand in hand in the Indian summer sun and shared a paper cone of cotton candy. He bought Destiny an antique painting of a whaling ship with their own lighthouse—his, he supposed, not theirs—all lit up in the background.

On the way back home, they stopped at Meggie's grave and left a bouquet of Chinese lanterns, bittersweet, and silver dollars, which Destiny had bundled with a big white bow before they left.

"Meggie says she loves it," Destiny said, butterflies marking the circle Meggie ran around her own gravestone. It hit him hard, then, that she was gone. She would never be an aunt to their—

God, he was screwed up today.

They later stopped at the same nursery for butterfly plants, and between them they picked garden stones for hope and love.

Did he want to spend his life with Destiny? Swell, yes. But why? Because he hated living on his own, or because he couldn't live without her?

Since she'd come to the lighthouse, he no longer felt that awful need to fly the earth screaming for something he didn't understand. He could finally land safely in her sheltering arms.

But who would shelter Destiny? Would a woman who needed a center as much as he did, a woman both as strong and goal-seeking as him—a kindred spirit—feel comfortable depending on him?

He thought he'd be comfortable depending on her. But permanently?

When they got home, Meggie disappeared right away, or so Destiny said, probably because he and Destiny were so filled with each other.

They went to bed that way, their emotions so fragile, sex had no place. Kisses, strokes, touches graced with reverence. Their gazes locked, they drifted into sleep entwined in comfort, support, tenderness . . . and love?

Morgan woke early, his need for her so enormous—his need, not his—well yes, his boner, too. But he wanted a spiritual, emotional, and all-encompassing relationship with Destiny. He wanted her beside him whether paddling a kayak, planting crazy-named asters, painting a door, or facing his parents.

He might be joking with himself, especially about his parents, but the whole loving Destiny thing scared the breath out of him, punched him in the solar plexus, and nearly brought him to his knees, because logic didn't enter into it. For a man like him, mistakes made more logical sense than an emotion as elusive and life-altering as love. He got up quietly, grabbed his sweats, and took the kayak out to think.

He would not run from love, but he did need to figure it out. He didn't fear it so much as he didn't understand it.

Maybe he was as mad as his mother thought. Maybe, maybe not.

Unsure how long he'd been on the water, he looked up at the sky and thought that dawn might not make as sunny a debut this morning as it had yesterday.

Eventually, dark clouds scuttled overhead, as if a storm might be brewing. Made him think of spending a rainy day in bed making lo—yes, making love with Destiny.

He heard the fog bell calling to him, and a great abiding forever love for the woman who sounded it welled up in him. Joyfulness infused him. He turned the kayak toward home—his *home*, if Destiny was there—surprised he'd come so far. Facing shore, the wind whipped at his jacket, and sea spray lashed like ice picks at his face and hands.

As if Destiny sensed his trouble, the Fresnel light went on, like a candle in the window leading him back to her. She must have awakened alone and gone looking for him.

He waved, assuming she'd brought the binoculars up there. "I'm coming," he shouted, grinning like a fool.

As if she could hear him.

Destiny, his beacon, sending rays of faith, hope, and love in dark and stormy seas. Maybe he'd fallen in love with the lighthouse because it was known for granting safe harbor to lost travelers, which he'd surely been when he first went there. Lighthouses directed lost travelers like him safely to shore, toward their destinies. His Destiny.

He loved her, and he couldn't wait to get back to tell her. When he'd come out here earlier, he hadn't been running from love but from need. It was scary to need another person as much as you needed your next breath. It implied a need for unlimited faith and trust. You had to believe your love would be there for you always.

Would she?

A sudden gust whipped the wind around him, making the water choppy and difficult to navigate. The kayak rolled, taking him by surprise. One minute above water; the next minute below. Morgan rolled himself and the kayak upright.

Thunder and lightning joined nature's frenzy.

His heart nearly pounded from his chest. The muscles in his arms clenched as he tried to paddle against the storm-tossed sea. He looked toward the lighthouse.

Knowing Destiny waited there gave him strength.

He rolled again, kayak side up, and got a premonition, a vision in slow motion. "No!" he shouted.

Chapter Forty-three

MORGAN rolled and resurfaced, again, pulling air into his lungs.

He'd lost his bearings, couldn't see the lighthouse anymore, but when he spotted it, he watched an instant replay of his vision in quick, terrorizing action.

Before his eyes, a lightning ball raced toward the lighthouse, hit the tower, and brick by slow brick, it collapsed. "Destiny!" he screamed, his mournful wail lost in the frenzied wind.

Had she stayed in the tower? Gone back down? Was she hurt? Safe?

The lens must have broken to form huge, heavy slivers of slicing glass. *Oh God, let her be safe.* He called her name as he fought the waves battering the kayak. It flipped him again, and this time he freed himself from its grip.

He floated to the surface too slowly because the tossing water fought to keep him down, his lungs about to burst. The minute he surfaced, he sucked in air, cleared his mind, and began to swim against the tide, in a lightning storm, by damn.

He looked in every direction, but he'd lost the shore.

Lost.

Hopeless. Exhausted. Frozen. It would be so easy to give up. Praying didn't even seem worth the trouble, except that Destiny needed him. He'd save her, but he needed to rest first, to gather his strength.

Morgan closed his eyes for a minute, just a minute, but water closing over his head woke him.

"Morgan," Meggie said. "Follow me."

"Meggie! I can see you. Your beautiful face. Finally, I can see you. Can you hear me? We're beneath the water, but I can hear you."

"We never needed sound to talk, did we?"

Morgan gave in to his fear. "Does seeing you mean that I'm dead, too? Did I drown?" He looked for Destiny, afraid she'd died in the collapsing tower, but he saw only water all around him. "Is Destiny okay? Did she make it?"

"I love you, Morgan," Meggie said. "I stayed because I knew that someone else you loved would be trapped in a tower, and I couldn't let you blame yourself this time. You couldn't have saved me. It was my time. I always knew I wasn't meant to grow up. But you're different."

"What about Destiny? I can't live without her."

"Destiny is buried alive, but Buffy is with her, so she has a chance, a *small* chance."

Denial. Loss. Rage. Sanity. "I'll do anything, Meggie."

"Can you believe in me enough to follow me?" his sister asked.

"I've always believed in you. I just got lost in the dark for a while, until Destiny led me to the light." And the thought of saving her gave him the physical strength to go on, while Meggie gave him the emotional strength. "Lead the way, Megs."

"Follow me."

Morgan no longer felt the cold as he swam after his twin—yes, Meggie did, indeed, walk on water, like Jake said.

Hours later, or so it seemed, when Morgan reached the island, he could barely stand, but he didn't have a choice. With bricks and a giant, battered Fresnel lens blocking the kitchen door out back, Morgan staggered to the front door. "I can't let Destiny die like you did, Meggie. If she's—if she—"

"Destiny," he shouted when he got inside. He stopped to call her from the bottom of the stairs.

"You're wasting time, Morgan," Meggie said. "She's in the tower."

Adrenaline surged through him as he stood in the keeper's room and tore bricks away from the tower entrance, Meggie encouraging him. He could see his dead sister, miracle of miracles. Now he wanted another miracle. He looked beyond the lighthouse ceiling and angry storm clouds. *Please, don't let there be a life limit on miracles or forgiveness.*

He resumed calling Destiny's name.

For every brick he removed, twenty fell. He couldn't move them fast enough, and for a minute, he wanted his world to end. Without Destiny, his life meant nothing. "No! I will not let the tower have her!"

"Morgan," Meggie said. "You're the logical twin. Think."

He took a minute to catch his breath, and he tried to calm enough to think logically. "The lighthouse keeper," he said. "Horace? Meggie, where's Horace?"

"Here he is," Meggie said, holding a uniformed man's hand.

"Thank you for taking care of my sister," Morgan said, shocked to see that the old lighthouse keeper was so young. "Destiny told me about a maze in the basement. Can you lead me through it?"

Horace nodded. "No one better. Follow me."

They crawled beneath the planking that led from the marsh to the porch to find a stone arch that seemed just above the ground beneath the plank, but it covered a set of stairs leading down to a door deep in the earth. "No wonder I never knew it was here. It looked like part of the foundation."

It wasn't so much a maze in a basement as it was a kind of landfill of pilings holding up the lighthouse. Horace, with Meggie behind him, led Morgan through the underground horror house, but the maze led to a dead end, or as good as.

"The hidden door is a trapdoor in the ceiling?" Morgan remembered and confirmed. He pushed against the metal square but to no avail. "It won't budge. It's covered with bricks. How can I get it open?"

"Pull on it," Horace said.

"What?"

"Don't push. Pull."

Morgan wedged his bloody fingers beneath an edge of the trapdoor and hung from it until he fell to the floor as it opened, bricks pouring down on him.

He crawled away as he got pummeled. Eventually, it stopped raining bricks, and Morgan climbed the brick mountain to wedge himself into the opening, shoving bricks aside, and slip through the trapdoor to come up in a corner of the ruined tower.

He faced Meggie and Horace, and shouted in surprise, as if he'd seen a ghost, well, two. "Hades. That's some trick. I just left you behind me, and now you're in front of me."

Meggie giggled, a sound he'd cherish forever, but right now, he needed to find Destiny. "Destiny? Darling, are you here?"

A good section of the circular stairway stood intact, though it was broken with great gaps in places and strewn with bricks. Not as many as in the entryway, which made sense, since the tower was hollow.

Samantha and Caramello came slinking through the trapdoor behind him, yowling and yapping. He bent down, and they jumped into his arms. "We gotta find her, guys. You gotta help me find her."

"Destiny?" he called again. "Destiny, where are you?"

No sound alleviated his anguish.

Chapter Forty-four

DESTINY drifted on the soft, feathery wings of a dream cloud.

Morgan walked toward her, almost as excited to see her as she was to see him. No hidden emotions for either of them. They were both putting their love, hopes, and dreams out there and lapping them up. Devouring each other with their gazes is what they were doing.

He spoke her name, but it came to her through a tunnel.

She opened her eyes and realized that the feathery wings of the cloud belonged to Buffy, Meggie's angel. Had she died in the tower then? Ooh, she'd died like Meggie. How weird.

Her heart raced. No, she didn't want to die. She wanted more time with Morgan.

She wanted a lifetime with him.

Fine place to realize she'd fallen head over heels in love. Not that they could ever be together, not forever, not in her wildest imaginings—not with him making peace with his faith and her being a witch—even if she could get out of here, but oh Goddess, did she love him.

She was so sorry his tower lay in ruins like in her painting. Sorry her vision had been correct.

Morgan? Her heart sped, her hands began to sweat. She remembered now that he'd been on the water in a thunder and lightning storm.

"Morgan?" she called, but she had no voice. She had to save him with the best means at her disposal:

> "God of fire
> No death bell.
> Save the man
> That I desire.
>
> "My heart he holds,
> For me, he's right.
> Though worlds apart,
> My soul needs his.
>
> "Air, fill his lungs.
> Water, wash to shore.
> Earth, bind to land.
> Spirit, pump his heart."

Destiny tried to move, but Buffy held her still. Her body ached almost everywhere, but she couldn't be seriously hurt, because Buffy had broken her fall.

"Destiny? Can you hear me?" Morgan called. "If you can, call out. Make a noise. Anything, so I know you're okay. Please be okay. Wait! Chant a spell to get yourself out. Can witches do that?"

Safe and asking for a spell. His own faith returning and maybe a little faith in her beliefs, as well. Two miracles, thank the Goddess. "Morgan," she called, but she'd swallowed so much dust she could do little more than whisper a gasp.

Make a noise? How could she make a noise, caged, or cocooned, as she was by buckled stair rails covered in bricks?

She looked around and found a small opening, like a window in her brick-and-iron cage, that allowed her to see a section of the stairs down below.

With difficulty, she raised her sore arm and tentatively pushed on a loose brick near the opening, afraid that dislodging it would cause another avalanche.

> *Angel bright,*
> *Wings so light,*
> *Guide my hand.*
> *Make it right.*
>
> *Protect my love*
> *Within my sight.*
> *Guide his eyes*
> *To me here, right.*

She didn't know what she'd do if Morgan got hurt as a result of her response to him.

Her brick let go, eased from its wedge, and fell down the stairs, actually widening her window and allowing her to see the separation—a big break—in the stairs.

He would never be able to reach her.

"Do you think Destiny did that?" she heard Morgan ask. "I mean, it was only one brick. It could have fallen by itself."

One minute he was talking, then there he stood, on the last step before the split. Destiny looked up, beyond her angel cradle and gasped, as much as she could. Vexing vetiver, it looked like she was hanging on a section of stairs severed at both ends yet still connected to the wall by a steel thread.

Sweet sassafras tea. A flying trapeze cage.

Wait. Morgan was talking to Meggie and Horace. He

could see them, which meant he remembered, believed, embraced his psychic ability, or he wouldn't be able to see his sister, never mind Horace. Somehow, in the midst of this, he'd been set free, totally free, of his past.

Destiny heard a ringing in her head. That couldn't be good.

She closed her eyes against her headache and thought of how Meggie must have felt in the same situation, a worse situation, where fire surrounded her. Poor Meggie . . . who must sense her presence.

Wait. Had the clever, clairvoyant Meggie stayed here all these years, because she *knew* this was going to happen? With a second collapsed tower, Morgan must feel like he was reliving a nightmare.

"Destiny?" he called again.

She squeezed her eyes shut against the pain of moving and nudged another brick. Several fell . . . and Morgan shouted her name.

She heard other shouts, different men's voices, banging, pounding, sledgehammers, jackhammers.

Destiny croaked Morgan's name again and pushed her hand through the mini window so he could see it.

Caramello jumped the break in the stairs, came closer, and yowled at her. Great, her cat could see her waving, but Morgan couldn't. Then her dear, sweet Caramello yowled at Morgan, and Samantha the schnoodle barked and ran back and forth toward him and the stairs, so Morgan would look up at Caramello.

Morgan whooped. "Destiny! I see your hand. I'm coming, Kismet. I'll save you."

But he couldn't reach her, because he didn't know yet that this part of the stairs wasn't attached at the top. If he put any weight on this section she was trapped in, it would break away from the wall, and she would fall . . . about sixty feet to the floor, and maybe take him down with her.

She'd rather not think of it as a death trap, but a cocoon,

a chrysalis of her very own. She couldn't reach her butterfly necklace, but she'd pretend to be a growing butterfly, and she'd bide her time until she could emerge and fly free.

Shouts erupted from several directions. Destiny got a peek of a seaman with a pickax breaking through from the keeper's room.

"Coast Guard," one of them said. "What happened?"

Morgan explained from the break in the stairs while Destiny rested her tired hand. One of the seamen suggested that Morgan go back down to the bottom, because she might be safer if he got off the stairs. Sounded smart to her, except that she liked being able to see Morgan. Made her feel connected to him. She needed that connection right now.

He said something she couldn't hear, then he cupped his hands around his mouth. "Kismet, they're going to brace the section of stairs you're on, then set up some scaffolding to get you down. You might be up there a while."

She touched her thumb to her forefinger, giving him an okay signal, telling him she understood, then she let Buffy rock her to sleep.

DESTINY opened her eyes in time to see the stranger who lifted her from her open cage. How had they opened it without her hearing them? The first stranger handed her to another, then another, down lower, and so forth, until someone finally handed her to Morgan.

His amber eyes were full. A tear slipped down his cheek. "I love you," he said. "I realized it on the water before all Hades broke loose."

"I love you, too," she croaked, pleased that he was still trying to use positive words after all this, but he had to lean close, and she had to repeat herself before he heard her.

Their tears mingled when they kissed.

"I'm carrying you up to our bed where a medic is wait-ing to check you out. Do you understand?"

"Not deaf," she croaked, her voice a bit less raspy. "You?"

"Not deaf either."

She made a fist at him but couldn't raise it.

He raised it himself, to his lips. "I have scrapes on my hands and cold feet from my icy swim. That's all."

He was bruising as she watched. "Kayak?" she asked.

Morgan shook his head. "Sleeping with the fish."

She rolled her eyes.

A half hour later, the medic shook his head. "No broken bones," he said. "Miss Cartwright is extensively bruised and has a few scrapes." He packed away his stethoscope. "But it's a bloody miracle nothing is broken."

Morgan made a flying motion behind him, as in wings, à la Buffy, and she nodded. He must know, probably from Meggie, that Buffy had been with her.

"How did you know to come to our rescue?" Morgan asked the medic.

"We got a call from Miss Regina Paxton who was on the dock and saw it happen. Ball of fiery lightning skimmed the water, she said, and headed straight to the lighthouse for a dead hit."

Morgan tilted his head her way.

"Storm," Destiny mouthed and she practically saw the lightbulb go on over Morgan's head. Her sister, Storm, could literally see the psychic present, though her specialty was finding lost children, but they were siblings after all—an identical three-pack—and each of them sensed when one of them was in trouble.

The medic picked up his bag. "I'd like to take you both to the hospital and get you checked by a doctor."

Destiny shook her head almost as adamantly as Mor-gan.

The medic growled. "See your doctors for a checkup as

soon as possible, then. Will you? Tomorrow? I can't find anything wrong, but I'm *not* a doctor."

"We'll be fine." Morgan started to walk the medic out the door as she thought about getting up. He turned to her. "Stay," he said, "under penalty of severe punishment."

She guessed she dozed, because when she opened her eyes, Morgan was placing a bowl of soup on the nightstand. Meggie, Horace, and Buffy were with him.

"Thank you, Buffy," she said. "Morgan, the Fresnel lens would have crushed me if Buffy hadn't pushed it over the edge. Then she caught me in her arms and covered me with her wings, and we rode out the tower collapse together."

"I'm glad you're okay," Meggie said.

Destiny wished she could hug her. "I'm glad you stayed with Morgan. I love you, Meggie."

"I love you too, Sis."

"What?" Morgan said. "Another sister? Meggie, you wouldn't believe all the sisters Des has, but you're the best by far."

Meggie winked at her. "We're gonna go now, so you can sleep." That fast, they disappeared.

"They're not totally gone, are they?" Morgan asked. "I mean forever?"

"Not yet," Destiny said. "But I think they've fulfilled their unfinished business on this plane. They'll tell us when they're ready."

His eyes full, likely at the thought of losing his sister again, Morgan took her sweats off her and put her in his flannel robe. "It'll be loose on you, but it'll keep you warm." He proceeded to try to feed her some soup.

"Hey, I can do that. I'll sit up and eat off the night-stand."

"Okay," Morgan said, crossing his arms and moving the vase of wildflowers she'd put there. "Go for it."

Destiny got the spoon into her hand, but she ached too much to raise it to her lips. She hated that she had to put it down and look up at him, but he didn't crow; he just fed her.

"Don't even pretend you're not hungry. Somehow we managed to miss breakfast, lunch, and dinner."

"When are you eating?"

"The Coast Guard fed me after I changed into dry clothes, while they were putting up the scaffolding."

"You left me to go and eat?"

"No, I ate a couple of hot dogs that the cook brought to the tower while the Coast Guard worked to rescue you. I only left you long enough to fetch dry clothes at a run. Twelve seconds. Then I made Meggie turn her back and got buck naked in the tower in front of the rescue crew so I'd be near you."

"Thank you." She took another spoonful of soup. "I can't believe I didn't get soaked in all that rain."

"It had stopped by the time I reached shore," Morgan told her. "I was lost out there. Meggie brought me back. I don't think we need to protect her anymore. I think she's figured out what's up with us."

"What *is* up with us, exactly?"

Chapter Forty-five

DESTINY got nervous waiting for Morgan's answer. He ran his hand through his hair, either uncertain or scared.

"We're in love, Kismet, and when we're not bruised and beaten, we're having überhot beginner sex."

"You hardly perform like a beginner."

"Thank you, but I'll need a lot more practice."

"Glad to hear it."

"I want to practice only with you. Marry me, Destiny."

"Whoa. I think you got hit on the head with too many bricks." Though his aura certainly radiated the bright blue of love.

He looked stumped. "How do you know about the hail of bricks?"

"I'm psychic?" She smiled and fingered one of the many bruises on his temple. "I love you so much, Morgan, but I don't see how we could possibly have a life together. Our beliefs; we're too different." Neither could she imagine living without him, but she didn't want to ruin him either.

"I don't want an answer tonight," he said, rubbing a topical anesthetic on her bruises, while she bit her lip against the pain.

"You've been through a traumatic experience," he said. "We both have. We *are* from different worlds, different faiths, which I think we can handle. But you need time to think, especially after yesterday at my parents' house. I understand."

Destiny felt the pain in her muscles receding. "I appreciate that."

He got into bed with her. "I want to hold you, but I don't want to hurt you. How would you be most comfortable?"

"In your arms," she said.

He held her loosely, and she relaxed. "Just so you know," he said, "I'm offering my unwavering devotion and my heart, my whole heart. You are my missing center. You understood me when I couldn't understand myself. You saw my vulnerability, my psychic ability, and you saw my dirty aura and cleaned it up."

"Sure, I'm handy that way, but marriage?"

"You helped me come to terms with my guilt and my past."

"I think I was always meant to save you," she said, sleepy again. Maybe he was her psychic mandate. Who knew? A tender and gentle lover with a heart that needed healing. She wasn't surprised when he said he loved her in the tower. Joyous, grateful, and elated but not surprised, though the marriage proposal, after everything, *was* a bit of a shock. "I knew you'd save me today," she said. "As scared as I was, I knew."

Morgan kissed her brow and stroked her hair. "I think we were meant to save each other in different ways."

"Hmm."

Destiny opened her eyes. Again, she was being cradled, minus the feathery cloud. "Where are you taking me?"

"To the bathroom."

"Very good idea."

He set her down.

"You don't need to stay with me."

"I don't want you taking a header into the tub."

"Out. Now. I'm drawing the line at peeing as a spectator sport." She ignored the sound of his doubtful cough as he left the room. "Ow, ow, ow," she said, as she lowered her body.

"You okay in there?"

"Just peachy."

"I'm heating water so you can soak in a hot tub."

"I love you!"

A few minutes later she bit her lip as she walked into the kitchen. "What a mess," she said.

"Yeah, the stovepipe popped at the elbow, hence the soot, and a few things fell off the shelves, but the outside wall is intact, and every other wall is structurally sound, too. We're lucky it's just the tower."

"Morgan, I'm sorry my painting was right."

"Any chance that you'll feel like painting the lighthouse again sometime soon?"

She looked into her mind. "There is that chance, actually."

"What would the tower look like this time?"

"Exactly like the old one did, erect and proud, because this superior architect I know is going to rebuild it in keeping with the integrity of the original structure."

"Glad to hear it. Here ya go." He helped her sit. "Toast. Orange juice. Aspirin. Hot water's nearly ready for the tub."

A short while later, he helped her stand in the gorgeous French claw-foot bathtub, so out of place in a lighthouse, stenciled as it was on the outside with gold filigree scallops and pink teacup roses. Morgan climbed in after her and sat first, settling her so she rested on him, not on the hard tub bottom.

"Oh my Goddess. This feels sooooo incredible. I needed this soothing heat, this man muscle body mattress, too. Sooooo fine."

"You sound like you're having great sex."

"I think I'm about three hundred or so ouches away from sex, but somebody forgot to tell your big guy."

"Sorry about that. Reflex. You naked. Me naked. He's primed."

She sighed. "What time is it?"

"You're not going to believe this, but we slept for thirteen hours."

"How long is a flight from Scotland?"

They heard the front door open. "Hello? Anybody home?" Harmony called.

"Holy triple decker," Morgan swore and lowered them deeper into the water. "You sensed them coming, didn't you?"

"'Fraid so."

"Sis, are you okay?" Storm asked, probably from the top of the stairs.

"Morgan, old man, are you here?" Aiden called.

"Maybe they got taken to a hospital," King suggested.

The bathroom door opened. "Shit!" Morgan said, pulling more suds up to cover Destiny's breasts.

Her brother-in-law, Aiden, whistled and grinned. "I found them."

Morgan growled. "Why don't you just sell tickets?"

Aiden shrugged. "Why should I, when the show's free?"

And there they gathered in her open bathroom door, her sisters and brothers-in-law smiling at her and Morgan in the bathtub together.

When they'd left for Scotland, she and Morgan were trying to get away from each other, and at least two of them knew they'd end up here. *They* probably even knew that Morgan had been a virgin.

"You're a bunch of intruding, grinning buffoons," Morgan said. "I could get you for breaking and entering."

"No you couldn't," King said. "I still own the place. You haven't bought it yet."

"That's right!" Morgan said snapping his fingers. "Brother, do you have an insurance claim to file."

"We knew the tower was gone," King said.

"But did you know about your new kayak?"

"It came?"

Morgan shrugged. "And went."

Chapter Forty-six

MORGAN liked that Destiny rested her head on his chest, as if it was them against the world. "Dearest gawking friends and grinning sisters-in-law," he said. "Would you care to shut the door so we can get decent?"

"Bit late for that," Storm said, wiggling her brows.

Destiny raised her head, though he held it because moving it must hurt her. "Storm, thanks for calling Reggie when you got the vision."

"I can't say it was a pleasure. I nearly had a heart attack. Seriously, are you okay? I mean, I knew you were, but it was scary."

"Yeah, it was. I'm okay. A little sore."

"I'm okay, too," Morgan said, "in case anybody cares."

When he and Destiny came out of the bathroom, Aiden, King, and her sisters were cleaning the kitchen. Good friends, no, family. He walked Destiny up the stairs slowly, an occasional "Ouch" escaping her.

"Des, do you need help getting dressed?" Harmony asked from the bottom of the stairs.

Morgan tightened his arm around Destiny's waist. "I've got her, Harmony," he said. "Thanks."

"No kidding?" Harmony asked.

"What?" Destiny said without turning. "The tub wasn't a clue, you matchmaking brat."

"Who me?" Harmony gave them an innocent, cat-that-ate-the-cream look. "I'll be cleaning the kitchen."

Fifteen minutes later, Destiny's sisters stood in the parlor and watched Morgan walk their clone down the stairs. He could see how much they loved each other by the way that Destiny's pain was reflected in their eyes.

Harmony held the chair for Destiny. "We were thinking that since tonight is Halloween, and we're home in time, we might celebrate Samhain together, but maybe you're not up to it, Des?"

"I'm up to anything." Destiny lowered herself into the chair by biting her lip. "Tonight at the castle? What time?"

"You can't walk to the castle," Storm said. "You can't even sit in a chair without pain. I don't think this is a good idea."

Morgan cleared his throat. "We could celebrate Halloween here, or Samhain, I suppose I mean. If that would be all right with you?"

Storm did a double take. "A witchy Samhain ritual, Morgan? Here? We don't want to chase you out of your own home."

He shoved his hands in his pockets, embarrassed by the way he'd acted at Harmony's Midsummer ritual. "I won't leave this time. I'd like to take part, if you don't mind?" He looked down to catch Destiny's pleased expression. God, he loved her. Then he saw Meggie, Horace, and Buffy standing behind her, and he grinned. "Tonight's the night that the veil between the living and the dead is the thinnest, isn't it?"

Destiny followed his gaze, but apparently her sisters didn't see what they did. Morgan rather liked having a psychic gift her sisters lacked. He cleared his throat again. "There's something you should all know about me."

Aiden waved away his explanation. "We told the girls that you'd been a priest."

"There's more, something I was hiding even from myself. I'm psychic. Clairvoyant. So was my twin sister, Meggie. She died when we were twelve."

"Meggie's here right now," Destiny said. "Morgan was on the water when the lightning storm began, and she saved him and led him to me after the tower collapsed."

"No way." Storm looked around. "Can you see her, Des? Morgan?"

"We do. But that's not the point," Morgan said. "Samhain ritual here tonight, right, so Destiny doesn't have to walk all the way to the castle, though I *could* make her a soft bed in the wheelbarrow and roll her there."

Destiny winced. "Over my bruised body."

Morgan sipped his cider and winked. "That's what I thought. What do we have to do to get ready for Samhain? I'll do whatever I can, but Destiny's not up to anything except a preparatory nap."

King stood. "Do we need to get the Oak King altar over here, or will the gateleg table in the kitchen do?"

"We'll make do," Harmony said. "Storm and I will bring the ritual supplies, and you and Aiden are going to bring one of the fainting couches from the castle, so Destiny can rest in the ritual circle. Great job of decorating for Samhain, though, Destiny."

King looked around and nodded. "The place looks like a home for the first time in years."

Morgan realized it was true. "It feels that way. Des and I plan to dress as Horace the lighthouse keeper and his wife Ida tonight. What kind of costumes are you all wearing?"

King raised a brow. "I guess we'll have to find something. You're a new man, Morgan. Sounds like something went down here while we were gone."

"You set us up." Morgan raised his chin. "But what went down here isn't a story *you'll* ever hear."

Harmony herded a protesting King out the door.

"Don't forget your ritual baths," Des called after them. "Morgan and I have already taken ours."

Chapter Forty-seven

SHORTLY before midnight, with Morgan by her side, Destiny welcomed her sister, Harmony, dressed as Lisette, the gentle ghost who'd helped Harmony rid Paxton Castle of the spirit haunting it. Harmony's husband, King, dressed as his many-greats grand-uncle Nicodemus, who bought and settled this private island, Paxton Island, where the castle, the windmill, and the lighthouse stood.

Aiden and Storm had also found their costumes in the Paxton Castle closets, outfits belonging to second-generation relatives, once removed, descended from Nicodemus's brother, King's many-greats grandfather, who inherited the castle and passed it through the generations to King.

None of the Samhain ritual participants wore anything belonging to Gussie, wife of Nicodemus, the castle's dark spirit, who Harmony had tamed and banished. Why take the chance?

At midnight, with the veil between the realms gossamer

thin, Destiny played the sound track from *The X-Files*. Perfect background music for a Samhain ritual.

Harmony, their high priestess, announced that they should begin, then she consecrated the ritual space and its participants, blessed the elemental tools they would use, and cast the circle with her athame.

Harmony and King, Storm and Aiden, lit the four tapers for earth, air, water, and fire, while Harmony called the quarters: "North, south, east, and west."

Morgan lit the fifth taper, the one in the center of the gateleg altar. "For spirit," he said. "The spirits of our friends and relatives—but especially my sister, Meggie—who have passed from this earthly plane."

Destiny and Morgan lit the two sweet-scented pillar candles, one for love and one for peace, respectively. Destiny suspected that Morgan chose the candle engraved with love as a message to her, and she appreciated it. She wanted it, except that she didn't see how a life together could possibly work between them.

She'd always been attracted to him and wanted him for a boy toy, a playmate, because forever never seemed possible, given their different beliefs, which had changed but not.

He may no longer debunk witches and ghosts, but he'd always retain his basic faith. Yes, he was participating in their ritual, but how did he really feel about it?

She was so confused right now. She'd ask the Goddess for guidance as the ritual continued.

Harmony blessed the altar while she and her sisters walked the circle three times clockwise, Caramello and Samantha following them and amusing Morgan.

Harmony circled and cleansed with salt; Storm circled and cleansed with water, each invoking the Goddess of death and rebirth on this special night.

Destiny circled and cleansed with incense:

> *"I invoke Meggie's spirit of joy.*
> *You have a brother and sister for eternity.*
> *I invoke Buffy's protectiveness,*
> *And thank her for her protection.*
>
> *"I invoke Horace and his family,*
> *Dear Ida and their babe.*
> *Horace will soon be with you.*
> *You have a family for eternity."*

That's when Destiny realized *why* she hadn't been able to say yes to marrying the man she loved. Yes, they could be together in this realm, but there would be no single place for a couple of their diverse faith and belief systems in other realms for eternity.

Not being able to move on with Morgan didn't bear thinking about.

When the circle walk ended, Destiny retired to the fainting couch, where Morgan waited for her. Would he always be forced to wait?

In her heart, Destiny prayed for a miracle.

> *God, Goddess,*
> *Those who've gone before,*
> *Help us find a way*
> *To a life evermore.*

The ritual circle had been outlined with colorful crystals, alternating with vases of orange and gold bittersweet, to honor the harvest; red and green holly to honor the Holly King; and red, yellow, and orange oak sprigs, to honor the Oak King. Marsh grass had also been added to honor their ritual location.

Morgan sat on the edge of her fainting couch and took her hand.

"Are you okay in the middle of a witch circle?" she whispered.

"Nearly content," he whispered leaning close, "except that I'm on pins and needles waiting for my fair witch to say yes."

"Pray for the right answer during the ritual."

"Oh, I am," he said, kissing her brow.

She cupped his cheek. "So am I."

On the altar, candle colors and scents honored the season as did the orange altar cloth, the wooden bowl of apples, pomegranates, pumpkins, and gourds—gifts of the harvest— and a pentacle made of bittersweet branches. The ritual cauldron held a smoking smudge braid of sweetgrass, which gave off a soothing scent. Also on the altar, Harmony's ritual knife, her athame, their three wands, one tipped with amethyst, one with aquamarine, one with citrine, and a blue ceramic chalice. On this particular day of the dead, a cornucopia of candy also sat on the Samhain altar for Meggie, their child ghost.

In the dark parlor, candles shed the only light from every corner, creating a spiritual and ghostly ambience. Floating tea lights stood on each dark, invisible stair, tapers on mantels, and pillar candles in harvest wreaths on tables and chairs.

Caramello purred in Morgan's arms, and Samantha snored in Destiny's lap. Family filled her heart and mind.

Meggie, with Buffy and Horace, stood quietly to the side, watching.

Destiny sent a nod their way, and Meggie waved as Destiny began her chant:

> *"Call down the moon,*
> *Lift the veil,*
> *Call down the sun,*
> *Let us hail.*
> *The spirits are here*
> *Of those we hold dear.*

> *"Call down the stars*
> *For those we love,*
> *Call down the angels*
> *For those we've lost,*
> *Journey's end, a place to spend*
> *Eternity in the Summerland."*

Harmony waved her wand over the feast of the dead to bless the harvest vegetables, fruit, pumpkin bread, and pomegranate wine, which they would share with each other, the deities, and the spirits, in celebration on this Samhain night.

> *"This feast we leave*
> *This Samhain Eve.*
> *Those passed to nourish*
> *As they slip the veil."*

Storm lit a black tea light.

> *"This year dies*
> *On harvest skies*
> *But life takes place*
> *In Goddess grace."*

Destiny lit a black tea light.

> *"Good come to us each one*
> *Negative from us begone*
> *May the new season bring*
> *Love, light, and blessings."*

Harmony lit a black tea light.

> *"Each beginning an end*
> *Each end a beginning*

Bless us here and those apart
Blessed be; you hold our hearts."

Morgan stepped up and placed Meggie's doll on the altar. "On this night, I remember my twin, Meggie. Meghan, my sweet; my heart that was broken and hollowed at your loss is now mended and full. I loved you then. I love you now. I always will. I will love you until we meet again—"

He turned to Destiny. "Where?"

"In the Summerland," Destiny replied.

"Megs, until we meet again in the Summerland. Godspeed."

Destiny brought Horace's uniform cap and a baby bonnet that Ida had embroidered. "I remember my friend Horace, who led Morgan through the tunnel maze beneath the lighthouse to find me. Blessed be, Horace, Ida, and baby makes three. Peace dear family for eternity."

Harmony placed one of their nana's mirrors on the altar, the one in which she had seen Lisette wearing the gown that brought her to Paxton Castle, to the love of her life—had brought each of the triplet triad to the loves of their lives, Destiny realized. "Nana, we missed you in life and mourn you in death," Harmony said. "We've lived in your home, worked in your shop, known you better, and loved you more. Thank you for preparing Vickie to receive us. You carry all our hearts in the Summerland."

Storm placed their many great-grandmother Lili's diary and book of shadows on the altar. "Lili of Clan Lockhart, grandmother, matriarch, Pictish witch, your message we heed, and your heritage we keep. With the laird of Mackenzie, may your love bloom sweet in the Summerland."

Destiny looked to see if, by any chance, Nana or Lili had joined them this night, but they had not, yet she knew that all their ancestors were smiling down on them in spirit.

Storm and Aiden, together, brought to the altar a copper seahorse necklace fashioned by the mother of Aiden's baby daughter, *their* baby now. "Claudette," Storm said. "We're raising Becky so she knows that you gave her life. Bright blessings."

Aiden cleared his throat. "We're raising her with love, Claude, and with a big sister named Pepper. Your mother is with us, too. Rest in peace."

Destiny swallowed hard. Most of their loved ones were still with them, praise the Goddess, though their babies and some of their siblings, whether by birth or adopted, were either asleep nearby, or elsewhere, by necessity.

Harmony blessed and included each in the celebration by name:

"We thank the Goddess and ask for blessings for our half sister, Vickie, her husband Rory, and their little Rory in Scotland.

"For our half sister, Pepper, for Aiden and Storm's baby Becky, and Becky's grandmother Ginny, all here on the island at the windmill.

"Bless Regina and Jake, King's daughter and grandson, our dear friends, Melody and Logan, Kira and Jason, and their children. And bless our own babes soon to come."

Destiny and her sisters regarded each other with inquiry, their triplet telepathy running rampant. "Not me" became the mantra, with a wink and a "yet" after each, except for Destiny who abstained from adding "yet," the omission nearly breaking her.

Harmony changed the music to the golden moldy "Monster Mash" for an upbeat ritual celebration of life and afterlife, to which they could dance in the circle with the spirits.

Harmony and King, Aiden and Storm, swung their booties with enthusiasm, but Morgan took her tenderly in his arms, so tenderly that Destiny fell deeper in love, if that were possible, and he waltzed her in place so as not to hurt her, his love for her shining in his eyes.

How could she resist? And yet they were so different.

She wanted to weep for what they could never have.

To end the ritual, they a shared a feast to thank God and Goddess, with pumpkin bread, honey, apples, and pomegranate wine, leaving a piece and sip of each on the altar for the deities.

Before her sisters and brothers-in-law left, they placed the bowl of harvest fruits and vegetables on the porch for the wandering spirits of their loved ones to refresh themselves during their earth-side journey this night.

Neither her sisters nor Morgan would let Destiny off the fainting couch to say good-bye, so she accepted their blessings and kisses from there.

Morgan saw them to the door, and they left, flashlights in hand, Aiden and Storm for their home at the windmill, King and Harmony for their home at the castle, all here on the island.

"For the first time in years," Morgan said, as he closed the door behind him and turned to her. "I feel as if I'm home and nearly whole and happy. I want only one thing more to make life perfect."

He sat beside her and took her hand. "Kismet, marry me. Be my wife."

Destiny had never wanted anything more. She cupped his cheek. "Morgan, you've often placed more emphasis on my being a witch than a person."

"As it turns out, I'm proud to have a witch who loves me. An outstanding *woman* who loves me."

"But a witch and an ex-priest, Morgan. It'll never work. Be reasonable."

"Do you know what Destiny and Kismet also mean?" he asked her. "They mean *pre*ordained. You were meant to be mine before I made the wrong turn in my life that led to my being ordained. They also mean inevitability. Before I met you, I recognized my ordination as a mistake. Give me credit for knowing when I was on the wrong path, but also give me credit for knowing when I'm on the right one. *You* are my right path."

"Oh, Morgan."

"Kismet, call us what you will, a witch and an architect, a woman and a man. Whatever I call you, like witch, and whatever you call me, like grumblestiltskin, I love you. I'll respect your beliefs; you know I will, as I know you'll respect mine, for witch or for poorer, for as long as we both shall live."

"And into eternity," Meggie's angel said. "My father's house has many mansions."

Destiny gasped.

Morgan grinned. "I forgot, but it's true."

Destiny welled up. "There is a place for us, now and forever. Here, and in the Summerland, or in heaven, Valhalla, the promised land. Whatever it's called, it's a place on a plane in whatever realm we visit from here."

"That about sums it up. Marry me, Destiny. You *are* my destiny. She is, isn't she, Buffy? Meggie? Horace?"

Destiny's heart overflowed as their specter spectators, and the angel she would always remember, gave their approval. Yes, Buffy nearly did smile.

"A place for us together, for eternity. Thank you, Buffy," Destiny whispered. "That's what I needed to hear. Forever is important to me." Destiny took her love's hand and kissed each battered knuckle. "Yes, Morgan, I'd be honored to be your wife."

Morgan hooted, his aura a bright wide band of blue— love—and he crushed her gently to him and kissed her with an amazing enthusiasm, considering their audience.

When he finished, Buffy nodded her approval. "It's time for me to take Meggie and Horace home now."

"Oh no," Destiny said, sadness welling up in her until it overflowed and wet her cheeks.

"No, Meggie, not when I can finally see you," Morgan

pleaded, panic cracking his voice. "I love you, Megs. We'll be together again. All of us."

Destiny grasped his trembling hand.

Meggie looked sad yet strangely elated. "I love you, Morgan, but it's time. The empty place in your heart is full again. Destiny, thank you for filling it. I love you, too."

Buffy spread her wings to a span that filled the parlor, a magnificent sight. "Horace and Meggie have fulfilled their entwined destinies," the angel said, "to set Morgan free of guilt and loneliness and to give him the soul mate he yearned for but wouldn't allow himself.

Buffy nodded her way. "Destiny, we were also here to protect you in the tower for reasons that will soon become clear to you. Know, too, that your psychic reason for being is entwined with Morgan."

The angel opened her hands over their heads.

Destiny and Morgan knelt and clasped hands to receive her blessing.

"No more guilt," the angel said. "No regrets. May love, light, laughter, and bright blessings be yours now and into eternity."

Buffy stepped away and raised her wings toward her charges.

Morgan clasped Destiny in his arms as they watched Buffy, Horace, then his sister turn to vapor.

But Meggie's parting words lingered like a kiss on the cheek and a song on the wind.

"There are three. Safe as can be. Name one after me."

Annette Blair's award-winning paranormals owe their beginnings to a root canal and a reluctant trip to Salem, Massachusetts, where she stumbled into the serendipitous role of Accidental Witch Writer. Magic or destiny, Annette's bewitching romantic comedies are national bestsellers. With twenty-two novels sold to date, Annette will have four new releases and begin two new series in 2009. Contact her through her website at www.annetteblair.com.

Turn the page for
a peak at the first book in
a brand new magical series
from bestselling author Annette Blair

The Naked Dragon

Coming soon from Berkley Sensation!

TIME to cast the spell. Andra, Goddess and sorceress, took a long, last look at Bastian, her huge, shimmering, tawny gold dragon.

"Why the earthen plane?" he asked.

"It is where you came from, and no place needs white knights more." They were quick studies, her dragons. They could ape anyone, learn languages and customs, though they locked their emotions in thick-walled cells. Living earthside would fix that.

Reluctantly, she raised her arms toward the firmament to chant her spell:

> "Cloaked by the gatekeeper moon
> From Killian, Crone of Chaos and Doom.
> Knight to beast, now back again.
> Make Bastian dragon a splendid man."

Pain seared Andra. The palm trees began to undulate. A warning storm. Killian had cast a counter spell and bound it to hers. She might never know its effect, but every dragon she turned would suffer it.

Whatever Killian's stigma, the time had come for her to send Bastian, the first of her knights, to safety. If anyone could establish a Dragon community on Earth, he could.

Only if Bastian survived, could she send his fellow dragons—his fellow knights—by turning them back into men, one by one, moon by moon, to save them.

Somehow, Killian had failed to destroy the man Bastian had once been. It appeared as if, between Andra and Killian, they'd created a stronger man. Earthside, he would be the tallest of the tall and the broadest of the broad. His strapping back, roped with muscle, looked smooth as welk skin. Pleased with his firm man-buttocks, she began circling him. She skimmed her gaze down a brawny arm and faced him, his tapered feet, his muscular calves, his hard thighs, and—"Oh, dear!"

The result of Killian's counter spell pointed her way in firm accusation.

Bastian frowned at his flawed erection. "Do Earth men have such long . . . what is it called?" His man-voice sounded like warm quarry stones scraping one against the other.

"A penis," Andra said.

"Ah, yes, but I do not recall such length or that man-penises have scales beneath the skin, or arrowed tips like dragon tails."

Andra denied her envy. "The better to please the earth woman whose true heart speaks to yours."

As if chiseled from cliff rock, Bastian frowned. "How will I know her?"

"The one you seek will likely be alone. She may have rivers flowing from her eyes and will seem shunned by men. Her figure might be rounder than some, her face plainer, but her heart will be pure and beautiful, and it will speak to yours. She will not like who she is or what she looks like. You will change that. Part of your task is to make her quest your own. As you struggle toward that goal, the dragon in you will clamor to be set free. Resist with all the strength in you."

"If I fail?"

"You will perish. As will your brother dragons. If you succeed, you will live as a mortal man again. Free from Killian's evil forever. Then I will send your brothers, each with his own quest."

"When will you join us?" Bastian asked.

Andra tossed him into the mist. "Earth is not my home," she whispered.

"Neither is it mine!" Bastian shouted on the wind.

HE landed naked upon a thorn bush.

No longer protected by armor or scales, Bastian roared at the searing pain and shot to his feet. Dreadful notion. He'd retained his strong dragon leap. After downing three trees and cracking his skull, he landed flat on his back, his bones rattling, the earth trembling beneath him.

Pain teased his inner dragon, but he'd keep the beast in check, or suffer the consequences.

In the trees that survived, a banquet of birds cawed with laughter. A delicious-looking morsel with long ears landed on his chest and wiggled its nose in disdain.

Wishing for his long, pointy dragon teeth, Bastian dislodged the haughty, puff-tailed meal as he rose and shivered. So this was rescue? Prickly trees, crisp air, cold feet, and a flawed man-spike?

Yes, he'd breached the veil between the planes, but at what cost? Except for a cozy cave or two, Earth appeared to have little to offer.

A cloaked and hooded being approached, short, and soft

of hand, her appearance chiding him for his ingratitude. Female. Human. Odd. Dozens more snacks whirred around her head and followed behind her—bats and tiny red and green birds.

"You are not my heart mate," Bastian communicated. Words would not work. Telepathy served most evolved species, humans and those who were more and less than.

"I am not. My name is Vivica Quinlan," she said. "I own Works Like Magic, a safe house and employment agency where I will acclimate you to our world and prepare you to take your place among us to earn your keep."

Odd but friendly. "Do you not fear me?"

"I have the sight. You're bold of spirit, fiercely protective, and pure of heart. Do you have a purpose on this plane?"

"I am the first of my kind to arrive and am duty bound by my rescuer to make way for the rest. Time is of import. Our island is shrinking." Which could not be said for his man-spike. Bastian wished for a very big fig leaf.

He had forgotten, as a dragon, what he now remembered as a man . . . in the presence of a woman for the first time in centuries. He *loved* women. The shape of them, their tastes and scents, the way they felt beneath him, above him, gloving him.

She handed him a cloak like her own. It fit perfectly, though he towered over her. Impossible for her to know, unless— "You have magic of your own. Else, how did you find me?"

Her smile further stirred him.

"When the air shivers and the bats awake by day," she said, "they come for me with the hummingbirds, often a source of embarrassment. I know only moments before they appear that the veil between the planes has been breached. But together, we greet the chameleons of the universe and offer hospitality."

"Which I humbly accept." Holding his cloak together, he bowed. "Your magic is a gift."

"Some call it a curse. I'm a descendant of a witch who remained undetected in the burning times because she hid in one of these caves."

"So the veil is thinnest here?"

"Oh no. You're one of the lucky ones."

Considering the thorns in his nether regions, he doubted it.

"My ancestor was known for acclimating the magical, supernatural ancients," Vivica said. "Though there were fewer of you back then. Human magic has thinned the veil to a mist. But enough of my ancestry; I find myself trying to guess at yours."

"I come from the Roman army that went missing. Surely someone must have noticed that we vanished?"

"More than one Roman Legion vanished over time," she said.

"Did they? I wonder what they became and where they are."

"Pardon?"

"We, as a legion, happened upon an evil sorceress who turned us into dragons and banished us to an uncharted island on a plane our rescuer often called Purgatory."

"In that case, you'll need the full mainstreaming culture package—language, customs, technology, etc. You do realize that you brought a fairy in with you?"

Bastian growled and turned to find something that looked like a palm-sized human female with sun-kissed hair and stardust wings. Endearing in looks, but she could be an enemy in disguise. In true form, she might be a roach with red pig bristles and a reeking stench.

She could also be a beacon signaling his presence to good and evil, alike. Killian's scout, perhaps. Bastian regarded his acclimater and supposed that he should know where he'd landed before anyone else did. "Where exactly do I find myself?"

"Salem's End. Earthside plane."

CONN ap Llyr had not had sex with a mortal woman in three hundred years.

And the girl grubbing in the dirt, surrounded by pumpkins and broken stalks of corn, was hardly a reward for his years of discipline and sacrifice.

Even kneeling, she was as tall as many men, long boned and rangy. Although maybe that was an illusion created by her clothes, jeans and a lumpy gray jacket. Conn thought there might be curves under the jacket. Big breasts, little breasts . . . He hardly cared. She was the one. Her hair fell thick and pale around her downturned face. Her long fingers patted and pressed the earth. She had a streak of dirt beside her thumb.

Not a beauty, he thought again.

He knew her name now. Lucy Hunter. He had known her mother, the sea witch Atargatis. This human girl had clearly not inherited her mother's allure or her gifts. Living

proof—if Conn had required any—that the children of the
sea should not breed with humankind.

But a starving dog could not sneer at a bone.

His hands curled into fists at his sides. In recent weeks,
visions of her had haunted him from half a world away,
reflected in the water, impressed upon his brain, burned
like a candle against his retinas at night.

He might not want her, but his magic insisted he needed
her. His gift was as fickle as a beautiful woman. And like a
woman, his power would abandon him entirely if he ignored
its favors. He could not risk that.

He watched the girl drag her hand along the swollen
side of a pumpkin. Brushing off dirt? Testing it for ripeness?
He had only the vaguest idea what she might be doing here
among the tiny plots of staked vines and fading flowers.
The children of the sea did not work the earth for their sus-
tenance.

Frustration welled in him.

What has she to do with me? he demanded silently.
What am I to do with her?

The magic did not reply.

Which led him, again, to the obvious answer. But he
had ruled too long to trust the obvious.

He did not expect resistance. He could make her willing, make her want him. It was, he thought bitterly, the remaining power of his kind, when other gifts had been
abandoned or forgotten.

No, she would not resist. She had family, however, who
might interfere. Brothers. Conn had no doubt the human,
Caleb, would do what he could to shield his sister from either sex or magic.

Dylan, on the other hand, was selkie, like their mother.
He had lived among the children of the sea since he was
thirteen years old. Conn had always counted on Dylan's
loyalty. He did not think Dylan would have much interest
in or control over his sister's life. But Dylan was involved

with a human woman now. Who knew where his loyalties lay?

Conn frowned. He could not afford a misstep. The survival of his kind depended on him.

And if, as his visions insisted, their fate involved this human girl as well . . .

He regarded her head, bent like one of her heavy gold sunflowers over the dirt of the garden, and felt a twinge of pity. Of regret.

That was unfortunate for both of them.

LUCY patted the pumpkin affectionately like a dog. Her second graders' garden plots would be ready for harvest soon. Plants and students were rewarding like that. Put in a little time, a little effort, and you could actually see results.

Too bad the rest of her life didn't work that way.

Not that she was complaining, she told herself firmly. She had a job she enjoyed and people who needed her. If at times she felt so frustrated and restless she could scream, well, that was her own fault for moving back home after college. Back to the cold, cramped house she grew up in. Back to the empty rooms haunted by her father's shell and her mother's ghost. Back to the island, where everyone assumed they knew everything about her.

Back to the sea she dreaded and could not live without.

She wiped her hands on her jeans. She had tried to leave once, when she was fifteen and finally figured out her adored brother Cal wasn't ever coming back to rescue her. She'd run away as fast and as far as she could go.

Which, it turned out, wasn't very far at all.

Lucy looked over the dried stalks and hillocks of the garden, remembering. She had hitchhiked to Richmond, twenty miles from the coast, where she collapsed on the stinking tile floor of a gas station restroom. Her stomach lurched at the memory. Caleb had found her, shivering and puking her guts into the toilet, and brought her back to the echoing house and the sound of the sea whispering under her window.

She had recovered before the ferry left the dock.

Flu, concluded the island doctor.

Stress, said the physician's assistant at Dartmouth when Lucy was taken ill on her tour of the college.

Panic attack, insisted her ex-boyfriend, when their planned weekend getaway left her wheezing and heaving by the side of the road.

Whatever the reason, Lucy had learned her limits. She got her teaching certificate at Machias, within walking distance of the bay. And she never again traveled more than twenty miles from the sea.

She climbed to her feet. Anyway, she was . . . maybe not happy, but content with her life on World's End. Both her brothers lived on the island now, and she had a new sister-in-law. Soon, when Dylan married Regina, she'd have two. Then there would be nieces and nephews coming along.

And if her brothers' happiness sometimes made her chafe and fidget . . .

Lucy took a deep breath, still staring at the garden, and forced herself to think about plants until the feeling went away.

Garlic, she told herself. Next week her class could plant garlic. The bulbs could winter in the soil, and next season her seven-year-old students could sell their crop to Regina's restaurant. Her future sister-in-law was always complaining that she wanted fresh herbs.

Steadied by the thought, Lucy turned from the untidy rows.

Someone was watching from the edge of the field. Her heart thumped. A man, improbably dressed in a dark, tight-fitting suit. A stranger, here on World's End, where she knew everybody outside of tourist season. And the last of the summer people had left on Labor Day.

She rubbed sweaty palms on the thighs of her jeans. He must have come on the ferry, she reasoned. Or by boat. She was uncomfortably aware of how quiet the school was now that all the children had gone home.

When he saw her notice him, he stepped from the shadow of the trees. She had to press her knees together so she wouldn't run away.

Yeah, because freezing like a frightened rabbit was a much better option.

He was big, taller than Dylan, broader than Caleb, and a little younger. Or older. She squinted. It was hard to tell. Despite his impressive stillness and well-cut black hair, there was a wildness to him that charged the air like a storm. He had a strong, wide forehead; long, bold nose; firm, unsmiling mouth; oh my. His eyes were the color of rain.

Something stirred in Lucy, something that had been closed off and quiet for years. Something that should *stay* quiet. Her throat tightened. The blood drummed in her ears like the sea.

Maybe she should have run after all.

Too late.

He strode across the field, crunching through the dry furrows, somehow avoiding the stakes and strings that tripped up most adults. Her heart beat in her throat.

She cleared it. "Can I help you?"

Her voice sounded husky, sexy, almost unrecognizable to her own ears.

The man's cool, light gaze washed over her. She felt it ripple along her nerves and stir something deep in her belly.

"That remains to be seen," he said.

Lucy bit her tongue. She would not take offense. She wasn't going to take anything he offered.

"The inn's along there. First road to the right." She pointed. "The harbor's back that way."

Go away, she thought at him. *Leave me alone.*

The man's strong black brows climbed. "And why should I care where this inn is, or the harbor?"

His voice was deep and oddly inflected, too deliberate for a local, too precise to be called an accent.

"Because you're obviously not from around here. I thought you might be lost. Or looking for somebody. Something." She felt heat crawl in her cheeks again. Why didn't he go?

"I am," he said, still regarding her down his long, aquiline nose.

Like he was used to women who blushed and babbled in his presence. Probably they did. He was definitely a hunk. A well-dressed hunk with chilly eyes.

Lucy hunched her shoulders, doing her best turtle impression to avoid notice. Not easy when you were six feet tall and the daughter of the town drunk, but she had practice.

"You are what?" she asked reluctantly.

He took a step closer. "Looking for someone."

Oh. Oh boy.

Another slow step brought him within arm's reach. Her gaze jerked up to meet his eyes. Amazing eyes, like molten silver. Not cold at all. His heated gaze poured over her, filling her, warming her, melting her . . .

Oh God.

Air clogged her lungs. She broke eye contact, focusing instead on the hard line of his mouth, the stubble lurking beneath his close shave, the column of his throat rising from his tight white collar.

Even with her gaze averted, she could feel his eyes on her, disturbing her shallow composure like a stick poked into a tide pool, stirring up sand. Her head was clouded. Her senses swam.

He was too near. Too big. Even his clothes seemed made for a smaller man. Fabric clung to the rounded muscle of his upper arms and smoothed over his wide shoulders like a lover's hand. She imagined sliding her palms through his open jacket, slipping her fingers between the straining buttons of his shirt to touch rough hair and hot skin.

Wrong, insisted a small, clear corner of her brain. *Wrong clothes, wrong man, wrong reaction.* This was the island, where the working man's uniform was flannel plaid over a white T-shirt. He was a stranger. He didn't belong here.

And she could never belong anywhere else.

She dragged in air, holding her breath the way she had taught herself when she was a child, forcing everything inside her back into its proper place. She could *smell* him, hot male, cool cotton, and something deeper, wilder, like the briny notes of the sea. When had he come so close? She never let anyone so close.

His gaze probed her like the rays of the sun, heavy and warm, seeking out all the shadowed places, all the secret corners of her soul. She felt naked. Exposed. If she met those eyes, she was lost.

She gulped and fixed her gaze on his shirtfront. Her blood thrummed. *Do not look up, do not . . .*

She focused on his tie, silver gray with a thin blue stripe and the luster of silk.

Lucy frowned. *Just like . . .*

She peered closer. *Exactly like . . .*

Her head cleared. She took a step back. "That's Dylan's tie."

Dylan's suit. She recognized it from Caleb's wedding.

"Presumably," the stranger admitted coolly. "Since I took it from his closet."

Lucy blinked. Dylan had left the island with their mother when she was just a baby. Four months ago, he'd returned for their brother Caleb's wedding and stayed when he fell in love with single mom Regina Barone. But of course in his years away, Dylan must have made connections, friends, a life beyond World's End.

Lucky bastard.

"Dylan's my brother," she said.

"I know."

His assurance got under her skin. "You know him well enough to borrow his clothes?"

A corner of that wide, firm mouth quirked. "Why not ask him?"

"Um . . ." She got lost again in his eyes. What? Crap. No. No way was she dragging this stranger home to meet her family. She pictured their faces in her mind: steady, patient Caleb; edgy, elegant Dylan; Maggie's knowing smile; Regina's scowl. She blinked, building the images brick by brick like a wall to hide behind. "That's okay. You have a nice . . ."

Life?

"Visit," she concluded and backed away.